CORALEE TAYLOR

I Hear You, Charlotte

Ties That Bind Series- Book Two

To all those who have been fucked over by love. Don't ever give someone the power to make you feel less than the absolutely magnificent human you are.

Shine on, you beautiful bitch. The world needs your light.

Contents

II   Part Two

Preface

This book contains dual POVs, and occasionally, the timelines go back and forth. Please note the date stamps at the beginning of the chapters.

Prologue

Dear Grayson—aka "Dad",

Fuck you.

I

Part One

Part One

Chapter 1

Zach

Leaning down, I place the plate filled with lava pockets on the table to cool. You ain't catching me slipping again with those fuckers. They feel cool enough to eat, but pop one in your mouth, and it explodes in pepperoni-speckled napalm. The resulting burn makes you want to rip off your own tongue.

Falling back on the couch, I firmly grasp my video game controller. The familiar mold of the plastic settles in my bones like a long-lost friend.

As I flip through the bevy of weapons at my disposal for my next match, my mind drifts to the short, sassy blonde who crept into my life. The beautifully broken shadow searching for its missing light.

The TV flashes with game still shots as it loads. A soldier covered in blood, poised to shoot, coiled tight like a snake preparing to strike its prey. Always ready to take down its adversary at a moment's notice.

Laying my head against the back of the couch, my eyes flutter shut as a memory surges forward of the shattered

3

enchantress who smashed her way into my chest and claimed my heart as her own. Jesus Christ, I sound like such a pussy.

Her gorgeous, long, blonde hair is splayed out on the black satin of the pillowcase. Flowing in soft wisps across her skin as she turns her head slightly to the side to allow my lips to graze along her flesh at my leisure.

Kiss-swollen lips quirk up into a heart-stopping smile, a smile just for me. Her tantalizing tongue snakes out to wet her full bottom lip before sinking her teeth into it as her hands map my body like her favorite route. Making their way down to my waist, where my dick takes it as a call to action and perks up at the barest of touches.

"Uh-uh, Little Bit," I whisper in her ear, loving the shiver that overtakes her body. I grab both of her wrists and bring them above her head, firmly holding them in place so I can continue my mouthly exploration.

Her little moans and whimpers have me harder than Stone Mountain obsidian. For fuck's sake, I can't help the groan that leaves my throat.

"Please, Zach. I need you, please." She begs in a breathy murmur.

I like to think I'm a generous man when it comes to pleasing a woman. Through my experiences, I've found that if you can bring her to the edge over and over, not only will she beg for it, but in the end, it's a goddamn explosive, blissful experience that shatters around us like orgasmic raindrops.

I bite down on her shoulder, reveling in the tightening of her muscles at the pain, knowing she loves it. "Mmm, say my name again."

My tongue darts out along the mark I just made, down to her collarbone, and I give it a hard suck.

She inhales sharply, "Zach." Her eyes fly open to search mine. I give her a smirk and tighten my grip on her wrists when she begins to struggle.

I press my nose against the middle of her bare chest and slowly drag downward. My voice is raspy and deep, "I can smell how much you want me, Little Bit."

Her thighs press tightly together, searching for the friction that her jeans are failing to give her.

I chuckle and move both of her wrists into one of my hands. My free hand traces a feather-light trail down her body until I reach the waistband of her pants.

"You want me to make you feel good? Hm?"

She nods, still clenching her thighs tightly against one another.

"You gonna come on my fingers like a good girl?" I swirl my forefinger against her bare navel, making a painfully slow descent to just underneath the button of her jeans.

She makes a greater–yet unsuccessful– attempt at getting her hands loose. I love it when she starts to lose control. "Yes. Fuck. Yes, I want your fingers inside me now." She breathes out in a heavy pant.

I tsk at her needy form, "Patience, darlin'. I'm gonna play that pussy like a fuckin' fiddle. Then you're gonna sit on my face and let me claim all that sweet honey drippin' just for me," I cup her pussy over her pants and press my mouth against her ear, "Because this is fuckin' mine, Little Bit." I slide two fingers along her slit, feeling her warmth through the material. I press harder, "Say it." I command, "Tell me who this belongs to."

It's fucking mine. We both know it. I need to hear that mouth admit it. Own it. Own me.

I lick the shell of her ear, moving my fingers softly over her clit. "Say it, baby. Tell me who owns it." Who owns you?

My heart nearly shatters when her soft, melodic, enraptured voice sounds out, "It's yours, Zach. It's yours," her eyes lock onto mine, and I know without a doubt I'm a fucking goner for this girl. "I'm yours."

"Shug!" My mama's booming voice shocks me back to the present.

With a jerk, I turn my body towards her. She's standing in the kitchen behind me, her hand covering her mouth and her brows furrowed in concern.

I set the controller on the coffee table and entered the kitchen. "Mama? What's wrong?"

She's shaking her head but hasn't looked away from the small TV on the counter. I put my hand on her shoulder, "Mama, are you okay? What's goin' on?"

She finally looks over at me, her eyes glassy, and waves a hand at the TV. "Have you seen this?" she asks.

My hand falls back to my side as I look at the screen; the scene is unfamiliar. I look back at Mama, confused. "What is this?"

Before she can answer, the news caster's voice fills the air.

"... Michael Cochran with Channel Six News at Six. Thank you for joining us tonight. We have some breaking local news. Late last night RVPD, along with the assistance of Federal Law Enforcement Officers, raided a highly sought-after drug den in River View. We have our own Sandra Techmeyer on the scene to give us the latest. Sandra, can you let us know what occurred and what the residents of River View can expect moving forward?"

"Yes, Michael, I have contacted some local LEOs about tonight's incident. They can't divulge much as it is an ongoing investigation, but we have learned that this was part of a sting operation that has been in the works for months.

The source I spoke with assured me they wanted to impact the neighborhood as little as possible and take down the suspect without incident.

Unfortunately, there may be a fatality in tonight's events. We are still waiting for more information, but we have gathered so far that there were only two people in the house. Which you can see behind me is now riddled with chaos and caution tape.

Gunshots could be heard from all around. Ultimately the suspect, who has been identified as twenty-six-year-old Caleb 'Priest' Kirkpatrick, was apprehended and will be treated for a single gunshot wound to his right arm.

The other occupant was eighteen-year-old Charlotte Johnson. Her involvement remains unknown. Charlotte was found unresponsive in the home and had life-saving measures performed on her before being life-flighted to River View Harbor Hospital. Her condition is currently unknown.

Tune in to the eleven-o-clock broadcast for any possible updates on this story. Thank you for watching Channel Six News at Six. Back to you, Michael."

My heart thuds against my chest at a galloping pace as if roaming Cumberland Island with a herd of wild horses.

I gape at the small screen, silently begging for an explanation. A hand wraps around my elbow. "Sweetheart. Is that girl..." She brings her other hand under my chin, closing the gap and gently turning my face to look at her. "Is that the girl you've been seein'?"

I see her lips moving, but the words ain't making sense. They may as well be floating above us in a jumbled mess, plucked down in random order before me.

When I don't respond, she gives my arm a little shake. "Honey, are you okay? Isn't the girl you been seein' named

Charlotte Johnson? It is a fairly common name I suppose, but this is a small town so I can't imagine there are several eighteen-year-old girls with the same name. When have yo—"

Almost as if a lightning bolt struck down and jolted me out of my headspace's muddled mess, I jerk back and stare at her wild-eyed. No. "Mama, stop! Wha—" I thrust my hands into my hair and pull hard, looking around the room like the answers will pop out of the corners of the space.

Fucking *what*?!

I must've heard wrong. Charlotte? Drug den? Gunshots? Fatality? *My* Charlotte– My Little Bit? This can't be right.

My hands fall, and I force my gaze on Mama. "It can't be her." My voice sounds foreign even to my own ears; childlike, unsteady, and small. My shoulders sag, and I feel the onslaught of tears begging to be released, "Mama, please, tell me it ain't her."

I fall to my knees, my face buried in my hands, as the first tears burst forward. I'm engulfed by the scent of jasmine and cinnamon. A scent uniquely Mama's. Her arms tighten around my large frame the best they can. She whispers soothing words to me. Unfortunately, I hear none of them. My mind is a cyclone of questions, confusion, anger, and panic.

My train of thought flies through the air and bounces around like a tennis ball during a heated match at Wimbledon. Not landing on one thing or another.

"Shug, I'm sure she's fine. It's probably someone else," she sits before me, lightly swiping away the tears. Clearing her throat, sounding unsure, she says, "The girl you've described to me would have no business hangin' around with a low-life criminal like that."

She's right. Right? I know Little Bit's been going through some shit lately. I know she's been taking the edge off with something. She's not as good at hiding as she thinks she is, not from me.

Doubt starts to creep in.

But... why hasn't she answered any of my calls or texts?

I pull out my phone and look at the one-sided text thread.

Me: Wanna meet at Sky Ridge and take a ride on the Zach Express?? *wink emoji*

Me: The train's gonna leave the station without ya if you take too much longer to respond.

Me: My hand's got a first-class ticket!

Me:... you don't gotta ignore me.

Me: Okay, okay, you want romance, right? Let me try again. Little Bit, will you meet me at Sky Ridge and let me make sweet, sweet love to you?

Me: Darlin', you're gonna give me a complex if you keep ignorin' me.

Me: Where are you?

Me: I'm feelin' a bit like a stalker here. Can you just let me know you hate my guts and never wanna speak to me again or somethin'?

Me: Little Bit?

She never responded to any of them. They ain't even read.

With shaky fingers, I type out yet another text.

Me: ... just tell me you're okay? Plz. I love you.

I wait with bated breath for those three little dots to pop up.

9

I HEAR YOU, CHARLOTTE

She'll tell me to fuck off, that she's fine, and I'm too up her ass and need to chill. She'll tell me if I don't back off, she'll keep her mouth to herself. That's what she will say. That's what she has to say.

No dots. No response.

I fist my hands and press them tightly into my eye sockets. Shit, what do I do?

Savannah. She's her best friend, she'll know what's going on. I almost drop my phone, my hands are shaking so uncontrollably. It takes a few tries before my thumbs find the correct letters to fill out the words I need to say.

Me: Hey Savannah, it's Zach. I ain't heard from Charlotte in a couple of days. I seen some shit on the news about a girl named Charlotte found at a drug dealer's house and was taken to a hospital??? Can you please call me? I'm freakin' out here.

I open up the thread with Little Bit, staring at my unacknowledged words. They taunt me.

I've given her the space I thought she needed. I tried to be there when she wanted me, letting her set our pace. I hoped she would come out of this fog she'd been living in for months.

Did I miss something big? Should I have done more?

My ringtone echoes loudly throughout the kitchen as the contact flashes on the screen. I answer immediately.

"Tell me it ain't her." I plead. Knowing that her words will change my life forever, I still want to hold out a modicum of hope.

Savvy is silent for just a beat too long. I grip my phone with both hands as a tear slips down my cheek, "Please. Just tell me she's okay."

She takes a deep, shaky breath, and in the softest voice I've ever heard from her, she says, "She's not okay, Zach. She's not fucking okay. Nothing is okay."

Chapter 2

A little over one month later, September 2006

Charlotte

Tick, Tick, Tick

My eyelids fly open, and I shoot a glare at the offending timepiece on the wall to my left.

Tick, Tick, Tick

"Fuck off, you piece of shit! Jesus!" I scream as I hurl my too-flat pillow with the scratchy case in its direction.

Immediately, I regret my action as the tube that is connected to my forearm —with the world's largest fucking needle— begins to burn as it tears out of my flesh. I can't wait until I no longer need the additional fluids and can take my meds like a big girl.

Goddamnit!

I direct my ire at the sterile wall of the hospital-like dorm room I've been assigned to. When did this become my life?

"Ugh!" I slam my head back on the now pillowless mattress. The resulting insta-headache is just another cherry on top of a shit fucking cake that is currently my life.

The large metal door creaks as a head pops in. "Miss

Johnson, as I have already told you, if you cannot keep it down, we will be forced to sedate you." Nurse Hatchet-Face scowls at me with a poorly painted, raised eyebrow in challenge. "Have I been clear enough for you, or should I get the orderlies to join our little party here?"

I gnash my teeth into my bottom lip to keep the words I want to spit at her inside my body. I've already witnessed two people being "sedated" and then dragged— dragged by their arms, legs trailing on the ground behind them— to a secluded corridor on the other side of the facility. They were missing for days and wouldn't speak to anyone when they returned. They wouldn't look at anyone.

I don't want to discover what caused that emptiness in their eyes.

I nod wordlessly at HF. She clicks her tongue and looks down at me, smugness radiating from her evil frame. She closes the door behind her as she takes her leave.

A snort pulls my attention to the left.

I roll my eyes, "Fuck off, Cassie." I growl at my roommate.

The cutter. The nymphomaniac. The pathological liar. She's the fucking hat trick of this nut house— oh, I'm sorry, "Behavioral Clinic". What a joke.

Starry North. The Crown Jewel of Alaska's mental health crisis. A "State-of-the-art facility providing specialized inpatient care for mental health conditions as well as ground-breaking addiction therapy". Cue jerking off motion.

At least, that's what it proudly says across my welcome packet.

Welcome my ass. It's a fucking jailhouse itinerary.

13

- 6:00 AM: Wake Up
- 6:20 AM: Medication Disbursement
- 6:30 AM: Breakfast
- 7:20 AM: Morning Meditation/Journaling
- 8:00 AM: Group Physical Fitness
- 10:00 AM: Individual Therapy
- 11:00 AM: Creative Therapy of Choice (Music, Art, Writing... etc)
- 12:00 PM: Lunch with Additional Medication Disbursement if Necessary
- 1:00 PM: Self-Reflection
- 2:00 PM: Group Therapy/ Relapse Prevention
- 3:00 PM: Family Visitation/Phone Calls
- 5:00 PM: Dinner with Additional Medication Disbursement if Necessary
- 6:00 PM: Personal Time/Journaling/Evening Meditation
- 7:00 PM: Group Free Time/Movie Selection
- 9:00 PM: Bedtime- Lights Out

What a thrilling schedule they give to patients. Like I need seven hundred reminders a day that I've made shitty decisions and nearly ended up in a hole in the ground. I don't need to sit in a circle and sing Kumbayah while holding hands and sharing my problems.

At least, that's what I assume happens. I'm just going based on what I've seen in TV shows and movies.

The last week I've been here has been spent in the isolation of my room.

After the overdose and ICU stay, my body was still in a fragile state. My mind was even more brittle, so my lawyer advocated for a "trickle-in" effect for my entrance into therapy-dom.

14

Sometimes, I wonder if jail would've been the better option. Though I think it's bullshit to take someone who is on death's doorstep and not only interrogate them at diminished mental capacity but dare to threaten them with imprisonment if they don't agree to testify against the bigger fish. In this case, Priest.

I did get a little kick out of learning his real name, though; Caleb– sounds douchey to me. I hope *Caleb* drops the soap every fucking day and Big Thick Bubba is there to help him pick it back up. Asshole.

The detectives were relentless, and since I refused to see or speak to Grayson, Daddy's money was no help, and I was assigned a public defender, David.

I was sure the man –who can't be more than twenty-five– that entered the room with a spotless briefcase in his shaky hand, a coffee stain on his tie, and a crust of dried toothpaste on the corner of his mouth– that I couldn't stop staring at, *gag*– had absolutely no fucking clue what he was doing. I was resigned to the fact that I would definitely be going to prison.

David surprised me, though. His disheveled appearance clearly did not affect his negotiating skills. He argued that I needed to be in a proper facility to handle my "needs effectively".

He bargained for my livelihood with the District Attorney like I was a trading card—an old, unimportant, second-string playing card, complete with tattered edges!

Finally, my fate was determined: I must successfully complete the ninety days at Starry North without incident or spend two years in prison.

I traded one prison sentence for another. Either way, my life is not mine. Not that it has been for quite some time.

I don't remember much after Priest delivered the hot shot.

A loud bang.

Hands all over my body– like so many times before.

Some tube up my nose with mist– I found out later that it was the EMTs delivering Naloxone.

Lots of noise and activity, but nothing making sense.

Then, nothing. Pure, blank, quiet, nothing.

The hazy memory of waking up in the hospital threatens to come forth. There was so much pain. I was sure I was in Hell. Flailing around like a tumbleweed in the wind around one of the dreaded nine circles.

Flashing lights. Incessant beeping. Constant poking and prodding. Un-Godly tight squeezes from the blood pressure cuff every four fucking hours. Throat raw and throbbing from the breathing tube.

I want to erase it all.

* * *

"You know I was named 'most likely to suck a President's cock' by the boys at school, right?" *Lie.*

Her schoolgirl-like giggle fills the air. I imagine her standing there with one foot tucked behind the opposite leg, twirling a piece of her frizzy, bleached-blonde hair. Head tipped down ever so slightly in what she thinks is a demure pose but actually makes her look like a demented porcelain doll.

"That's how good I am." *Lie.*

A sloppy "pop" sound reaches my ears, and I cringe from secondhand embarrassment. "Want to take me to the Snack Shack and see for yourself?"

I don't look up from the notebook in my lap, but a snort erupts from me. Silence ensues for a moment too long. I brave a glance upward, and sure enough, Cassie glares at me while the orderly standing with her traces my body with lust in his eyes and winks. I make a gagging motion with my finger going into my mouth, "Not in this lifetime or any other, Horn Dog."

He's called Horn Dog (HD) for a reason. He will literally fuck anything and anyone that moves. He only has three requirements: warm, open, and willing. He doesn't discriminate by gender– or age. But from what I can tell, it's consensual-ish, which is more than I can say for some of the other douchefucks around here.

He shrugs at my dismissal and grabs Cassie roughly by the arm, leading her down to what I've coined as "The Pussy Pantry". Her basic white slip-on shoes squeak against the linoleum as she struggles to keep up.

When speaking in earshot of staff or management, we call it the Snack Shack. The term refers to the sign above the door with the name written in dried licorice ropes. No doubt, it's a craft left over from years past. The room is small—usually locked—but it's where the good treats are kept. Popcorn, candy, pretzels, juice... You name it, and you can find it in the Snack Shack.

The room is only open for *proper* use during movie time. The rest of the time, it's isolated and pretty soundproof, making it a popular place to take one's Tootsie for a roll, if you know what I mean.

Shaking the image of HD and Cassie plunging into each other's Fun Dip from my mind, I direct my attention back to my notebook.

As the plaques on the wall dictated, my new therapist, Dr.

Jensen Turner, gave me some homework after our first session.

I think he gave it to me as punishment because I literally said zero words to him for the entirety of the hour. We stared at each other for the first thirty minutes. For the next thirty minutes, I kicked back in the oversized sofa chair and played with the drawstring of my sweatpants.

"Well, Miss Johnson, it looks like our time is up for today. Perhaps at our next session, you could participate and make this time together worthwhile." He said as he stood and opened a drawer from his desk. He pulled out a basic black-and-white notebook—the same type of notebook that belonged to a beautiful heartbreaker with stormy eyes. Nope. I'm not going there.

He reached the notebook out to me. I eyed it as if it were a feral animal baring its teeth, sizing me up as its next meal.

"It won't bite, Miss Johnson," he sighed at me and wiggled his finger in my direction as if I were just a silly little girl avoiding vegetables at dinner.

I snatched the notebook out of his hands with more aggression than necessary. He quirked his brow at me, and I was certain he would write that little interaction down in his precious notebook. Note to self: get into that notebook and see what he keeps scribbling in there!

I tucked it in the space beside my thigh and the edge of the cushion without any inspection. Dr. Turner pulled the pantleg of his slacks up a bit as he crouched down to get eye level with me; he didn't touch me– and for that, I'm grateful– he placed his hand softly on the arm of the chair. "This doesn't have to be an unpleasant experience, Miss Johnson. I truly am here to help. To listen. To give direction," I lose the staring contest I was having with the wall and meet his deep brown gaze. Sincerity is etched all over his features.

I wonder how old he is. There's a slight dusting of gray along his temples, barely noticeable among his dark brunette tresses. His skin is smooth, nary a wrinkle, and a neatly trimmed beard. "You don't have to speak to me until you feel ready. We go at your pace," he tapped the toe of my shoe with a finger, "Got it?" he asked, but it was no question.

I tipped my chin down — the only answer he'd be getting from me. I peeked over at the notebook, begging the memories of a boy with stark black hair to stay tucked into the box in the back of my mind where he belongs.

Dr. Turner reached for the book, accidentally grazing my thigh as he pulled it out; neither of us acknowledged it. He placed it gently on my lap and tapped a finger to the top of it. "In your free time, you can use this for whatever you want: doodles, poems, origami, Harriet-The-Spy-ing…"

Ugh, I fucking love that movie. I tried to hide the small smile behind my hand. He stood to his full height, clearly amused with his ability to crack me just a little.

"However, I want you to pen some letters during morning and evening journaling time."

I cocked my head to the side and narrowed my eyes in question. He answered the question I didn't have to ask. "People have hurt you. People have let you down. People have abandoned you. You've felt small. Angry. Unseen."

He stared at me so intensely that it felt like he was searching my soul for these instances he spoke of. I felt uneasy that someone could know my weaknesses and insecurities, so I wrapped my arms tightly around my middle like it could deflect his penetrating observation.

"Tell them, Miss Johnson." He urged with another tap to the top of my notebook.

He walked back over to his desk and grabbed a cheap plastic pen. He turned toward me and threw it in my direction. I reacted quickly and fumbled to catch it before it hit the floor. When I looked back at him, his face was a blank, unreadable mask.

"When I see you again later this week, I expect at least one full letter to someone from your past. This will just be between you and me and will not be shared in group or with the letters' intended."

Well, that makes me feel a little better about it, even though it still seems pretty fucking stupid to write a letter that will never be read.

I nodded in acquiescence before gathering the two items and leaving his office. The door closed with a slight snick behind me, and I leaned against it, clutching the notebook tightly to my chest, and let out a large breath.

I guess the big question is... Who do I write the first letter to?

Chapter 3

Dear Priest,

I think this is stupid, but my shrink says I have to write some letters to people who fucked me over. And guess who's at the top of that fucking list? You. You absolute piece of shit. I wouldn't even be here if it wasn't for you.

Who hurt you, bro? Clearly, you didn't get enough love as a child because you are a horrific human being. I know I'm not blameless for the things that occurred during our time together. I don't know what else to call it. Seems better than "you and your friends raping me at a whim as payment for providing me with drugs".

Never again, you fucking douche canoe. Never again will you put your hands on me. Never again will you force me to take you and your friends simultaneously. Never again will you raise your goddamn voice to me like I'm a rabid fucking dog. Never again will you force drugs into my body. Never again will I do your bidding. NEVER. AGAIN.

I can't believe I got involved with you... I lost myself with you. I cowered in the corner. Maybe that's why you felt comfortable enough to treat me like an animal.

Did you even care that you nearly killed me? Did you give a second thought to that at all? I'm sure you didn't. I was just an experiment. Expendable. Just another warm hole to stick your dick in and a juicy vein to stick your drugs in.

Fuck you.

I hate you.

Why me? How many times have you gotten away with this? Have other girls fallen under your brutality? Why did you do this to me?

Why me?

Could you sense that I was already broken and decided you might as well scatter the shards to the corners of the universe? Split me apart and cast the battered pieces of my soul amongst the stars to burn in their endless flames for the rest of eternity?

How dare you. How dare you take me at my lowest and extinguish whatever remained of my light with your wickedness. How dare you mutilate any residual innocence within me to the point of unrecognizable despair and lifelessness.

I will never be whole again because of you. You ruined me. You executed the person I used to be. You ripped my body apart with your depraved desires. You shredded my mind with your constant psychological warfare.

Because of the deal I made with the District Attorney, I have to see your sadistic face one more time.

But guess what?

This time... I'm in control. I'm going to tell them everything. Every fucking thing I can to make sure they lock your ass away for life. I will look into those soulless pits on your face and smile when they read the guilty verdict.

I will smile because that's the night I will get to fall asleep, knowing that, for once, your asshole will never be safe again. Remember Priest: That soap be slippery, and you're awfully pretty.

Kisses– "Astra"

P.S. – When your eyes clench shut so tight in an attempt to block out the depravity happening to your body against your will, I hope it's my face you see in the white noise as that first– of many to come, I'm sure– big dick enters you dry. May your pillow always be hot and your belly always be full... of Big Bubba's seed.

Chapter 4

Charlotte

Closing the cover of my notebook, I attach the pen by the cap at the top. Smiling to myself as I envision a large, hairy man slamming Priest down on a cold, metal cot and fucking his ass raw until Priest begs his nonexistent deity for mercy and a swift death.

I feel the rugged hands that grip my ass cheeks and force them apart. I feel my
soul leave my body as some nameless, faceless monster takes what was not freely
given.

My teeth grit together, and I shake away the memory that surges forth. A tear carves a path down my cheek without permission. A salty reminder that, like everything else, I also have no control over this.

I swipe angrily at the unwelcome aqueous rebel and look at the clock on the wall—6:52 PM, almost group free time.

Standing, I stretch my arms above my head and lean to each side. The gurney-style beds we sleep in are basically cinderblocks with a layer of one-ply tissue paper as padding, and it is killing my back.

Movement catches my attention to my right. HD and his ward partner, "Small Dick Rick" are watching the gesticulation of my body with lecherous scrutiny.

I act like I'm stretching my neck to the side and take a sly peek around to see who else is in the meditation room with me. No one. Not a single fucking soul but me and these two pervy assholes. *Great.*

Mustering the courage to act chill as a cucumber, I begin to walk towards them– of fucking course, they're standing in the doorway. The only way through is to squeeze between them or for one of them to move out of the way. As I approach, SDR licks his chapped lips and shamelessly stares right at my chest. I clear my throat in an attempt to move them apart to let me pass.

The smirk on HD's face tells me they have no intention of moving. I swallow thickly, square my shoulders, and squeak out, "Excuse me." I think as thin of thoughts as I can and turn sideways to shimmy between them. Aiming to make my curvy body as slim as humanly possible. SDR takes the opportunity to also turn to the side and grind his junk against my ass while letting out a sickly moan.

I quickly force my way through their bodies and book it down the hallway like a fire was just lit under my ass. Their spine-chilling chuckles fill the echoey hallway as I approach the activity center.

A few patients are huddled in small groups in the hallway outside the activity center, gossiping, swapping stories, and swapping pills that have been cheeked at med time. Miss me with that.

The facility is separated into four wings by two categories: gender and age. The building has an "X" shape, with each of the four hallways leading to its respective wing. On the north side of the building is the younger group– known as the junior wing. Ages range from twelve to fifteen; boys dorms are located on the left wing, girls are on the right.

Then we have the older crew, ages sixteen to nineteen, taking up the south side wings—known as the senior wing. Boys are on the right, and girls are on the left.

The hallways all converge to the lifeblood of the facility. A circular center filled with a handful of therapy rooms and staff offices, a meditation room, an activity room, the cafeteria, a small gym, and a family meeting room. The compact laundry room is the last accessible space to patients before the long, barren stretch of hallway that leads to the Quiet Room.

A whimper from one of the closed therapy rooms draws my attention as I pass the closed door. The window on its right has tightly drawn shades, and no light emanates from the space. Female voices reverberate off the linoleum. Snickers and taunts float in the sterile air. Fuck, I hate this place. Rolling my eyes, I continue into the activity room.

The room is filled with black hard plastic chairs lining two long, rectangular plastic tables, intermingled with a few threadbare loveseats and four oversized tye-dye beanbag chairs.

Meals and group activities are the only times the ages and genders are simultaneously in the same place, so everyone tries to get here quickly to grab desirable accommodations for the next hour.

Even though I'm still a few minutes early, I'm late. There are two current seating options: a loveseat with a very sweaty, stick-thin boy. I'm not sure of his name, but I do know that he constantly tries to bite anyone who comes within arm's reach– no thanks.

The other choice is to sidesaddle Roman– Starry North's resident muff whisperer and King shit. All the girls in the senior wing get their panties wet over him, and he loves it.

I consider Bitey McBiter. His lip curls up at my glance, showing me his snaggled canine, and I'm pretty sure he let out a growl. Screw that.

Roman whistles to get my attention and tips his chin, beckoning me over like the complete tool he is. My gaze swings in his direction, and my brow quirks, thoroughly unimpressed.

He makes a show of widening his legs across the beanbag, opening a space to fit my body between them. The disgust crawls over my face, and I reevaluate the biteability of Chompy McChomperson.

Roman clears his throat, loudly, making a show of tucking his body to the side of the chair, leaving a decent space for me to sit on the side of him. He pats the now open spot, giving me his best impression of a church boy, a picture of innocence and pure intentions with rapid flutters of his lashes.

I scoff and unceremoniously flop onto the foam-filled sack. Something I didn't account for was our vast weight difference. His large form dips down lower than mine, bringing our bodies together against my efforts to do the opposite.

"Relax, Chantelle. I won't bite... unless you beg for it," he whispers hotly into my right ear. An unbidden shiver crawls up my spine as his meaty arm slings across my shoulders, bringing his fingertips to graze the tops of my breasts.

This fucker.

I bring my hand up to his, lightly running my forefinger across his skin, eliciting a shudder through his body at the contact. I lean closer to him, bringing our mouths a hairs-

27

breadth away from each other– no room for the Holy Spirit here– my tongue darts out to wet my lower lip, letting him feel the warmth of my mouth. He unconsciously tightens his grip on my breast.

"The only one who will be begging will be you when I jab my pen right in your disease-riddled shrimp dick–" the words come out so sensual and melodic that it takes their meaning a moment to sink into the useless gray matter floating inside his dome. When they finally do, his eyes widen comically large, and he shoves himself away from me at record speed. " – And it's Charlotte, you twat."

With a now respectable space between us, I settle further into my seat and drum my fingers across the cover of my notebook, trying not to chuckle when I see him continuously eyeball me in suspicion from the corner of my eye.

Commotion from the doorway commands the attention of the room. The three self-proclaimed queen bees saunter in.

Their leader is nonother than my dickmatized roommate, Cassie. Her stringy, bleach-blonde, shoulder-length hair is pulled back in a low messy bun; she wears the same facility-issued uniform we all do– basic white cotton tee, light teal zip-up hoodie, matching sweat pants, and white slip-ons. Her average height and lack of desirable "assets" make her pretty face and warm, willing holes the only appealing thing about her.

Flanking her on the right is Charity. Slightly taller and more busty than Cassie, Charity has long black hair braided in a fishtail down to her ass. She's definitely what the guys refer to as a "butter face", as in everything is fuckable, but her face. I've overheard some of the senior boys joking about how it would definitely be an act of *charity* to fuck her.

28

Finally, hoe bag number three on her left, Carina. She's the hottest of the merry band of skanks; she's also the quietest. With a svelte form, shoulder-length naturally platinum blonde hair, and curves in all the right places, it's a wonder she doesn't overtake Cassie for the head bitch in charge title. The triumvirate of cunts who bully together rule together, I suppose.

The menage-a-twats cackle as they walk up to an occupied loveseat. "Get the fuck out of our seat, rodent," Cassie hisses at a pair of junior girls who quickly scatter from the furniture and make a new spot on the hard floor.

Every part of me wants to jump up and pop that bitch right in her suckhole. *Without incident.* The DA's words play on a loop in my mind, halting my violent desires. I shove the need deep down and sit here like a good little criminal. I flip my notebook open to a blank page and begin to doodle.

A few minutes go by, and everyone is busy with their own conversations, games, or notebooks when a slight squeak of rubber on the floor draws my focus. No one else looks up, but I can't look away. The breath is stolen from my lungs. There's no fucking way...

In the doorway, a girl is making herself as small as possible. Her eyes dart rapidly around the space, looking for friendly faces, an invitation to join a conversation, or even just an acknowledgment of existence. She finds none of those. I watch as her shoulders sag in on themselves when she spots the trampy trio. Her gaze quickly leaves them and lands. Right. On. Me.

The change is visibly noticeable in her body the moment recognition strikes her. Those sky-blue eyes fill with unshed tears. Those freckled spotted cheeks stain red. Those flaming locks tangle around her left hand's long, black-painted finger-nails. Her chest rises and falls expeditiously as if building the momentum for battle. She wraps her free hand across her soft middle in a stance of vulnerability. As she tightens her grip on herself, a white bandage peeks out from under her sleeve.

I wish I had the audacity to be offended by her reaction to me. I wish I were delusional enough not to understand where her terror comes from.

But no, I have no such luxury. The last words I spoke to her slam into me with crushing force.

"You are a fucking joke, Aurelia. At least Jade is original and confident, even if she is a

horrid skank. You? You are nothing. Pathetic. You will always be a loser. You

could kill yourself today, and no one would even notice... You might be insignificant as yourself, but you are less than nothing *as someone else."*

My cruel words assault my memory as her observation turns to panic, and she spins around and takes off down the hallway.

The desire to chase after her plows into me with the force of a Mac Truck, but my body remains frozen in my seat as our history replays on a loop like mirrors in a fun house.

My internal deep dive into animal attacks is interrupted by a tap on my shoulder. I boredly look behind me and see one of the girls that hang out with Jason and Jade's crew. I think her name is Aurelia.

I've seen her throughout the year in this class, but we've never spoken. She keeps to herself, sitting in the back row with her headphones hugging tightly to her flaming auburn locks. Mr. Vale and the rest of our classmates seem to ignore her existence. She appears comfortable with being insignificant.

She's cute in an innocently Gothy sort of way. Like a baby Lucifer before his jealous rage sent him falling from the heavens. She has burnt umber freckles dotting a vast majority of visible skin. Her pale complexion is reminiscent of the fur on an Arctic Fox. I cock an eyebrow at her, questioning.

"Um, Charlotte? A–are you..." she stutters and lets out a nervous cough. "Are you okay?" her soft, kind, unsure sky-blue eyes meet mine.

I tilt my head slightly to the side and narrow my eyes, studying her. "Why do you fucking care, freak?" I bite back at her kindness. Fuck her. She's probably pretending to be concerned so she can gather information on me to take back to her Dark Mommy Overlord. Nope, not happening, Elvira.

She flinches as if I've struck her, and I guess, in a way, I have. She shrinks into herself as much as she can. Tucking her fists into the sleeves of her oversized sweater and slides down further in her chair. "I–I was just asking because you don't look like yourself. You seem really upset. I just t-think Jason isn't... worth it." her voice decreases even further, making me have to lean in her direction and strain to hear her.

I twist my whole body to face her and smash my palm down hard on the top of her desk, making her yelp and jolt in surprise. "You think that cheating bastard is the cause of this?" I swipe my hand up and down my body to indicate my appearance, "Fuck Jason. This has nothing to do with him."

Alright, that's not entirely true. But he is a very small part of my current state of mind. Very small. Aurelia gently shrugs one shoulder, still not meeting my eyes, and it's pissing me off. If she's going to talk about shit she has no business being involved in, then the least she could do is look me in the fucking eyes.

I curl my lip, ready to unleash more vitriol at her. I snarl, "You think you're invisible? Honey, I've seen you follow Jade around like a fucking dog. Begging for scraps of attention. Copying her look, trying to carry yourself with the same arrogance. Did you actually think if you looked and acted like her, Jason would look at you twice?" I cruelly laugh at her; I see the tears start to escape her clenched eyes, but I can't stop now. I knew I had seen that lovesick look in her eyes before. She has a thing for Jason.

I tip my head back towards the water-stained tiles on the ceiling and let out a deep, throaty laugh. "Oh, sweetie, you did, didn't you? That's hilariously sad," bringing my razor-sharp stare back to hers, I hiss at her, "You are a fucking joke, Aurelia. At least Jade is original and confident, even if she is a horrid skank. You? You are nothing. Pathetic. You will always be a loser. You could kill yourself today, and no one would even notice."

She sucks in a harsh breath and pushes back from the desk, grabbing her backpack off the floor. In her haste to get away, her foot snags on the metal leg of the desk, and she falls forward; the audible sound of her knee smashing against the hard tile perforates the now-silent classroom.

A few muffled laughs sound around the space, bouncing off the walls like an echo chamber.

I slowly move to a standing position and walk over to her. I gently bump her foot with mine, and she recoils, bringing her leg up to her body in a fetal position.

I look over her shaking frame and bend down to a crouch beside her.

Reaching my hand out, I gently part her cherry tresses to see her heat-bloomed, tear-stained cheeks.

She is sobbing silently and refusing to open her eyes. I softly run the backside of my index finger against the apple of her cheek as I lean down so close that my lips skim the edge of her ear, "You *might be insignificant as yourself, but you are less than nothing as someone else."*

Tears streak down my cheeks, and I watch in a trance as they fall on the white and blue-lined paper, their drops spreading, claiming the unblemished space as their own. I can't stop the torrent of emotion flooding through me, drowning me with intensity. I swipe the wetness away from my eyes with agitation and return my attention to the now-empty doorway.

"Aurelia?"

Chapter 5

Zach

Standing in the open doorway to my house, I flip through the stack of mail, searching desperately for the name I need to see in the top left corner. My heart nearly stops beating as the writing before me comes into focus. There's something off, though. The name in the left-hand corner doesn't belong to my sassy peach. It belongs to me. The letters "RTS" are stamped in large, red, bold print across the front of the envelope.

I stare down at the returned letters in perplexity. Skepticism creeps in and takes over all logical thought. Why would she refuse my letters? I've written her once a week since she was admitted to Starry North. Four letters sit before me, unopened, taunting me with feelings of unimportance. I wanted to see her with my own eyes to verify my Little Bit was okay. But that *place* only allowed family visits. I didn't want her to think I abandoned her, like everyone else in her life has, so I took to writing her.

I rush to the kitchen table to triple-check the address against the printout Mama brought home. I hold the envelope side-by-side with the paper, my eyes scouring every letter and every number, verifying it is indeed correct. When the realization sinks in that maybe she just doesn't want to hear from *me*, confusion makes way for rage.

Reflexively, I reach to my right, where Mama has a beautiful arrangement of pink orchids in a delicate, pure white ceramic vase – with intricate blue lines that curve around the clay in peaceful circles– and I hurl the flawless vessel against the fucking wall. Shards of the once piece of perfection litter the ground. I stare at them in irritation, waiting for them to form an answer, much like reading tea leaves in an empty cup. What the hell is happening?

The last time I saw her, she was laid up in a hospital bed with tubes and wires coming and going all over her body. She looked like an attractive version of Dr. Octopus. It would be amusing if it weren't so terrifying. Savannah's mama, Mary, was there just as often as I was, in opposite shifts. We passed each other like ships in the night. I let her know if anything of note happened on my watch and vice versa.

One thing that remained the same, day in and day out, was the man pacing the lobby repeatedly. I can see a lot of his daughter in his features. Mr. Johnson is a handsome man. Even if right now he looks ten years older with the stress of the current situation. I asked Mary why he doesn't ever come into Little Bit's room and sit with her. She got a real nasty scowl on her face and simply replied, "He's not welcome."

She was unconscious most of the time. On the rare occasion she was awake, she didn't speak much. I'm not family, so attempts to get the doctors to tell me anything were futile. But my eyes work just fine. The bruises that mottled her skin, the blown vein on her forearm, the thick handprint around her neck... They all told a story of unseen horrors. My baby had been through Hell and had the battle scars to prove it.

It was soul-crushing to watch the girl you love writhe in pain. Tossing and turning, always a fitful rest. The mere irony is enough to fuck with even the strongest of minds. But my girl has been struggling more than I ever realized. Over the last two months, I've spent most of my time blaming myself for not seeing what was right in front of me. How did I not see her opioid addiction? When I wasn't blaming myself, I was cursing every god I could name for doing this to her. To me. *To us.*

I was so enraptured by this enigmatic firecracker that I let myself be blinded to some obvious truths. Some truth Savvy had to drop on me during one of our many phone calls to discuss Charlotte's condition. It took Mary, me, and my girl during a moment of lucidity to convince her not to throw away her scholarship by dropping everything and coming back here. She could do nothing besides sit like a bump on a log at her bedside, and that title currently belongs to me.

My mama has tried to no avail to get me to come home and just visit every so often so I can focus on getting ready to head to college– well, that's not fucking happening.

Little Bit and I discussed our college plans a few months ago, but things were different back then; *we were different.* She wanted to get into the nursing program at Auburn. No way in hell I was going to let us be separated by states like that. I originally planned to attend LSU on a football scholarship, though I don't need a full ride due to Papaw's wealth and my dad's GI bill being available. I still wanted nothing more than to get there on my own with no help from that sad sack.

I hadn't told her yet, but when Little Bit and I started getting together, I applied to UA– *Roll Tide.* Their coach had sniffed around a bit when he visited with a scout during one of our last games. I told him I had plans already but thanked him for his interest. He left, telling me that if I ever changed my mind, I should let him know– and I did. After a few weeks of back and forth and some negotiating, I am now part of the Crimson Tide. A three-hour drive is much better than forty-two hundred miles.

I thought my mama was going to tan my hide when I told her not only had I changed schools—even though UA is D1—but also that I'd deferred entrance until the Fall semester, putting me a year behind. Her ire fell away when I tossed my brand new crimson and white jersey, embossed with the number "10" on the chest and back, and MORRIS stitched proudly across the shoulders at her. Boy, she grinned from ear to ear.

I know she means well; her concern is me and my future, but we're talking about the girl I love. I almost lost her. I have to know she's okay. I have to be here for her. I would never forgive myself if I left and she took a turn for the worse. Even though we've never had an official conversation defining our status, she belongs to me, and I belong to her. She is my girl, my Little Bit.

On one of her more lucid days, she stroked my face and told me she was sorry. For what? I have no idea. Mary told me they were giving her medicine to help her come off of the drugs, and there might be some side effects, but so far, all she does is sleep. After she had slipped back into unconsciousness, I stepped into the hallway to have a more candid conversation with her best friend.

I cleared my throat as I leaned against the dark blue hallway wall, my head tipped back in exhaustion. Bringing the phone back up to my ear, I let out a heavy sigh. "How did this happen, Savvy?

How did I miss this? What the fuck was she doin' with a goddamn drug dealer?" I whisper shouted into the receiver as I glared down the pocked ceiling tiles above me as if they'd personally wronged me.

"Zach," she breathed out my name in exhaustion. I could picture her sitting cross-legged with her hand holding up her chin. "Charls is very good at only showing someone what she wants them to see. This is not on you. Hell, if anything, it's on me. I'm her best fucking friend, and I was too busy living it up in Florida, worrying about making new friends, parties, cheer, and which frat guys were fuckable..." Her throat cleared, and I could tell she was fighting off a river of guilt. Guilt that's not hers to bear, not alone, at least. Silence filled the line as we both sat with shared shame and culpability.

After several moments of silence, she softly spoke, "Did you know she struggles with depression?" She does? I know she's dealt with some anxiety, and clearly, there was a drug problem, but I had no idea she was depressed. "I swear I'm only talking to you about this because I believe you truly care for her. She would be pissed as all get out at me for putting her business on blast. But I think you need to understand the girl you love, and then maybe you can understand how we got to this point."

For the next several minutes, Savvy delved into Little Bit's history. She'd be happy and bubbly one minute, pensive and withdrawn the next.

According to Savvy, this has been happening most of her life. She was medicated at one point but then seemed to be getting better and was taken off the pills. Savvy's of the mind that she didn't actually get better; she just became a pro at hiding it.

"There's more... I don't know the details because she'd never tell me what actually happened, but I saw..." she choked down a sob *and took a deep breath before continuing, "I saw the marks. I saw the bruises. I felt her light being snuffed out as we huddled together on the floor of the shower... He hurt her, Zach. He destroyed her in a way that I don't know if she'll be able to come back from." That last bit came out in barely a whisper.*

A tear snakes down my cheek and lands on one of the shards at my feet. I drop to my knees and reach for the delicate, jagged piece, letting it rest heavily in my palm. This little fragment will never be whole again. Even if I gather every single piece and attach them with the utmost care and precision, it will never be the same—just like my Little Bit. The acute comprehension of that fact drives a spike right through my heart.

My hand closes in a tight fist around the pointed wedge, and I scream to the heavens, "Fuckin' give her back to me! I can't lose her. Ain't no way. I'll help her. I'll be better. I'll be whatever she needs. I can fix it..."

My body heaves forward until my forehead is pressed against the cool hardwood. My bloody fist comes up to eye level, and I place the shard gently next to one of its scattered mates, "I can fix it..." I promise tenderly.

39

Chapter 6

Charlotte

I'm pretty sure I've cracked the code of the loony bin. They've strategically placed those incessantly loud ticking clocks in every room to drive us all mad and stir agitation. Ensuring a steady stream of wackos and junkies. Smart move, powers that be... smart move.

Tick

Tick

Tick

My back teeth grind against each other with such force that I know my jaw will be sore for the foreseeable future. Trying to distract myself, I focus on the small window in my room. The night sky is black as pitch, usually prime for stargazing, but we've had record snowfall this year. The city lights reflect off the snow, creating a faux daylight that settles like a heavy fog along the suburb. This excess lighting renders stargazing a no-go activity for tonight.

I sigh and roll over to my right side on this sad excuse for a bed. The room is never fully engulfed in darkness. Along the edge of the ceiling tiles, a slightly dim illumination fills the room enough to make out the main staples of the space.

Tucking my right hand under my head, I bring my left arm to rest along my chest. If I can't search the skies for my solace, I can find a suitable substitute right here.

My eyes trace the seven freckles on my left forearm. To an untrained eye, they are just a random, speckled pattern. Nothing of note... But if you know what to look for and were to take a marker and connect them, you would make the shape of a pot with a long handle– Ursa Major. *My very own Big Dipper.*

Juno was a spiteful bitch to turn Callisto into a bear– a twisted attempt to strip away her beauty and captivation. Just because Jupiter had a wandering eye and thought Callisto was a baddie, like, take it up with your man lady, damn.

But the joke's on Juno... I don't know what Callisto looked like as a woman, but among the stars? None compare.

Each enchanting celestial sphere glimmers with a brilliance that fills the expansive sky. They call to me—they always have.

I can only hope that one day when my earthly journey concludes, I might earn my rightful place amongst those radiant orbs that have guided me through darkness and stirred my soul.

Tracing the pattern repeatedly, my uneven nail carves a path of white. Through each pass, the once-white trail glows a vivid red.

Tick

Tick

Tick

My shoulders threaten to cave in on themselves as I cringe from the relentless ticking racket coming from behind me. I begin to hum an old favorite of mine –in an attempt to drown out the persistent drone of the clock– something about not wanting the world to see me because I don't think they'd understand. I press my nail a little harder along the fleshy route of stars. It should probably concern me that the pain is nonexistent. On the contrary, it feels... calming. Good even. It feels like *control.*

A rhythmic rustling sounds out from the bed behind me. My nail pauses its trek, hovering over the alleyway it has carved. *Please, no.* A soft moan accompanies the rustling, picking up pace and racing towards the finish line. *You've got to be shitting me.* Heavy pants chime in like low drum beats in the world's worst-ever Jazz rendition of "Porn de Cassie."

"Fucking knock that shit off, Cassie." I fume at my room-mate.

Not deterred in the slightest, her moans get louder and more dramatic as her hand works even faster beneath the prickly woven polyester blanket. A wet, squelching noise reaches my ear as she finger fucks herself to oblivion. A dry heave rocks my stomach. I latch my arm around it and beg its contents to stay put.

"Ah, fuck yeah," she proclaims to no one in particular.

The friction is audible as she grinds against the palm of her hand, alternating the friction with the penetration. Her moans speed up, and a series of "mmms" and "ahhhs" brings us to her uninspiring, lackluster conclusion.

As she pants satiated breaths into our shared space, my anger bubbles to the surface. She has no respect for anyone, and I'm over her shit. I thrust my blanket off of my legs and flop my body to the left, fully intending to give her a piece of my mind, when the sight of her freezes my movements.

She's moving into a sitting position in just her facility-issued white cotton tee and nothing else. My focus narrows in on her landing strip. I don't know why I assumed she'd be bare as the day she was born down there— she seems the type.

But somehow, I'm not shocked at all to see the shape of the pubic hair in a downward arrow. She follows my gaze down to her fully displayed beav and smirks, "You trying to get a taste, roomie?" she reaches down, gathering some of her own wetness, and brings the glimmering digit to her mouth, giving it a lick.

My lip curls in a sneer, "Not for all the money in the world, biotch."

She laughs and begins to walk towards our shared bathroom. She has to pass the end of my bed to get there. When she's right at the foot of the bed, she stops and reaches down to grab the edge of my blanket. I watch in horror as she lifts her right leg to rest on my bed as she wipes her juices off on my fucking blanket. *The fuck she just did.* My teeth grate against each other, and I slowly raise myself to a sitting position. With barely restrained rage, I grind out, "You did not just fucking do that."

Just as I'm about to spring from the bed and tackle this dirty shrew, she lifts her finger and tuts. "Ah-ah. You might want to check your tone, *roomie.* One word from me, and your ass will be headed to the Quiet Room." A smirk takes over her mouth. "Is that what you want, hm?" she taunts.

A shudder runs through my body at the thought, but I lean forward anyway, ready to smash her face in, "Oh, you fucking bit–" I can't get the rest of the words out because she opens her mouth to scream. I fist my hands and slam my back against the wall at the head of the bed, glaring at her. She shrugs her shoulder, throws me an evil grin, and begins whistling as she strolls off to the bathroom.

Fucking cunt.

43

The water flowing through the pipes behind my head drowns out the ticking enough to lull me into a relatively relaxed state. I close my eyes and try to picture being anywhere but this fucking room, in this fucking facility, with these fucking people.

I'm lying on a beach in Bora Bora. The warm sand sinks below my body, molding to it like a warm welcome home. My skin is damp with sweat from basking in the radiant bliss of the sun. My toes burrow into the sand, the little piggies eager to escape the unrelenting heat. The crashing waves weave their spell through my ears as they flow to shore. Errant cries of Black-Winged Petrels echo along the breeze as they coast along the surging tides. The wind whispers among the palms, a gentle serenade weaving through the fronds. I close my eyes to savor the sea-kissed air wafting around me...

The creak of the bathroom door interrupts my daydream. Her wet feet slap against the tile as she returns to her bed. Without opening my eyes, I calmly call out to her, "And Cassie?" I don't wait for her acknowledgment before I continue, "The next time you want to play digital DJ, do it in the fucking bathroom like a normal person."

She laughs as she settles back in her bed. Just as I'm about to drift off, she whispers, "And Charlotte?" I take a deep breath. "Mhmm," I offer dismissively. "Normally, I would go to the bathroom, but—" Something hard lands on my bed between my legs. As I reach down for the object, she declares, "Your batteries were dead."

My nostrils flare, and I drop the electric toothbrush like a hot jizz-coated cake.

* * *

44

"Well, Miss Johnson, will we have a dialogue today? Or shall we continue our parallel play?" Dr. Turner jests, wiggling his matching notebook at me. I roll my eyes at him and return my attention to the notebook in my lap, where I've been working on creating a tiny checkered pattern with my pen.

My eyes find the clock behind him on the wall, only twenty five more minutes to pass before I can get the hell out of here. It's not that I don't like Dr. Turner. On the contrary, he has a very endearing, trustworthy nature. But I don't trust myself. I've proven time and time again that my judgment of character fucking sucks.

This is our third individual session, and I've still yet to say a word. In our last session, he asked me to read the letter I wrote out loud. I gave him a *yeah fucking right* look with a cocked eyebrow, to which he chuckled and asked if he could read it himself.

I teetered back and forth on whether I was comfortable with him reading my letter to Priest or not. Ultimately, those soft, dark eyes got me, and I handed over the notebook. I watched his face closely for judgment, disgust, blame, or indifference, but the man was a steel trap of emotions. The only hint he was affected by my letter was the slight flaring of his nostril and sharp nod as he handed the book back to me. We spent the rest of the time in a shared silent transparency.

Dr. Turner is a patient man. He doesn't push. He's kept his promise on that– so far. We spend the hour sitting in companionable silence, him doing whatever he does inside his notebook and me doodling in mine.

As I'm coloring in another square to expand my chessboard pattern, Dr. Turner stands and heads over to his desk. I watch him out of the corner of my eye, not wanting to give away my interest in his actions.

He opens the top left drawer of his large wooden desk, rustles through some items, and clasps his hand around whatever he is looking for. He closes the drawer softly and makes his way over to me. His large body looms over me.

My shoulders stiffen instantly with the proximity. Feeling my discomfort, he lowers himself to my level—something he does often, like he knows I can't stand the feeling of someone imposing over me. I concentrate on the page in front of me, begging my heart to slow its cadence at the nearness of the man before me.

He lays his large hand softly on top of mine to stop the movement of my pen. I freeze and snap my gaze to his. He holds out his other hand, in a rock form, before turning it over and slowly releasing his fingers outward. There in his palm is a large gold coin. I meet his eyes and cock my head to the side in question.

A slight smile ticks up on his lips as he thrusts his hand closer to me like he is tempting a wild animal to take the tasty treat from a stranger's hand. "For you," he soothes.

My eyes dart from my checkered pattern to his reassuring eyes, to his offered palm, and finally, down to his left hand, which is still gently cupping my right hand. I slowly reach my left hand out and take the coin out of his proffered hand. I don't look down at it. Instead, my focus is solely on where our bodies are joined.

The delay in my response or acknowledgment must bring his attention back to what his hand is doing. He quickly pulls it back and clears his throat as if the sound could wash the awkwardness away.

Standing, he looks at the clock before heading to his desk

chair. "Looks like that's it for us today." He says almost dismissively. *Did I offend him somehow?*

I nod my head reluctantly. I close the pen inside my notebook and clasp my hand tightly around the coin. Dr. Turner's head is down, his sole focus now on the papers splayed out before him on his desktop. Guess that's it, then. I huff a breath and leave the room.

Making my way back to my room, I find it roommate-less—thank God. I set my notebook on the rickety nightstand beside my bed and take a seat with my back pressed against the wall at the head of the bed. I try not to give too much thought to the last hour, the way my breathing seemed to stutter with the bodily contact, and how Dr. Turner seemed to be affected by the interaction as well.

I tip my head back to the wall and pinch my eyes shut, bringing my fists up to rub at them. Now a heated essence in my palm, the coin begs for consideration. I bring my fist down to my lap and release my tight grip. The gilded medallion sits heavy in my hand as a sob works its way up my chest and settles thickly in my throat.

Etched in the disk are two squares – one inside the other– with words surrounding them. The words on the outside square read: **Self, God, Service, Society.** The inside square is adorned with the words: **Freedom, Goodwill.** The very center is inscribed with a "30".

My very first sobriety chip. I shouldn't be surprised that he gave this to me. He is a therapist at a clinic that specializes in rehabilitation for addiction as well as behavioral issues, after all. It's got to be a pretty common occurrence. So why does it feel like more than that?

Chapter 7

Dear Erick,

I just wanted you to know that you're a pussy-ass-bitch.

I hope you get a disease and your dick falls off. I hope Mommy and Daddy cut you off and you are forced to get a real job. I hope someone jacks your ride and crashes it into a guardrail, rendering it a total loss. I hope every shroom you get is a dud. I hope you get a bad batch of AstraMallum and are left with just enough remaining brain cells that you have to re-learn how to tie your shoes.

Most of all, I hope no girl ever comes to you seeking comfort again.

These were already more words than you're worth.

Choke on a dick and die, asshole- Charlie

Chapter 8

Charlotte

The smell of popcorn wafts through the air. My stomach clenches and begs for sustenance. I float towards the heavenly aroma like a cartoon dog being carried on the scent by its nose. My feet make their way to the movie room on autopilot. My hunger pains unwilling to settle for less than being stuffed full of buttery goodness.

I stop at the doorway and take inventory of the bodies in the room.

Bitey boy. *Check.* Junior crew. *Check.* Roman holding court like he's the king of the Oddball Wacky Losers. *Check.* The unholy trinity looking down their noses at everyone in the room. *Check.* The reserved girl peeking out timidly through breaks in her auburn hair. *Check.*

I make my way to the table in front of the Snack Shack, which is set up with styrofoam bowls and plastic spoons—our kind isn't trusted with forks, insert eye roll here. I grab a bowl, load it with the popped yumminess, and go in search of a seat.

Walking up to the small loveseat, I pause, suddenly losing the little nerve I had when I made the decision to come over here. I clear my throat, shaking off the hesitation, and sit in the open space. The girl beside me curls into herself further.

I don't fucking blame her.

I tuck my right leg under my ass and situate the bowl to balance on my thigh.

The TV at the front of the room displays tonight's choice in cinematic entertainment. A snort of laughter fills my chest as I take in the irony.

Surely, the staff knows the mental health implications of a movie about a girl chasing a white rabbit down a hole and her wild and crazy adventures in this wondrous land in which she finds herself.

As a very large, very intoxicated-looking caterpillar is blowing smoke rings of letters into the air, I keep my gaze on the screen but hold my bowl over to the apprehensive girl beside me.

The breath in my lungs freezes in anticipation of her response. We sit without movement for what feels like forever before I feel the bowl tip ever so slightly. I blow out my breath in relief. We don't look at each other. We don't speak. I move the bowl to sit between the two of us on the couch. A silent offer of peace, and we watch the rest of the movie.

When the credits roll, Aurelia scurries away without a second glance in my direction. Shaking my head slightly in disappointment, I pick up the few loose pieces of popcorn from the couch cushions. I cringe at the dark grease stains that have made themselves at home on the material, the pattern blending seamlessly with the other unknown marks on the cushion. God knows what kinds of fluids have been laid to rest here.

Thoroughly disgusted, my mouth pulls down in a frown, and I walk to the open plastic trash can by the door to throw away the snacky remains.

As I toss the bowl into the can —a slight swish is the only audible proof I wasn't a littering asshole like the rest of these heathens— a nasally rasp calls out from somewhere in the room behind me, "Yo, Chloe, think you could get fire crotch to meet me in the Snack Shack later? I want to see if the carpet matches the drapes." Roman laughs with a couple of the senior crew boys. He slaps the one on his right in the chest with his backhand as he asks me, like, *"Hey, watch me be a total D bag."*

I slowly turn to face him, "You will leave her the fuck alone," I stalk towards him, not stopping until we are literally toe to toe. He looks down at me, smirking. To anyone else, it would seem like he carries all the confidence in the world. But not me. I see that scared little boy behind his lascivious stare. I'm tired of guys like Roman thinking they can do, say and *touch* whatever and whoever the fuck they want.

From our little encounter earlier, he doesn't trust me—not that I blame him—but I'm banking on his ego being worth more to him than his common sense, so I press on.

I place my hand on his flat stomach and gently slide it up his chest before coming to a stop over the pounding nucleus of his being. I lift up on my tippy toes so my lips may graze the flesh on his neck, and goosebumps sprout along the fleshy trail my lips leave behind.

I keep my voice husky and low but loud enough for his gang of dickholes to hear, "You feeling needy, baby?"

My tongue darts out and licks a path along his earlobe before sucking it in my mouth, letting it go with a "pop".

"You want someone to meet you who can take care of those needs of yours?" I walk my fingers up his neck to just behind his ear. His eyes flutter shut. "Is that big cock of yours craving a tight, hot, soaking wet pussy?" I roll my lips together and release a small moan into his ear.

His body betrays his stoic face and dismissive attitude. He leans in my direction, seeking my touch and begging for the satisfaction only a warm hole can provide.

I press my whole body against him, feeling the effects of my words pressing into my stomach. *Gotcha.* "Hm," I sensually ponder, bringing my hand from over his heart down to the waistband of his sweats. I toy with the elastic with my finger and bring my lips to his stubbled cheek, "Forget the Snack Shack. How about I drop to my knees right here and take your majestic man meat to the back of my throat?"

"Damn, dude. If you don't take her up on that, I fucking will." Some faceless follower of his goads from behind him. Roman lets out a growl. No one dares question the king. "Fuck off, Masters. If anyone is getting their knob slobbed, it's going to be me."

I lean my head to the side, making eye contact with Masters, and give him a wink, "We'll see about that. Maybe Masters will know how to treat a girl right," my hand moves from his waistband down to cup his ever-growing shaft, it immediately twitches in my palm- a dickly *"hello".*

After I watch Masters' throat working, desperate to swallow the lump I created. I grin and look back at the toolbag before me. My palm makes small circles along his manhood, which is now harder than steel. He thrusts his hips into me in a steady rhythm, looking like he's going to pull a minute-man at any moment.

"What do you say, Rome?" I take my bottom lip between my teeth and give him my best sultry stare.

He narrows his eyes at me in smoldering uncertainty. On

one hand, he thinks I'm fucking with him. On the other, his dick is leaping at the chance to make acquaintance with my mouth.

I watch the battle war on in his bouncing gaze before he slowly nods– decision made then. His bravado getting the better of him, he reaches out and runs his hand to the back of my neck. He massages his finger in the area for just a moment, before he moves his hand to the underside of my ponytail. Fire blazes in his eyes as he grips my hair painfully, pulling me closer to him. He leans down and ghosts his lips over mine. I fight the cringe I feel and keep my face passionately indifferent. "I say get to sucking, whore."

Oh-ho-ho, okay. This fuckhead.

I throw a smile at him, dripping with sweetness and under-lying malice. I slowly sink to my knees, my eyes never leaving his. I blindly wrap my fingertips around his waistband. He looks over his shoulder to the left and nods his head in the direction behind me. His stare finds mine again immediately. I slide his sweats down his thighs until they pool at his feet.

I hear a click behind me, the large door to the TV room now securely shut.

I run my hands up his shins to his muscular thighs and finally to the elastic of his boxer briefs. Just as I lift them forward to pull them down, his hand covers mine. "Uh-uh, use your mouth," he demands.

Fuck you.

I push up on my shins enough to clasp my teeth on the springy fabric and drag it down. Grazing my nose against his purple-headed warrior, it quivers at the contact, and I shove down the eye roll that's dying to come out.

Still latched onto each other's observing orbs, I stick my

tongue out and run it over my palm. Roman sucks in a quickened breath at the sight. I grasp his sad excuse for a penis with my dampened hand, giving it a few test strokes. A bead of precum sits at the tip. I use my thumb to spread the moisture across the head and lean forward, letting him feel my hot breath across the saturated skin.

His hips tilt forward of their own accord, yearning for the dewy caress of my mouth. I smile up at him and wet my lips and wrap my mouth around the head of his cock. I desperately plead with my stomach contents to stay put. He grunts in gratification, the grunt quickly turning into an earth-shattering yelp as I sink my teeth into his fleshy rod.

My eyes shoot blazing waves at him, my lips contrasting the action by curving into a smile around his cock. I let him see how far my teeth are sunk into his sensitive schlong. His eyes have now taken on panic, with a side of murderous anger. My hand takes his family jewels in a vise-like hold, causing his eyes to widen and immediately glaze over with unshed tears.

I press my teeth tighter together in warning when his hands shoot out to grab my hair. My gaze bores into him, saying the words my mouth is currently incapable of saying, *"If you don't want to be known as Roman-The-Eunuch, I suggest you take your fucking meat hooks off my hair."*

"Fuck! Okay, okay. Stop. Stop. *Stop!*" He cries out.

I release his now flaccid peen, admiring the chuckle chomps I've left behind, but still keep a grip on his balls. I move to stand in front of him, his attention entirely on me. I steel myself and glare him down, "I said you will stay the fuck away from her. Have I made myself clear, Roman? Or do you need another demonstration of what I will do to your love stick if you go against me?" I quirk my eyebrow up and grip his balls even tighter. "Yeah. Fucking whatever, okay. I won't touch the bitch. Let me go." He pants.

I release his meaty sack. He immediately sags in relief. Before he can pull his pants up and cover his shame, I pull my leg back and knee him as hard as I can in the junk, "My fucking name is Charlotte." He predictably collapses like a sack of potatoes.

I straddle my legs on each side of his body as I stand over him, looking down on him in contempt. I bend at the waist and give him a sharp kick to the ribs, "You're going to want to put some ice on that." I laugh before flouncing out of the room with the echoes of Roman's cries at my back.

Chapter 9

Zach

"Shug, I just got off the phone with your Aunt Virginia,"

I roll my eyes and continue fucking shit up on my video game. I know what she wants to talk about. Aunt Virginia lives along the border between Georgia and Alabama. Mama wants me to go check things out early and move on with my life. When will she get it? I can't just leave. I can't leave *her*.

"Zachariah Thaddeus Morris. You will shut off that there video game and have a conversation with your mama right this instant," she scolds with an added foot stomp.

I make a show of slamming my thumb on the pause button and chuck the controller across the couch. She sits beside me, the pleat of her floral sundress being swallowed by the overused cushion.

I sigh and turn my body to face her. I love my mama to the ends of the earth, but the woman can be so frustrating. She has no patience and wants what she wants when she wants it with no excuses. Hmm, maybe that's where I get it.

"Mama, I don't wanna have this conversation again. We've already discussed my decision. I ain't goin' nowhere until Charlotte is out, and I can talk to her."

Mama's rough exhale fills the silence between us as she slides closer and laces our fingers together. Something she does when she's about to deliver bad news.

"Honey. I know you think you love this girl—"

"I know it, Mama. There's no thinkin' about it. I love her." I interrupt.

Her eyes soften, and she gives me the look that she's given me since I was a young buck, placating. Humoring. She pats the top of our joined hands, "Zachy, honey. Charlotte needs help. The kind of help you can't give her," she squeezes our hands lovingly, "Do you reckon she'd want this? You throwin' away your future? I don't think so, baby. I think she'd be slicker than a minnow in a mud puddle if she knew."

I shake off her hand and thrust mine into my hair, leaning my elbows on my knees.

"Before you say anything, let me speak," she softly demands. "Daddy and I discussed it with Mee-maw and Papaw as well as Coach Reynolds—" My eyes snap up to her unrelenting ones. She holds her hand up to stop me from speaking and sharply shakes her head once.

"We won't let you ruin your future. You are signed up for the spring semester. You will stay with Aunt Virginia while we wait for a dorm room to open. Coach Reynolds has assured us that you will get the very next one available."

What the hell? Who the fuck do they think they are? I'm eighteen. How can they make these major decisions about *my* life without me?

"You need to start packin'. Make two piles: one for your must-haves to take with you and the other for things we can mail to you later on."

No. To hell with all of this. They can't do this. I spring

57

to my feet, breathing in heavy pants as I look around the room. Surely, Ashton will pop out at any moment and scream, *"Gotcha!"*.

There ain't no way my family betrayed me like this. The depth of their deception slides inside me, filling me up, a toxic poison flooding my veins. Swallowing me whole. Stealing my breath. A pretty lie is still a lie. You can slap lipstick on a shitty pig, but at the end of the day, you still got just a pig covered in shit, smiling with lipstick stains on its tusks. You can't double-cross me while smiling in my face and tell me it's for my own good. To involve Mee-maw and Papaw? That's a new level of fucked up.

I look down at Mama, searching her eyes for something that tells me we can talk about this. That there's room for another option. But that's not what I find. The determination etched across her face tells me this isn't up for debate. This is a done deal, done in the shadows by the Judas' in my life. I huff out a scoff and shake my head.

"You can't do this, Mama. I won't go. I'll call Coach back and let him know you were mistaken."

"It's already done, Shug. Coach Reynolds had a long talk with your Papaw."

Fuck. My Papaw is a very respected man throughout the South. He's a formidable opponent. Most people try their damnedest to avoid being on his bad side.

Not only is he a powerhouse, but he's also extremely wealthy. His reach is as far as it is wide. So him taking the time to have a chat with Coach means... I'm super fucked. They hold my life in their hands. A poker chip to be exchanged in the game of who swings their dick around the best.

I've always been respectful to my mama. Ever since my dad's

affair, I've been fiercely protective of her as well. Right now, it's taking every bit of self-control I can muster not to have a full-on hissy fit. But I can't do that—not to her. So I grit my teeth and storm off to my room. Her voice pauses me at my bedroom door, "You leave in three days."

My shoulders tense, and I slam the door behind me so I can cool down before I turn around and give her a hearty what-for.

Collapsing on my bed, I stare at the pitted ceiling. The never-ending stream of shrunken mountains fills the expanse of the surface without a care in the world. Looking down with their sightless eyes on the destruction of my life.

This is a goddamn clusterfuck. This is what I've always wanted. To get out from under my dad's thumb. Do my own thing. Kick ass at football. Dick down all the jersey chasers I can.

But then *she* happened. It's not that I'm ready to throw my future away, but more that I want her to be a part of it. I want every part of our lives intertwined until I don't know where she ends and I begin.

It scares the fuck out of me that I feel this strongly for a girl I only met a few months ago. But my gut tells me this girl, she's the one. The one that's worth everything. The one that will *change* everything. I knew when I watched her stumble into those woods, eyes puffy with tears streaming down her face and her adorable nose bouncing up and down like a rabbit. I knew she would either be the beginning of me... or the end.

Looking over at the stack of returned mail on my nightstand, I grab the one on the top and tear it open.

Little Bit,
  This is letter number three, without a response from you. What's

going on, darlin'?

I took a run up to Sky Ridge this mornin', and I stopped at our table. As I looked out over this little town, all I could think of was the last time we were here together. It was early afternoon, and there were a few random folks mullin' about the area. I've never been as homicidal as at that moment. I wanted nothin' more than to devour you right there on the spot. But all those fuckin' people.

So you sat your pretty ass on top of the table, with me in between your luscious thighs. We embraced as we stared out at the picturesque settin' of River View.

This mornin', as I ran my fingers over the etched words in the wood, I recalled how flushed your skin was at the thought of my hands roamin' all over you.

How it felt when I pressed my palm against your chest to lay you down, the drumbeat of your heart loud enough to dance around us in the breeze. Watchin' the pulse throb in your neck as I ran my tongue along its path. I kissed you with an urgency that stemmed from the pooled desire buildin' from deep inside me. I wanted to own your body right on that table, Little Bit.

One day, I will.

The little mewls and sighs of desire coming from your mouth made me feral. And then you wrapped those gorgeous legs around me, pullin' me further into you. It took every ounce of control I had not to tear your clothes right from your body and slam into you with no regard for the public indecency.

The only thing that stopped me was utter possession. Every noise that comes from that delicate throat is mine. Every arch of your back is mine. Every curl of the toes is mine. Every wanton look is mine. Every sordid request that leaves your sultry lips is mine. Every flash of satisfaction on your beautiful face is mine. I will not share you.

You. Are. Mine.

Well fuck. Now I'm sittin' at the DMV with a hard-on.

I miss you, Little Bit. Not just your captivatin' lady garden, but you. I miss holdin' you in my bed. I miss you runnin' your fingers through my hair. I miss your sassy ass mouth. I just miss you.

I can't wait until you're home. We've got time to make up for. Make sure you prune the garden, sweetheart. I've got some seeds to plant. Okay, that was bad. I admit. Disregard the shitty come-on.

You know that girl that works at the Gas'N'Go? The blonde one? I stopped in the other day to get a "blue-motherfucking-raspberry" slushy, and she went on and on when she was checkin' me out... while checkin' me out. I'm serious. She looked me up and down so hard I was a little afraid for my safety. I thought she might try to pull a Dahmer on me when I turned her down. I tried to tell her I was spoken for. She basically said she didn't give a fuck if I had a girl, that it could be just between us, and my girl would be none the wiser.

Earlier, one of the rings on my keychain had broken off and was inside the left pocket of my jeans. I covertly slipped my hand into my pocket and put the metal ring around my finger.

When she continued to come at me, I finally lifted my hand up and said, "Look, missy, my wife is my whole fuckin' world, and not in this life or any other would I screw that up by so much as breathin' in another woman's direction. You go on and call me Casper because I might as well be a ghost to you. Don't speak to me. Don't look at me. Don't even think about me. Or next time, I'll send her down to set you straight."

The saucy minx doesn't take no for an answer, does she? At her age, you'd think she should know that no is a full gosh dang sentence. She just kept poppin' that godawful gum and twirlin' her hair, smirkin' at me. When she finally rang me up, she jotted her number on the back of the receipt.

Are you gettin' green as a June bug in July yet? Come on now, Little Bit, you know you're the only one for me.

When I was walkin' out of the Gas'N'Go, a very large, hairy gentleman in his fifties passed by me, and I slapped the number into his palm and told him the little lady inside would love to hear from him.

I reckon we're gonna need to find a new place to get those bangin' frozen treats.

Fuck, I want to see you.

I miss you.

I'll be here, waitin' for you. As long as it takes, Little Bit. I ain't going nowhere.

I love you, Charlotte.

–Zach

I crumple the pages in my fist. She may not have gotten the letters, but I know what they said.

I fire the parchment filled with my hollow words at the wall. I said I'd be here waiting. As long as it takes. I promised.

My parents just made me a fucking liar.

Chapter 10

Charlotte

Hands tighten on my hips, a bruising force keeping them in place as the faceless man slams into me from behind. Another set of hands fists my hair in an unyielding grip, forcing my head down to an unrecognizable dick, pummeling my mouth repeatedly until I'm choking for air and drool runs out of the sides of it.

The one in front commandingly holds my head down to his pubic bone with one hand and pinches my nose closed with the other. He's cut off my oxygen supply with his cock in my throat. I can't swallow. I can't speak. I can't breathe. Just as blackness dots my vision, he lets go, thrusting backward with such force as the man behind me slams forward that I feel like he could split me in half at any moment.

Loud clambering commands my attention to the right. There's a window with a beautiful stained glass picture etched into the lower half. A semi-circle pattern with intersecting lines that lead to a single star. A flurry of blues and greens meld together, creating an Aurora Borealis throughout the glass. On top of those luminescent colors lies a beige crescent moon, donning an all-seeing eye, with its gaze trained on the single star. Mouth set in a line. Like the moon is disappointed in the star.

The grunts of the unwelcome invader of my body reverberate off the walls around us. A symphony of my torment to echo on repeat.

The malevolent, red, glowing-eyed demon before me has moved to a throne of broken glass. Shards stick out in all directions, and the chipped edges are flooded with blood, which trickles slowly down the smooth surface.

His face is completely covered in shadow. Only the crimson gleam stands out against the pitch. The strike of a match flickers in the room as the demon brings a cigarette to his mouth. The flame attaches to the end, bringing the slender wand of destruction to life, conjuring forth its whispers of death. As he sucks in a breath of the filament, the flame chases down the length, setting everything in its path ablaze.

When the ember has been extinguished, the smoke billows from the obscurity on the throne. As the thrusts behind me continue, the grip crushes my bones as my head falls limply between my arms—the only thing keeping my body upright.

Blood traces a path along the milky skin, matching the stains of the shards on the throne. Jagged, deep cuts allow the meat inside to dangle flaccidly from my body. Pools of my life force surround my hands.

The monster behind me grabs a fistful of my hair, jerks my head back as far as it will go, and turns it back to the window and the enchanting celestial art decorating it.

A hand slams on the clear half of the window from outside. Frantic, verdant eyes stare back at me. A second set of panic-laced, smokey eyes latch onto my lifeless gaze. Unheard pleas radiate from the turbulent orbs.

The monster forces my fixation back on the infernal presence. The smoke begins to form into letters. **H**. The letters flow straight *to me one at a time, disintegrating once they hit my face.* **I**.

The smoke burns my eyes. **A**. *I blink quickly, my globes begging for relief.* **S**. *Tears gather and give momentary respite.* **T**. *My lungs are filling with the deadly plume.* **R**. *I choke on a cough and blink hard, the tears washing the burn away.* **A**. *My psyche oscillates around the letters, lining them up in my mind's eye.*

As the puzzle pieces snap together, I wrench my focus back to the aberration. A spotlight shines on the tabletop beside him, and I follow it to its origin, the star, and back to the table. The light reflects off of the shiny metal of the large needle. Beside the needle, a vile. Beside the vile, a tourniquet.

Hi Astra.

* * *

I wake with a start, panting and covered in sweat. I stare, unseeing, at the water-stained tile ceiling. The nurse said this new med could cause vivid dreaming, but *fuck*. I wasn't expecting it to be that intense. I can almost feel the oppressive force behind me and the taste of smoke on my tongue.

I swallow down the vomit that threatens to relieve itself from my body and take deep breaths in an attempt to calm my galloping heart. I press my palm to the overworked ticker, rubbing slow circles to coax the calm that I don't feel to come out.

Buzzing sounds out from the shared bathroom. I force myself to sit up and let the damp sheets pool around my waist. I kick out of them and grab some fresh clothes. A moan echoes from the bathroom, and I roll my eyes.

Once the dry clothes cover my body, I look at the clock on the

65

wall. 5:56 AM. My nightmare-addled brain finally catches up with the noise filling the room, goddamnit Cassie. She doesn't have a fucking electric toothbrush!

I slam my notebook on the med counter. Janice, the nicer of the nurses in this dreadful place, blinks back, surprised at my ire. She fixes a smile on her face. "Charlotte, good morning. Here's your morning dose." She slides over a small white paper cup with two small round pills inside – not the fun kind either. One is to help me wean off the opioids, and one is to manage my depression– even though I never accept it, she holds out another small cup of water. I'm no noob to dry-swallowing pills, honey.

She raises her brow at me expectantly. I open my mouth, moving my tongue in all directions so she can verify I have ingested them both.

"Thank you," she praises.

She begins to busy herself with other tasks, and I clear my throat to grab her attention. "Uh, Janice?" She turns back to me with a smile and tilts her head slightly forward, allowing me to continue. "I need a new toothbrush."

"Certainly, but I just have to warn you, they have wooden handles and can sometimes splinter out if they get too wet." She warns as she places the plastic-covered toothbrush in my palm. I grin at her, "Perfect."

The food here sucks especially breakfast. Metal prison trays full of bland, thick, sticky oatmeal. A third of a very bruised banana. A cardboard carton of skim milk. Barely a spoonful of rehydrated eggs. Sometimes, a mystery meat that somewhat resembles bacon but tastes suspiciously like fish. Like I said, it fucking sucks.

I'm already in a bad mood with the shitty wake-up, the

toothbrush debacle, and now faced with food that is doubtfully fit for human consumption. The last fucking thing I want to hear is the irritating prattle of the spiteful triad.

"You're so ugly. It's a shame you failed at killing yourself. The world really doesn't need any more ginger uggos. Are you that dumb, too? Couldn't even do suicide correctly." Ironic statement coming from her.

Charity cackles, followed by the grating giggle of my bitch-ass roommate. The third groupie stays stoic. Their bodies imposing over whatever unfortunate soul that drew their attention at 6:30 AM.

"Hey, are you fucking deaf? I'm talking to you, bitch," she goads. A whimper sounds out from the object of Charity's wrath as she leans down and shoves her off of her seat.

Snickers from the audience around us echo off the linoleum, filling Charity with renewed bravado. She presses her white canvas shoe against the leg of the body, now cowering on the floor. Carina shakes her head and walks away, leaving enough of an opening for me to catch eyes with the frightened redhead.

Tears fill her pleading eyes. My body remains paralyzed in place. My eyes slam shut, allowing a familiar memory to flash along my eyelids.

She sucks in a harsh breath and pushes back from the desk, grabbing her backpack off the floor. In her haste to get away, her foot snags on the metal leg of the desk, and she falls forward; the audible sound of her knee smashing against the hard tile perforates the now-silent classroom.

A few muffled laughs sound around the space, bouncing off the walls like an echo chamber. I slowly move to a standing position and walk over to her. I gently bump her foot with mine, and she recoils, bringing her leg up to her body in a fetal position. I look over her shaking frame and bend down to a crouch beside her.

Reaching my hand out, I gently part her cherry tresses to see her heat-bloomed, tear-stained cheeks. She is sobbing silently and refusing to open her eyes. I softly run the backside of my index finger against the apple of her cheek as I lean down so close that my lips skim the edge of her ear, "You might be insignificant as yourself, but you are less than nothing as someone else."

Jeering from the crowd around me recalls me from the past. Just as Charity lifts her foot to stomp down on Aurelia's leg, I lift my tray and slam it down on the hard table top.

The crashing sound immediately calls everyone in the room's attention.

Cassie's smile slides off her face as she meets my infuriated stare. She unconsciously pulls her hand back from Charity's shoulder and takes a step away.

I direct the full weight of my wrathful stare at Charity. "If you touch her one more time, you and I are going to have a problem," I warn, my knuckles turning white from the forceful grip on the tray.

She laughs nervously and takes a look around the room. Looking for backup, maybe. She won't find it. I've created a certain reputation for myself with my frosty demeanor, and I suppose the scuffle with Roman solidified the fact that I am not to be fucked with.

She straightens her shoulders and flicks her onyx braid over her shoulder, the weight slapping across her ass as she stares at me in challenge. Like a true fucking idiot, she decides to test my gangster and slowly lifts her foot over Aurelia's knee. I close the gap between us in an instant and brick her right across the face with the metal tray.

Charity screams as we fall to the ground. I quickly straddle her, reaching my hand down to each side of her head. I pick it up and slam it backward to the floor with enough force to rattle her brains a little bit. I'm not trying to kill the bitch. Just teach her a lesson.

Blood careens out of her nose, I pull a fist back, ready to pop her one, when my arm is stopped mid-air, and my attention flies to Cassie – who has clearly lost her fucking mind– we both look at where her hand is clasped on my wrist.

I bare my teeth at her. If she wants some of this, too, I'll gladly share. She must think better of her decision to intervene because she drops my arm and backs away. I pull back once more and deliver a solid blow to her left cheek.

Charity sputters and cries below me, begging for me to stop. She didn't give Aurelia that courtesy so she could take what was coming to her.

I cock my arm back to give her another one when my body is jerked off her. SDR and some other orderly are dragging me away from the bloody, crumpled mass. I give her a smarmy grin as she watches me being hauled off.

I look over at Aurelia, who is now sitting up but still on the floor, staring at me in disbelief and awe. I offer her a soft, genuine smile and wink at the shock on her face.

Rough hands squeeze my now sore arms, and my feet dangle lifelessly against the floor as we make our way down a hallway I'd hoped never to see.

Nurse HF stands sentient at the doorway to my hell. Arms crossed over her stickly arms, talons digging into the white linen of her scrubs with force. She scowls down at me before a cruel smile lifts her wrinkly lips.

"In." she barks at the orderlies before turning on her heel and strolling back down the hallway.

Creaking hinges groan as the large metal door is thrust open, and the orderlies heave my body into the padded room.

I quickly crab crawl to the back wall and bring my knees to my chest. My gaze turns frantic as I take in the severe lack of decoration in the space. The floor and the walls are covered in what looks like blue wrestling mats. That's it. There is no window. No bed. No toilet. No clock. I never thought I'd miss that incessant ticking device, but knowing I won't have any frame of reference for passing time makes shivers run down my spine.

SDR crowds my space. I press my body against the wall as much as I can. Attempting to blend into the insulated material, unsuccessfully. He leans down to me, pressing one large arm to the wall, partially caging me in, and pressing his other hand to the rigid line against his linen trousers.

His lustful eyes roam over my body, pausing on the blood stains dotting my chest. His tongue darts out and wets his lips. He palms his growing erection while examining my chest like he suddenly became Cyclops. The urge to punch him in the balls is strong, but my desire to not get the shit kicked out of me is stronger, so I stuff the urge deep down and clench my jaw, pressing my fists into my shins.

Putrid breath fills my senses when he brings his mouth to a grossly close proximity. I fail at holding back a full-body cringe. He smirks at my reaction, "On your feet, girly," he quietly demands. When I don't move fast enough, he jerks me up by my already sore bicep and spins me around, pressing my face harshly against the buffered wall.

He kicks my feet apart and presses his lips to my ear while shoving his rough left hand between my legs, "Contraband check." He snickers while stroking me through my sweats.

His stiff member grinds against my ass, pulsing against the soft skin.

His teeth latch onto my earlobe, and he bites down *hard*. The right hand, not to be left out of the exploration, finds its way to my breast. He cups it with vigor, painfully squeezing my nipple between his forefinger and thumb. My hands curl into fists, my nails finding their familiar settlement on the crescent shapes permanently etched in the soft flesh.

A kaleidoscope of grotesque visions and unsettling scenarios circles my mind like a demented carousel. Each round is more disturbing than the last. Revulsion wraps around me like a suffocating cloak of nightmares and vile intentions.

He continues grinding against me, alternating his grip between my battered nipple and the sensitive globe of my breast. The rhythm gains speed, and the pressure of his body against mine increases. My mind immediately dives into escape mode. Producing a picturesque cabin in the woods for me to hide in until it's safe to come out again.

All at once, the pressure behind me is lifted, and the sound of the heavy metal door slamming shut gives me a slight reprieve. The screeching of a small window towards the top of the door has me jerking my head towards it, fear creeping down my spine. The window slides open, and SDR leans in with a wicked grin, "Welcome to the Quiet Room, little girl. See you soon."

Chapter 11

Charlotte

The silence is maddening. The Quiet Room is aptly named, for sure. The rest of this place echoes like a sound chamber. From my bed, I can hear footsteps tip-tapping as they creep along the hallway in the dead of night, but not in here.

In here, the intruder would open the door before you even knew they existed.

Time is but a fanciful concept within these walls. Have I completely lost my mind? Every time I take the meds, things get fuzzy, but it's also the only time I get darkness... and through darkness comes clarity.

Light, yet the heaviest weight I've ever felt.

Hazy, yet the clearest I've ever seen.

Quiet, yet the most deafening sound audibly possible.

The light buzzes. My heartbeat echoes in my ears. I feel the rigid thumping against my chest. The hinges squeak. My throat bobs as it swallows. The metal scrapes. The darkness calls.

Rinse and repeat.

The orderlies never speak to me or answer questions. They bring their trays, watch me ingest whatever they brought, and then leave.

Always alone.

Just me and my spectral darkness.

Food. *Darkness.*

Pills. *Darkness.*

Thoughts. *Darkness.*

No matter what, it always comes back to nothingness.

* * *

"I don't know what's happened to me, Momma," I admit, lying on my stomach with my face pressed against the padded floor.

My fingers find the now familiar nail marks left over from the lost souls who occupied the space before me. Their madness becomes my comfort. My nails trace their hopeless routes, walking in their proverbial shoes of despair and agony.

A loose thread of the material lays flaccidly along the top of the pad. I lightly pluck it up and let it fall again. "I don't know how to live without you. Everything hurts. Nothing makes sense. Why didn't you tell me sooner?" I ask, desperately trying to keep anger from my voice.

I don't want to be angry at her. But fuck, how could she keep such vital information from me? Why would she wait until it was far too late to tell me that she was sick? If I had known sooner, I could've convinced her to do treatments. We could've looked into clinical trials.

In the weeks after her death, when I was lucid enough to work my fingers properly, I scoured the internet and found multiple trials happening all over the country. Why did she rob us of that chance?

73

I tightly wrap the loose tendril of string around the tip of my finger. As I ponder the reasoning, I observe with a detached gaze as the flesh gradually swells, taking on a deep shade of purple, completely devoid of emotion.

Was it money?

I would have begged, stolen, sold... anything to get it. Even if it meant facing Grayson and faking "the good daughter" routine to get it out of him. Fuck, I would've sold everything we had. I would've sold myself if it meant saving my mom.

Why her?

Anger surges through my body like a relentless tide as I reflect on the betrayal my sperm donor inflicted on not only me but my mom, too. The emotion, fierce and consuming, engulfs me. Each thought of his betrayal intensifies the flood of resentment and disgust. For what? The whore of a secretary? Was she worth destroying our whole fucking world? Does she have a pussy made of Corinthian leather or something?

She doesn't hold a candle to the beautiful person my mom was, inside and out. Amelia Johnson was a step above all the rest. Truly, she was a coveted soul that this world will forever suffer without.

A storm begins to brew within, with each wave of anger crashing against the shores of my emotions. His actions sullied what should have been a solid foundation of trust and left behind the wreckage of broken familial bonds. The weight of his deceit drowns me in a fiery turmoil threatening to consume any remnants of fondness or understanding I've ever possessed for the man.

I wind the string tighter around my already numb finger, punishing the digit for the sins of the father.

Fuck him.

74

"I would've done anything, Momma... anything," I croak, my throat dry and raw from the recycled stale air in this small box.

I roll onto my back and trace the blemishes filling the ceiling over to the silver ballast holding the large fluorescent tube. I fixate on the chiseled edges of the metal cage surrounding the glowing bulb. Sharp lines run the length of multiple ceiling tiles, probably about the length of my body.

I slide over, position myself directly underneath the cage, and pray, "Lord, I know I never talk to you. I'm not even sure if I believe you exist. I have at some point, but how can I continue when all this fucked up shit keeps happening to me?" I wave my hands out wide in the air above me, beckoning an answer to appear before me.

"If you could do me a solid, I'll never ask you for shit again," I beseech in a secret whisper with a sly smile on my face. If He granted this one wish for me, I *wouldn't* be able to ask for anything again.

My lids flutter shut, watching as the dots behind my lids dance in the darkness and bring my hands together in a prayerful motion against my chest. "Please, give us one of those 1964 earthquakes right now. I'm talking the force of eight thousand atomic bombs because I need that case–" I pull my right hand out of prayer to point to the light above me. " – To come loose and make everything stop. Please make it all stop."

Squeaking hinges have me rolling my head towards the door. I peek through one eye and see a set of black tennis shoes coming into the room, the recognizable tinkle of tablets rocking against one another in their paper cup.

I squeeze my eye shut once more and shake my head, "Guess

that's yet another fuck you from you, huh, big guy?" I snort with a sarcastic huff of laughter, aiming my words at the God who either doesn't exist or finds it amusing to fuck with me.

"What did you say to me?" Anger floods the voice of the burly, unamused orderly.

I wave him off with my right hand and then hold out my palm expectantly. "Not you, Tiny." I curl my fingers back and forth in a "gimme" motion. " I was just having a chat with our Lord and Savior."

He slams the cup into my waiting hand and scoffs, "It's a little late to play the good girl, don't you think?"

As the tablets work their way down my throat, I shrug my shoulders as much as the unforgiving floor allows. "Don't most people beg for forgiveness as the Devil drags them to Hell?"

Chapter 12

Charlotte

I don't know how much time has passed by when I'm thrust feebly into my bed by yet another unknown orderly. They change out staff here like faulty lightbulbs. Except for the worst ones, those seem to be the keepers. Make it make sense. The cramps in my stomach have started to ease up.

With no clock or window, I had no idea what time of day or even what day it was. Meals seemed to come at random intervals. I tried to keep count of the seconds between them but always fucked up in the thousands somewhere. The harsh fluorescent lighting never dimmed, which made sleeping a remarkably arduous task.

I would stare for what seemed like days at the slight flickers coming from the glowing tubes. At one point, I convinced myself that it was the ghost of a patient who died in that room trying to communicate with me via Morse code.

After a while, everything started to blend together. Colors were no longer distinguishable, and textiles were all the same. The ceiling became a floor, and the floor became a wall. The wall became the entrance to my Hell.

I know a few things for sure. I had seven meals and six cups of meds, but each cup had three pills instead of the regular two and four bathroom breaks. The rest is a hazy recollection.

"Are you okay, Charlotte?" A timid voice calls from my left. My head feels fuzzy and heavy, and it's a feat of strength to turn in the direction of the sound.

I blink a few times, trying to clear the veil obscuring my vision. My brows furrow in confusion, "Aurelia?" I question, wondering why she's sitting on Cassie's bed.

She nervously pulls her hands into her sleeves and nods. A flash of the bandages wrapping around her thin wrists catches my attention, and I make a mental note to revisit what happened there.

I look around the barren space. All Cassie's little knick-knacks are gone. The bedding is made up flawlessly, very not Cassie-like.

Aurelia chews on her lip, her gaze focused on the floor between us. "Where's Cassie?" I ask. Because what the fuck is going on.

"She's been moved to another room," she explains. *But why?* "She asked to be moved because she felt unsafe with you as her roommate. Her words, not mine." She adds as if I had posed the question aloud.

Well, whatever. Fuck Cassie. Maybe now I'll be able to get some sleep without the sex fiend flicking her bean all night.

"And you? Why are you here?" I ask, my eyes boring into hers with uncertainty. She rolls her lips together, gaze darting around the room.

"I asked to take her spot."

I damn near roll off my bed. Shock fills every part of my body.

"B-but, why? Aurelia, you should fucking hate me for what

I did to you—" I ask, my eyes begging her to see reason. She shouldn't want to be near me. " – I hate me." I admit quietly.

She leans back against the wall, sitting sideways on the bed to face me. Her chest expands with the deep breath she inhales. I watch the motion, flabbergasted by her admission.

"No one has ever defended me, Charlotte. Never. I've been picked on my whole life for one thing or another. I'm too pale, too skinny. My hair is too red, too frizzy. I have too many freckles. My style—" she pauses, looking at the door, no doubt plotting an escape route in the event I turn into a feral animal and pounce on her.

Her eyes find mine again. She gulps and continues, "I'm used to being everyone's punching bag. But when you came after Charity like that... Charlotte, you saved me. In one of the darkest moments of my life, you came crashing in, a shining, blonde beacon of hope." Her sky-blue eyes gloss over from unshed tears as she gives me the accolades that I absolutely do not deserve.

I sit up on the side of my bed, facing her full-bodied. Leaning forward, I rest my elbows against the top of my thighs, "I did the bare minimum of what should have been done. You know that, right? It was no act of heroism. It was basic human decency, and the fact that no one else stepped in just goes to show that the whole human population is garbage. We need another plague..."

She huffs out a small giggle at my comment. "I agree with you. In my experience, a vast majority of people do indeed suck. But in my book... you are no longer part of that group. Thank you, Charlie. For real. Thank you."

I shake my head, staring at her in disbelief. I don't deserve her forgiveness or reverence. I deserve her hatred, detestation, and fists.

"Ari–" I choke on the words I want to say. That I *need* to say. My feet carry me across the room and stop in front of her of their own accord. I kneel at her bedside and place my hands over the top of her feet, " – I'm so, so, so fucking sorry." I apologize. My eyes implore forgiveness with tears streaming down my face. Aurelia leans forward and cups my cheek with a soft, one-sided smile, "You're forgiven, Charlie."

We both move simultaneously, standing and embracing each other, the depth of our bond solidifying in the hold. Whispering apologies and gratitudes, we sink into each other, two lonely, broken souls desperately seeking repair and understanding.

Maybe that's why I threw so much of my hate at Ari.

She *is* me. My fated sister. My cosmic companion.

* * *

Tick, Tick, Tick

A soft chuckle interrupts my mental formulation of clockly destruction worldwide. I'm seconds away from pulling a Hook and slamming the face of the insolent timepiece with the nearest hard object.

My eyes narrow at Dr. Turner, and a scowl sits firmly on my face. His tongue runs along his perfectly straight, white teeth as his lips curve into a smug smile. "A little loud, eh?" He tips his head toward the clock. I shrug a shoulder in response and focus back on the doodle on my lap.

Movement interrupts my focus, and my perusal stops short at the comical sight.

My very professional, very grown-up shrink is scooting his chair towards me on the thick carpet in small bursts as the wheels struggle to gain traction.

His large frame thrusts forward as much as the dense material will allow. Not only are his actions fucking hilarious to see, but his face of focus has me full belly laughing before he reaches me.

His arms flail outward beside him. Slicing through the air like he's competing in a breaststroke heat to gain enough momentum to propel ahead. His face is screwed up in concentration, his brow is furrowed, and his gaze is narrowed on the floor. His bottom lip is tucked in, and his tongue has tipped out to cover his steep cupid's bow.

Our eyes meet. Mine misty with laughter-induced tears, his with pride, determination, and arrogance. He finally comes to a stop in front of me, knee to knee. I simply shake my head, a small smile playing on my lips as I press my ballpoint pen back to my paper.

A line begins to appear before me. Ink flows out of the fountain pen in a straight line, gliding gracefully across its canvas. I watch transfixed as another line is duplicated at its side. The fountain pen elegantly weaves a lattice on the lined parchment.

I glance up at Dr. Turner, my eyes questioning. He looks down, his pen still moving. Without words, he merely tips his chin down at the paper. When I look back down, my shoulders shake with barely restrained laughter.

There's an "o" in the top right corner of the grid. I humor him and place my "x" in the top left corner.

Dr. Turner scoffs at me like I just made the gravest of mistakes. Yeah, okay, Mr. I-Have-A-Masters-Degree. That degree doesn't mean shit in the house of Charlotte, Reigning Queen of Tic-Tac-Toe. You can take your little "o" and go cry alone in the corner when I stomp your ass at this game.

Completely ignorant of the trash talk flowing throughout my brain, he marks the next "o" in the center. I inwardly punch the air in celebration. He's fucked now. I place my "x" in the bottom left corner and smirk at him. He simply shrugs a shoulder, not bothered by the move, as he puts his next "o" in the bottom right corner. "Checkmate, biotch!" I declare as I put the winning "x" in the middle left column.

I pause the small victory wiggle sesh I'm having in my chair when I sense eyes fixated on me, and I remember I'm not alone.

Heat blooms over my cheeks, and I shrink into myself a little. I chance a look up, and sure enough, Dr. Turner is watching me with amusement −and a little something undefined− dancing across his handsome face. *Jesus Christ.*

I clear my throat, pretending the last ten seconds or so didn't happen. I didn't just perform an embarrassing shimmy for my therapist. That was simply a shared hallucination... nope, didn't happen at all.

"Ah, she speaks," he jokes, reminding me of the vow of silence I had entered with myself. I internally kick myself for breaking said vow.

I scoff at him, "I speak when there's someone worthy to listen," I sassily refute.

"I take it you haven't designated me into the worthy category yet. Tell me, Miss Johnson, how does one find themselves in your good graces?"

Yet? The balls on this man. Why would I talk to him? He's one of *them.* Anything I say will be jotted down in his little notebook, surely to be passed around like a shared joke between staff members. My eyes roll of their own accord at his audacity.

A gentle hand rests on my knee. I look up to its owner, distrust filling my gaze. "I would *never* break your trust. What goes on inside these four walls is strictly between you and me. Unless I fear for your safety or the safety of others, I am a steel vault of secret keeping. You can trust me, Miss Johnson," he avows, pleading with his words and eyes for me to open up, to let him in.

Can I?

Should I?

My lips purse, as if the secrets that beg to stay locked up came down to guard the entrance into their sacred tomb. They are trapped in the deep recesses of my mind. Secured in a box, wrapped in barbed wire, and tucked in the forgotten corner of my anguish and avoidance.

Do I want to filet myself open for yet another person? Will the sight of my flayed, darkened soul send him running for the nearest straight jacket and a shot of Lorazepam?

I have nowhere to hide, nothing to numb the pain. I'm forced to sit with my thoughts and memories, day in and day out. This place is supposed to help me get better? All it's doing is bringing my worst traits to the surface, placing them on display for those who wish to get a gander.

Might as well place me in a pretty clear box to sit atop a pretty shelf with a placard that reads: Here sits the poor depressed girl whose mom died. The girl who went crazy and wanted to kill herself, but she was too much of a coward, and she almost died anyway. She pushed away the boy who wanted to love her and ended up in this shit hole, alone. Or, you know, something

83

shorter that's bright and shiny.

My lips roll together, tightening the entrance to the covert echoes that dwell beyond. The grip on my pen increases, the cylinder embedding itself into my flesh. My jaw clenches repeatedly, the indecision playing out on my molars.

A deep breath flows from my lips, an unsealing of the tomb beginning.

"I've fantasized about my death since I was little. Do you know how many ways you can kill yourself, Dr. Turner?" I turn my focus to the death grip I have on my pen and bring my other hand to it, rolling it back and forth between my palms. Like I could light a fire of acceptance in my hands.

"In my mind, I've died a thousand times. Each time, more imaginative than the last. I've lived a thousand lives, and they all end the same way. At my hand," my voice flows steadily as the darkness ebbs out of me.

Dr. Turner is silent, his presence looming but not imposing.

"Do you know what it's like to be scared of your own thoughts and have those in charge of protecting you act like nothing is wrong? Brush it under the rug and take you to some quack who throws a bottle of pills at you and says, 'Okay, take these, and you should be good to go'," I laugh, though the sound carries no humor, "I'll tell you what, you get used to hiding your real feelings for the comfort of others real quick. I've spent my whole life pretending to be someone else just to make everyone else feel better. They couldn't tell that I wanted to fucking die inside. That I *was* dying. As long as I fit the mold of the normal, presentable girl, no one dared to peek further,"

My head shakes, the disappointment flaring up inside at the thought of those closest to me overlooking my wounds for the sake of ease.

"You know what my last thought was as my body was shutting down from the drugs that were forced inside me? My vision was hazy, and I kept going in and out of consciousness. Pain like I've never experienced before coasted through my body as the poison settled into my veins. Sounds of my rescuers whomped in and out of my ears, and all I could think was– "

The pen continues to roll between my palms as I look up at Dr. Turner, our eyes locked onto one another. He instinctively leans forward ever so slightly.

" – fucking finally."

Chapter 13

Dear Mom,

I'm so angry. I don't want to be. Not at you. But I am. Fuck, how could you leave me? This isn't how this is supposed to go.

I miss you. So much.

I can't stop thinking about all the things you will be missing out on—my college experience, the heart-stopping midnight phone call telling you I've been picked up by campus security for streaking—but you'll forgive me because it was a drunken dare, and Johnsons don't back down from dares.

Meeting Zach. He's a good guy. You would've liked him. He would have charmed the shit out of you. You would've threatened him. He would've pretended to be scared like the gentleman he is. I think I may love him, Momma.

Something holds me back. I don't know what it is, but I can't give him all of me. He deserves that, a whole person. Not this broken, mismatched mess that I've made of myself.

My graduation. My career. The first time I get written up because I'm irresponsible and, as you like to say, "will be late to my own funeral" and have a "problem with authority".

My wedding.

My children.

Fuck. fuck!

There was a rift between you and me. I know I caused it, but I wish you were here. I need you, Momma. I don't know how to do this without you.

How do I move forward? How does the world continue without Amelia Johnson?

You were a bright spot in my dark world. I'm afraid, Momma. So afraid that the darkness will swallow me whole and I'll never find my way back out.

You've left a huge void in my life, and nothing will fill it. I'll always have this emptiness with me.

So here I am. Empty. Angry. Confused. Devastated. Numb.

I just miss you. So much. I love you.

–Lola

Chapter 14

January 2007

Zach

"Morris! Get off your ass. I'm tired of watching you mope around all the time. You are coming out with me. It's fucking Friday night. You've been here for a week and have yet to leave this damn room if it isn't for a meeting with Coach," my roommate, Tucker Lewis, harasses me. I groan and roll away from him on my bed to face the wall laden with posters of half-naked chicks on various vehicles.

"Fuck off, Tuck. I ain't goin' to a fuckin' frat party. All that sweat, bravado, and sausage just ain't my scene," I lob back at him. I know this is college, but damn, there is a party literally every day. Not that I've ever been huge into the party life, but especially lately, my mood is shit.

That'll happen when you're forced to move across the country at a moment's notice and can't tell the girl you love that it's happening.

She's going to think I abandoned her. That she isn't important to me. That I'm a liar like all the other men in her life. Goddamnit.

Three more weeks. She's out in three weeks. But my parents couldn't be bothered to wait any longer. Now, here I am in Alabama. Attending a prestigious college with a promising football career ahead of me, and I couldn't care less about any of it. I just want my girl. Fuck, I am a sad sack. Maybe I do need to get out of this room and out of my head for a while.

Rolling to my back, I flick a look at my roommate hovering in front of the mirror on his dresser. It's too short for his 6'4 frame, so he has to duck to see himself as he runs gel through the tips of his short, frosted hair.

We lock eyes in the reflection, and a slow, sinister smile takes over his mouth. "Hells yeah, dude. Let's fucking go!"

His lip curls up slightly, his nose flaring as if he smelled a dead animal or something. "Uh, bro, maybe run through a shower first. You're becoming one with the bed. I'm trying to get laid tonight, and I don't want your stank ass running off the ladies."

I roll my eyes and sit up. Lifting my arm over my head, I take a whiff of my underarm, and I'll be damned if he ain't right. I huff out a breath and go to my dresser, pulling out a plain white tee, my ripped black jeans, a pair of boxers, and socks. With an arm full of my clothes, I grab my toiletry kit in the other and head off to our shared shower.

As we pull up, the music pumps through the walls, seeping into the air surrounding the frat house. Tuck parks his two-seater along the curb of what is dubbed "fraternity row", and we exit the car.

Walking up the paved walkway to the front of the house, red plastic cups and bits of trash litter the front yard. Fucking animals. I hate frat boys.

I shrug off my piss-poor attitude and slide into the good ol' southern charmer I'm expected to be.

As we approach the front door, it swings inward, and a smoking hot brunette stumbles out, her heel catching on the door frame. I reach out and catch her before she eats shit. She giggles and looks up at me like I hung the damn moon. Cartoon hearts in her eyes and all.

I chuckle, "You alright, darlin'?" She groans and closes her eyes. When she reopens them, they peruse my body slowly. I move to stand her up straight, her body unsteady due to the copious amount of alcohol if the stench of Eau de Vodka has anything to do with it.

Holding my hands at her shoulders to steady her, I lean down to eye level. Her glassy sea-foam eyes stare back at me with uneven blinks. I take the moment to look over her attire. Confused as to why she's wearing a tee shirt that seems to be four sizes too big that hangs down to her knees, leaving only her bare legs on display. She looks like she played dress-up in her daddy's closet before the party.

"Top-smop," she slurs out with a cackle and a snort, her small hand slapping my chest at what she must think was the funniest joke ever. "I mean top-SWAP," she corrects herself while still leaving me confused as hell.

Tuck huffs a laugh beside me. His elbow taps my rib, and he tips his chin towards the house, "That's the theme tonight, newb, top-swap. The girls pick guys' names out of a jar, and they swap tops... and usually bodily fluids." He throws his head back, howling laughter.

I throw a lop-sided smile down at the drunk co-ed, "What's your name, sweetheart?"

She lowers her lashes, staring up at me with sex written all over her face, "Kierra." She answers in a slurred whisper.

"Well, Kierra, do you have a safe way home tonight?" I ask, ever the gentleman. She nods softly at me while tucking a loose strand of hair behind her ear.

"Kierra!" A shout behind us interrupts the conversation. We all turn and see a black car with two girls in the front and one hanging out of the window in the back seat, hollering her name.

"That your ride darlin'?"

"Mhm, unless..." She leaves the answer open-ended, the invitation clear in her voice. She doesn't need to, not for me. She won't get what she's looking for here. But I'm not a complete asshole, so I let her down easy.

"Maybe another time, sweetness. You better get goin' now. Have a good night, Kierra." I whisper in her ear as I walk past her, throwing her a wink and start into the throng of bodies. Tuck catches up to me and hits my stomach with the back of his hand, "What the fuck, man? That chick was eye-fucking you hardcore. You coulda had that." He huffs.

Looking back at him, I shake my head, "Ain't happenin' Tuck. First, she was drunk as fuck, and I ain't that guy. Second, I don't want 'that'."

I pause in the middle of the foyer to take in the scene around me. Looks pretty much like every college party movie I've ever seen, minus the room with dog semen-filled doughnuts. Wall-to-wall bodies. Guys in bras, halters, some even in dresses. A couple of the dudes are just rocking their bare chests. Chicks wearing jerseys, tees, button-downs, and a few topless. Now the half-naked guys make more sense. Can't swap a top if there's no top to be had.

Tuck bumps into me from behind, propelling me towards a room behind the large stairwell. As we pass the kitchen, he

91

grabs two beers from the red and white cooler. I crack the top and take a swig. I tilt the bottle towards the back door. I need some air already. We step out onto the back patio.

Glancing up at the sky, a pang of disappointment floods my chest when I can't spot that pot-shaped constellation. The distance feels greater and greater every day.

"Yo, Lewis!" Someone shouts at my roommate from across the yard. There's a group of people gathered around a small bonfire. Most sit in white plastic chairs. Some are mulling around in small groups chatting, and a few girls are sitting on some of the guys' laps.

Tuck nods in their direction, and I follow him over. The group expands outward to absorb us. We smoothly assimilate into the collective. Tuck immediately engages in conversation with a few dudes I recognize from the team. He may be one of the best defensive linemen I've ever played with, but the dude is a jabber mouth. Most big boys tend to be strong silent types, in my experience, but not Tuck. The man is a goddamn social butterfly.

Finding an empty chair, I plop down in it, stretching my long legs towards the fire. I tip my beer back, taking a large pull. Flames dance across the night, embers flowing towards the sky, their light extinguished early in their journey. The longer I stare at the flames, the more they come to life: a phoenix gliding through the walls of fire, gathering strength to take flight, the guarded snarl of a wolf melting away to a rigid skull bathed in the glowing inferno.

"What's up? Haven't seen you around here before. You new?"

I glance over at the girl to my right. If her thin, skin-tight black tank top is anything to go by, she must not be participating in the top swap. Bringing my bottle to my lips, I take a slow sip as I slide my gaze down to her black pants, which may as well be painted on. I chuckle at the tattered hot pink Chucks on her feet.

Can't a man enjoy a fucking beer at a party without someone trying to get all up on his dick?

I meet her eyes. They're alright if you like the endless ocean type. Her curly, dark strands fall loosely over her heart-shaped face, stopping at her shoulders. I can tell she's tan and fit, even in the firelight. In another life, I'd be all over it. Probably would've already dragged her to the side of the house and slid my fingers inside her pussy, while covering her mouth with my hand to keep her from screaming her pleasure for the whole party to hear.

Hell, in another life, I would've already had the brunette from the front and this chick taking turns choking on my cock in a shadowy corner of the house.

But these days, my dick only gets hard for the blonde sasshole with honey eyes that owns my heart and soul. My Little Bit.

"Not interested." I bite out, a little harsher than I intended, as I keep my focus on the fire.

"Okay, pretty boy. First of all, no one fucking asked. Second, you aren't my type, so why don't you lock up that blimp-sized ego and chill the fuck out." She rebuts with a scoff.

I glance over at her. She's crossed her arms to sit firmly on her chest. Don't know if she's trying to thrust them out and call further attention to them, but that's what she's doing. I snort a laugh and shoot her my most cocky smile, "I'm every girl's type, darlin'. What's wrong," I gesture to the frat house behind us, "not douchey enough for ya?"

93

She tips her head back and barks out a loud laugh. Okay, it wasn't that funny. What's this chick's problem?

After a good twenty seconds or so of her laughing in my face, she looks back at me and swipes a tear away from her full cheek. "Oh honey–" she starts and pats my hand condescendingly, " – I'm afraid you have too much equipment for me." She aims a pointed glare at my crotch, "I like my partners to have a little less cock and balls and a little more tits and clit."

Oh.

I narrow my eyes at her in suspicion, "For real?" I ask.

She raises her eyebrows and nods at me like the fucking idiot I am, "Yeah, big boy. Sorry to disappoint." She rolls her eyes and takes a drink of her own beer.

Well, shit. I'm a dick. I shrug my shoulders and shake my head. A defeated smile plays on my lips. I hold my hand out for her, "Zach." She looks over at my outstretched hand, debate warring on her face before she clasps her hand in mine. "Morgan."

"How long you been goin' here?" I ask.

Morgan tilts her head side to side as if calculating the time. "I'm a sophomore, but I took a gap year before starting, so I'm a little older than most folks in my class. You?"

"Nice. I also took a bit of a gap, but I'm startin' my freshman year. I ain't as far behind as I shoulda been since I took a few courses in high school, but here I am, nevertheless."

My fingers nervously peel at the label on the neck of my beer bottle. The din of conversation around us increases in volume like someone is turning the knob slowly up. The tension in my neck forces me to roll it side to side, desperate for relief. I could really use a joint and a blow job. Neither of which I can fucking have.

"Whoa, wound up pretty tight, ain't cha?" Morgan jests at my obvious discomfort with a pointed look towards the destruction my fingers are wreaking on the label.

My first instinct is to tell her to pound sand and leave me the fuck alone. But ain't that why I came tonight? To get out of the room and out of my head for a night. I could use a new friend. Not that Tuck ain't good, but he's a lot to handle all at once. It would be nice to have some options. It might be nice to have a woman around to chill with that I don't have to worry about getting weird or making shit something that it ain't.

I relax my hand, resting the bottle on my thigh and flicking what's left of the label towards the flames. Turning to Morgan, I force a smile to my face and lean my beer bottle towards her. "I'm workin' on it, Morgs." She laughs at her new nickname and clinks her bottle with mine in cheers. "Well, okay then, Pretty Boy. Let me go grab us another round."

"Morris, you good?" A tipsy Tucker wraps his arm around my shoulder, squeezing me in a little too tightly to his side. Man, this fucker doesn't know his own strength sometimes. I shove his big body to the side, moving him very little, "Yeah, man, I'm alright. I'm gonna have another beer or two and then head out. You gonna be ready to go, or do I need to make it back on my own?" I ask.

His eyes are locked onto a dancing group of girls across the yard, not paying me no mind at all. I nudge his rib with my elbow to get his attention back, "Tuck! Did you hear me?" Eyes never leaving the writhing bodies, he nods his head, in answer to which question I have no fucking idea. I roll my eyes and shove him with more force. He stumbles away, laughing. Guess I'm on my own.

I lean back in the chair, hoping the cheap plastic holds up against my weight, and stare at the dotted clouds lining the pitch-black sky.

Hands thread through my hair and scratch along my scalp. My head jerks forward, and I swing around to see a petite girl dressed in a men's ribbed A-shirt, clearly no bra and possibly no panties. If she is wearing panties, it's a G-string or flesh-colored. The sharp lines of her platinum blonde bob complement the softness of her jawline.

She's probably one of the most attractive chicks I've seen on campus. Full plump lips, lined in blood-red lipstick. Smokey tones cover her eyelids. A sweet floral smell that isn't overpowering wafts off her warm, silky skin. And it does fucking nothing for me. Nothing but cause me irritation.

Before I can tell her to get her damn claws off me, a voice from beside her barks out, "Back the fuck off, Hooker Barbie. I see you touch my man again, and I'll rip that dusty ass wig right off your head and shove it up your ass. You got me?"

Blondie stares at me in horror. Half expecting me to stand up for her and half expecting me to let Morgan follow through on her threat. I just shrug at her and turn my attention back to Morgan. She looks down at me with a wink and slides onto my lap, "Here's your beer, baby," she purrs just loud enough for Blondie to hear. Apparently, she takes the hint as she stomps her foot and huffs before storming away.

Morgan laughs loudly before shoving off of me. She sits back in her chair and tips her bottle to clink with mine. "You're welcome."

I laugh, fit to split at her performance. Clinking my bottle with hers again, I offer her an earnest, heartfelt grin. "I think we're gonna be good friends, Morgs."

Chapter 15

Zach

How the hell can I have this much homework already? It's the second damn week of the semester, and my shit is overflowing. I throw my History and Foreign Language textbooks in my bookbag.

Looking around the dorm room I share with Tuck, I find myself smiling at our messy little slice of life. It's small, it's a disaster, and it smells like an old jock half the time, but it's ours. No Lieutenant Colonel to order me around. No random spot checks. No hospital corners. Just pure fucking chaos, and I love it.

I nod to the librarian, Claire, as I pass her to head to the table that I've unofficially claimed over the last two weeks. Sitting at the large circular table, I spread out my texts, notebooks, and pens. Ready to tackle some of these assignments.

An hour later, only one assignment has been completed and I'm a blank canvas. All the scholarly knowledge I may possess ain't nowhere to be found.

So, I do what I always do when I need to get my mind right. I pull out a blank sheet of notebook paper and start writing.

Little Bit,

Man, you would not believe how much homework you get in college. I thought Mr. Vale's class was the be-all-end-all to mountains of lessons, but nope, Professor Allen tops them all. Dick face looking asshole. During his lecture yesterday, some chick was talking in my row, and he kicked ME out of class. Wouldn't hear a fucking word of "excuses" from me about who was or wasn't talking. So, not only does my history professor already hate me, but now I have to find someone to get notes from about whatever I missed after he kicked me out.

Honestly, I was hoping school would be kind of like RHS, with the teachers catering to the athletes. I'm not saying I wouldn't do any hard work, but it would be nice to have a little bit of a break. My goose is cooked, sweetheart, between strength training, team meetings, practice, and assignments.

Here I am bitching about my course load, and you're there. I miss yo–

"Oh, who's Little Bit, Pretty Boy?" Morgan teases as she falls into the chair beside me with a thud.

I quickly shove the letter into my notebook, away from prying eyes.

"None of your fuckin' business, nosey," I answer, good-natured amusement coating my tone as I reach my pen over and tap the back against the tip of her nose.

She slaps my hand away in jest, "Aha! Pretty Boy's got a girlfriend." She cups her mouth and sings, "Pretty Boy and Little Bit sitting in a tree, F-U-C-K-I-N-G."

I swat at her arm and shush her, "What are you, five? Act like you got some damn sense, woman. We are in a library, for God's sake." I chance a look at Claire, who is indeed staring daggers at me and my uninvited friend. I ain't gonna let her ruin the good rapport Claire and I got going on. I kick her shin in warning when she continues loudly giggling.

"Ow, what the hell, Pretty Boy?" she grumbles.

I shoot a pointed look toward the librarian. Morgan meets Claire's death glare and shrinks back in her chair, holding her hands up in apology.

"I didn't take you for such a goody-good." She whispers.

I close my textbooks, gather my papers, and start putting everything in my bookbag. It's clear there will be no more studying going on right now. "I ain't a fuckin' goody-good. I just wasn't raised in a damn barn and have some respect for my elders," I meet her eyes and wink at her so she knows I'm just giving her a hard time.

"Now, since you ruined my study time, how about you treat me to one of those yummy chocolatey shits you brought to Comp Ed a few days ago."

"It's called a Frappucino, you fucking caveman." She retorts.

"Yeah, whatever, that. Get a move on, youngin'," I shoo her with my hands out of the library, and we make our way to the campus coffee shop for a fucking yummy chocolate shit. I'll be damned if you catch me ordering a fucking frappelattcino bullshit.

* * *

My muscles are screaming for rest. The tendons are wound so tightly that they may snap at any moment, but I refuse to stop. My body takes the punishment my mind can't stand. I pump the bar again, down to my chest, bumping off the inflated muscle and back up to full arms-length, and over again.

Sweat drips down my face as the cadence of my heavy breaths echoes throughout the gym with each rep.

Just ten more, I tell myself.

It's never just ten more. I'll go until my arms resemble jello and shake from the relentless force. Each descent of the bar is another controlled plunge into my control and resistance. Down. Up. Down. Up. The war against the iron is long and hard-fought, but iron always wins in the end.

My arms tremble as I slam the bar back on the rack. The metal thunk reverberates throughout the room.

"Whoa, bro. Who pissed in your Cheerios this morning?" Tuck asks with a snap of his hand towel against my thigh.

I lay panting on the bench press pad, staring at the ceiling, waiting for my heart rate to return to a normal speed. I flip him the bird.

"Seems like someone needs to get some pootang," he ribs, standing in the spotter area of the bench press, peering down at me. "Good news for you, we don't have practice tomorrow. So your lame ass ain't got no excuse for not coming down to the Pit with me and the guys."

The "guys" make up half of our defensive line. From what I can tell, they're mostly good dudes, but I haven't made much of an effort to get to know them, except one: Keegan "Key" Hostead. Key is the Crimson Tide's best defensive tackle, and he knows it. He's a force to be reckoned with on the field—a wall of rage and dominance.

Off the field, he revels in belittling everyone around him. Carries himself with a disdainful swagger, and condescension drips from every smile he offers. Such a prick.

He's the only teammate we hang out with that has a steady girlfriend and will still fuck everything that moves when we go anywhere while lying through his teeth to her. She has to hear the rumors. Hell, maybe she's even seen some of the nudes that he saves proudly on his phone, and she still chooses to stay. Maybe she thinks she can cash in on an NFL payday if she rides his coattails long enough. Keep them jersey chasers far the fuck away from me. Little Bit is nothing like these desperate ball sluts.

I don't like explaining what I have with Little Bit to anyone here, but both Tuck and Morgan know I've got a situation back in Alaska. I don't like to talk about it, but I'm not interested in getting with anyone. Morgan accepted it as fact without any further conversation. Tuck is Tuck and believes having "hoes in different area codes" is okay. I just ignore him. He doesn't push it too much... so far.

I reach for my water bottle on the ground beside me and pop the mouthpiece open. I give it a solid squeeze, sending a stream of cold water right into his face. I thrust myself into a sitting position before any of it can drip back onto me and laugh heartily at his shocked face.

"Fine. But you're payin' the fuckin' cover this time, ass-hole." I point my finger in his face as I agree.

The Pit is a local club. Of the dancer variety... Alright, it's a titty bar. The bouncers are Crimson Tide fans – not many folks who ain't around these parts– and forgo checking our IDs at the entrance. They don't, however, wave the twenty-dollar cover charge to get in. Something about them supporting us all season long so we can support the dancers when we come in. All for a good cause, I suppose.

"Welcome back, fellas," the burly, Billy Bob-looking

bouncer says as he parts the blackout curtain covering the entrance.

We stand at the entrance, taking in the glowing strobing lights, neon attire, and poofed-up hair of the dancers and servers. The guys and I throw questioning looks at each other before the bouncer interjects, "80s night, boys. Music is a steady stream of hair bands. Drinks are two-for-one until 2 AM."

We nod and make our way to a large booth in the center of the room.

A dancer gyrates against the floor-to-ceiling length pole on the stage. Her neon green bikini bottom glows under the black lights around the room. A beacon of sex and secrets, daring you to imagine what lies beneath. Her blonde Farrah Faucett-like hair bounces with each of her ministrations, her dewy skin shining like a radiant morning glow against the metal.

The dancer drops to her knees and crawls to the edge of the stage, her eyes locked on Jimmy Floyd, our defensive end. Like a lamb to slaughter, he struts to the chair before the stage. Heart full of hope, head full of lust, and hand full of cock and singles.

A server with waist-length brown pin-straight hair, dressed in a neon pink tube top with matching booty shorts and neon yellow fishnets, on roller skates, rolls over and sets a tray of cherries on the stage. She pops one in her mouth and sends a wink my way before rolling back to the bar.

Another server, dressed like the other girl, rolls up to our crew, "Hiya boys, welcome to the Pit. I'm your server for the evening, Chastity. Can I get y'all something to drink?" The group lets out a collective snigger at her stage name before listing their orders.

Picking up my Miami Vice, I take a tentative sip. The pineapple and cranberry juice pair nicely with the rum and go down smoothly. I have to watch it, or I may find myself inebriated by accident. This shit is delicious.

I excuse myself to hit the head. The long, dark hallway is a shocking contrast to the blindingly light bathroom. My eyes take a moment to focus. The walls are covered with titty shots. No faces. Light ones. Dark ones. Members of the IBTC with little chocolate chip-sized nipples. Tig ol' bitties with large gum drop-sized nipples. And my personal favorite, sagging wrinkly ones with no discernable nipple to be seen. This place has seen all kinds, and they clearly don't discriminate.

After I take a piss and wash my hands, I look at the man in the mirror. I look normal. My hair gelled and tousled to look like I just got out of bed. White tee, snugged tightly across my muscular chest, short sleeves wrapped firmly over my biceps that seem to bulge out of the thin material. Black ripped jeans, fitting like a dream down to my signature skate shoes. But my eyes. Melancholy lingers, and lightness is dimmed.

As I walk down the hallway, the speakers overhead blare out a ballad about a sweet cherry pie. The previously quiet and calm hallway fills with the raucous noise from the ever-growing crowd. Hooting and hollering for the girl on stage, who I gather is about to do some unsavory things with that tray full of cherries.

Debauchery and neon fill every corner of the club. Alabama may be on the Bible belt, but these girls keeping their bottoms on doesn't stop the filth that goes on between clients from time to time. By the looks of things, Floyd hopes this will be that time. I watch with a smirk as he rises from his seat and makes his way to the stage. His fit form allows him to jump up with one hand on the stage with ease.

Floyd's got one handful of Cherry's tit and one of her ass when he's tackled by one of the security team. Cherry quickly grabs the singles, still flowing slowly to the ground from the force of his takedown, before she scrambles to the back behind the red glittery curtain.

The security guy throws Floyd off the stage. He staggers as he tries to stand back up. The guy jumps down beside him and grabs him by the collar, "Y'all are done for tonight. Out!" He shouts at our group.

Tuck looks like someone just kicked his puppy as he gently pushes the dancer off his lap and adjusts his boner before sulking out after us.

"Can't have anything nice, can I? Fuck, Floyd, I'm gonna have blue balls for a month. You're such a dick!" Tuck complains as we pile into the bed of Key's pickup truck and head back to campus. Laughter flowing in the wind behind us.

Chapter 16

January 2007

Charlotte

" – The courage to change the things I can, and the wisdom to know the difference." Our hands clasp together and raise up and down with the chant, "It works if you work it, so work it because you're worth it!" My enthusiasm is not on the same level as the other four in this meeting, but I get away with it by mouthing the words and making eye contact.

Ninety days.

Ninety days without drugs.

Ninety days without Priest.

Ninety days.

Should be a joyous occasion. I should be celebrating my accomplishment. But all I can think of is how I traded one toxic relationship for another.

I'm still being told what to do daily by an oppressive prick with a small peen.

I'm still being forced to take drugs. Even if these are legal.

My body still isn't mine. My wants still don't matter. How can I celebrate that? Even when I get out of here in a week, it doesn't just end. I have court-ordered therapy sessions twice a week, random drug testing, and must stay on the medications I'm currently taking for two full years.

"That's it for tonight, guys. Thanks for a great meeting." Joe, the drug counselor who runs our NA meeting, says while the rest of us gather the chairs and stack them together in the corner.

I'm almost out of the room before he calls out to me, "Hey Charlotte, hang back a minute, would you?"

I hold my blue book tightly against my chest as I make my way back to him. He's tall, maybe six feet, with shoulder-length gray hair and a full Santa beard. He's thin and wiry, always wearing rainbow suspenders over his checkered button-ups. He's a hot mess, but he's nice, and that's a rarity in this place.

I glance up at him expectantly. "I just wanted to thank you for your share tonight. Trust me, I know what it's like to divulge some of your darkest moments of horror to total strangers. I commend you for being brave enough to tell your story. You're being released next week, right?" he asks, a genuine smile on his face.

I nod, emotion clogging my throat. I'm afraid of the sound that may escape if I choose words.

"Excellent. Here," he reaches into his back pocket and pulls out a crinkled yellow brochure. I take it and read the top **RIVER VIEW NA MEETING SCHEDULE.** I look back at Joe, and my eyes fill with the tears I refuse to let fall.

He places a hand gently on my shoulder, a reassurance. "I know a few people who make some of those meetings. I put a star next to the ones I think you would benefit from attending. I would tell you their names, but you know..." he gives me a knowing look before we both answer, "Anonymous."

I thank him and tuck the brochure safely inside my blue book, heading back to my shared room.

Ari sits on her bed, adding to the ever-growing chain of gum wrappers that she's laced together in a lattice pattern over the time she's been here.

"How was the meeting?" she asks, not bothering to raise her eyes to me and disturb her focus.

I set my book on the nightstand, kick my shoes off, and lay across my bed on my stomach. "It was... a lot," I admit, recalling giving the group the cliff notes version of my descent into indulgence and immoral behavior.

She pauses her fingers and looks up at me, concern on her cherub face. I wave her off, "I'm fine, Ari. I just talked about some shit that was hard to remember. But I do feel a little better," I offer her a placating smile, which she accepts and returns to her project.

"I'm starving. Let's hit the caf. I heard it was taco night. You know how I feel about tacos, Ari. They rarely feed us anything with a spice palette in this place, and I'm not missing it!" I stand, slip my shoes back on, and walk to the end of her bed. I bend down, grabbing her shoes, and thrust them in her face, "Move your ass, Red!"

* * *

Fucking pain.
    Shit.
    Bile.
    More pain.

Mouth vomit.

Ass vomit.

Agony.

The cool tile is a balm against my heated, sweat-soaked cheeks. As another cramp hits my stomach, my nails search for anything to dig into on the hard surface.

Which fucking way is it coming out this time? Neither end can handle much more. My throat is raw from the acidic bile expelling out of it repeatedly. And my ass is on fucking fire. I wouldn't be surprised if my rectum has eroded and bloody shits await me at the next round of ass vomit.

A soft knock on the door calls for my attention, but I can't move. I grunt and think I may get out a "Uhn" kind of answer. Aurelia's gentle voice flows through the door, "Charlie, are you okay? You've been in there for almost two hours."

When I don't answer, she opens the door. Her gasp tells me the sight before her is not a pretty one.

I am buck naked, curled around the toilet with my ass pointed towards the shower area of the bathroom. Thank God this place is set up just like a hospital, and the shower isn't in its own room. There is no separation between the toilet, sink, and shower tile. The only thing that creates the illusion of a separate space is the track on the ceiling, which allows a small sliding curtain to protect part of the room from getting soaked when the shower is on.

"Oh my God, Charlie," she kneels down behind me, her hands hovering over my body. She's not sure what to touch or not to touch. "What can I do? What do you need?" she asks urgently.

I squeeze my eyes shut, another cramp rolling in, this one making its way up my chest. I thrust myself forward over the toilet bowl. Heaving over and over as the cramps roll up and down my chest to my stomach. There's no material left in my stomach to come out. But that doesn't stop the action.

When the heave lessens, I lay my cheek against the toilet seat and meet Ari's concerned gaze. "Get help." Is all I get out before the next cramp hits. This time, it rolls south, and the ass volcano erupts once more.

I must have lost consciousness. I'm in my bed with a hospital gown on. The one with the wide open backside.

A soothing hand glides over my back, "Charlotte, honey, I need you to roll onto your side and tuck your legs as close to your chest as you can," the sweet nurse, Janice, instructs me. Every part of my body is in distress. My legs feel like they are encased in cement as I draw them up, putting myself in the fetal position.

"Very good, thank you. You're doing great. You're going to feel my fingers on your bottom," she walks her fingers gently across my ass, parting my cheeks. "Now, I am going to insert a suppository. It shouldn't hurt, but due to the... affected area, you may feel some discomfort. It will be quick, and you will feel better much quicker this way," she assures me as she inserts the small cylinder into my bum.

I would be humiliated if I could muster any energy to give a single fuck.

"All done. You did great, Charlotte. Do the best you can to get some rest. The medication will work quickly. I will excuse you from morning activities. Someone will be by to check your vitals every two hours." I groan, not looking forward to constant interruptions of whatever sleep I may get. "Don't worry, dear, they won't have to wake you to take your temperature and blood pressure." She pats my arms in a

109

comforting manner.

The snap of her glove removal makes me jolt, and I immediately regret my response. My muscles balk at the action and burn with rebellion.

Janice delicately rolls me onto my back and tucks the blanket around my chest. Smoothing away the hair glued to my forehead with sweat and other things I refuse to acknowledge, she whispers, "Rest, dear. It'll be over soon."

* * *

A clatter startles me from slumber. I peek an eye open and catch Ari frozen in mid-stride with a food tray in her hand. Her face is pinched in irritation. "Fudge," she curses under her breath. We lock eyes, and I raise an eyebrow at her.

"Heck, Charlie, I'm sorry. I was trying to be quiet." She sighs as she continues her trek across the room and places the tray on my nightstand.

"Bang up job, Ari." I tease.

She pats my side with the back of her hand in a "move over" gesture. "You need to put something inside your stomach. I brought you soup and apple juice with pretzels,"

My stomach roils at the thought of food. "Don't make that face at me, Charlie." She huffs. I wasn't aware I was making a face. "That one. Stop it."

I roll my eyes and start scooting upwards, taking way too long to enter a sitting position against the head of the bed. Ari lifts the soup bowl to me, my lip curls, and I snap my head to the other side. "Okay... not the soup. How about a little juice, hm?"

I take my stomach's lack of outward protest as a sign of consent and accept the cup.

Taking small sips of the apple juice, I decide maybe I can handle the pretzels.

Ari holds out a handful of the crunchy snack like she's reading my mind. I close my eyes and take a tentative bite, praying with everything I have to every God I've heard of that it decides to settle in my stomach and fucking stay there.

A few minutes pass, and everything that goes in stays in. Thank whatever God made it happen.

"You know, Red? You're alright. I think I'll keep you around for a while," I tell her, pointing a pretzel in her face. She leans in and bites it from my fingers with sass, "You're damn right. There's no getting rid of me now. I've seen all the crap you have to offer, literally, and I'm still here. You got me for life, sis."

"You cussed! You're turning into quite the rapscallion, Red. Maybe you shouldn't hang around me after all," I cackle, the look of pride beaming from every part of my being. She's finally coming out of her shell. And man, she's glorious.

"Do you know the worst part of all of this?" I ask her, a wave of seriousness weaving through my words.

"What?"

"This fucking place ruined tacos for me, Ari. Tacos! If I never see another taco in my life, it'll be too soon." I shriek.

She pats my arm condescendingly. "There, there, Charlie. You'll make it through this. I know you will. You'll live to enjoy tacos once again. Someday."

I glare at my roommate, "Fucking tacos, Ari. Tacos!"

* * *

"How are you feeling about tomorrow?" Dr. Turner asks, knowing damn well the answer is not fucking good.

How can I feel okay about walking into that courtroom and seeing *his* face again? I thought I would look forward to this. As a matter of fact, I have been looking forward to this. The day I get to have his future in the palm of my hand.

I've rehearsed my words over and over. Sometimes out loud to myself in the bathroom mirror. I would make sure to hit the jury right in the feels with my facial expressions as I detailed every sick and depraved thing he did to me while shucking out his drugs to their children. It would be amazing. They would lock him up and throw away the key. Problem solved.

But the closer the day gets... The more I lose my nerve and dread going.

"Not good," I answer simply.

Dr. Turner closes his notebook, placing it off to the side with his pen on top. "That's to be expected. Is there anything I could do to help? Do you want to go over your testimony?"

I shake my head. "My lawyer went through it with me yesterday at our meeting. And again today on the phone. I'm sure we'll go over it again before I actually take the stand." I nervously fiddle with the drawstring on my pants, not making eye contact.

Tears cloud my vision, and I blink them back furiously in a futile attempt to keep them from falling. The tear streaks down my cheek and settles in the corner of my mouth. Its saltiness floods my senses like it is the secret key to unlocking the safeguard. And the surge begins.

Dr. Turner crouches before me, placing a hand on my knee and tilting my chin up with his other hand. Blearily, I meet his fretful gaze. "What can I do?" he begs.

His strong hand is the only thing holding my head up as the onslaught of tears continues. Each sob escaping my body in a visceral expression of pain. My body trembles with each convulsion of anguish, echoing the weight of my grief.

I cling to his steady hand with both of mine. Small enough to fit in his palm, I latch on like he's the last lifeline I have.

"Be there?" vulnerability shows through my question.

His eyes soften, and he moves his palm to cup my cheek, "Of course."

Chapter 17

Charlotte

David scurries into the conference room, looking around to verify that we are the only occupants. We sit at the large table. He spreads out tons of documents along its surface, arranging them in a way that must make sense to his chaotic brain because it sure as hell doesn't make sense to me.

"Okay, let's go through it again." He declares.

After going through everything a bazillion times, he finally decides I'm ready for the real deal. He gathers all his documents and stuffs them haphazardly into his pristine briefcase. The man is a fucking enigma.

We enter the courtroom, and shock hits me right in the gut. This is nothing like those court shows on TV. Everything is... *more.*

You could fit the entirety of RHS's graduating class of 2006 in the gallery. The judge's bench is huge, at least one and a half of my body tall and at least that wide.

The jury box sits regally in two neat rows of six. A line of windows aligns the top of the wall behind them. Letting light shine upon the dark cloud that seeps into this room.

All of this grandeur for a scumbag like Priest. I shake my

head in annoyance. Taking a deep breath, I scan the expanse of the space, slowly letting it out as I look around the area. My heart stops at the tripods set in each corner behind the gallery. Large news cameras are placed on top of them, pointing at the front of the courtroom.

My heart beats like an out-of-control metronome with no rhythm to be seen. My lungs seize, not letting air in freely. An iron grip locking down my chest, making inhaling nearly impossible.

"Hey, hey. It's okay, Charlotte. You're ready. We've gone over this time and time again. You. Are. Ready." David assures me while holding on to my arms, his face level with mine.

I shake my head, hoping that if my body agrees first, my mind will follow... eventually.

David takes my arm and leads me to the prosecutor's table, where the DA will sit. I have the option of sitting behind him throughout the trial or waiting in the conference room and only being led in when it's time for my testimony.

I've debated this for so long, but I've finally decided that I want to be here the whole time. I want to see Priest's face when his crimes are laid out before him in front of a jury of twelve of his peers and broadcast nationally for everyone else to get a glimpse of this waste of skin.

I settle into the hard wooden pew, brushing the nonexistent lint off my knee-length black skirt. My hands glide down the length of my white blouse. I don't want a single crease in the material. I promised myself there would be zero signs of weakness from me today. Priest doesn't get anything else from me. Not ever again.

I lift my right leg and gently bring it over my left, letting my ankles cross over one another. The immaculate, shiny material of my black Mary-Jane's reflects the area around me in a warped, dark echo of reality.

Armor in place.

Shoulders braced and straight.

Hair and makeup on fucking point.

Let's do this shit.

* * *

I fantasized about this moment long before Priest was arrested.

I also... had nightmares about it.

In my fantasies, he's led in wearing full-body chains. His feet shuffle in tiny steps, reminiscent of an elderly man. His head drooped in shameful remorse, and when his eyes met mine, fear shone brightly in the reflection of the tears pooling in their sockets.

He knew I would be his undoing. The power was mine. The control was mine. I had control of him, for once.

But in my nightmares... He strolls in, untethered, bumps fists with the guards, nods at the prosecutor, smiles at the judge, and when his soulless gaze lands on me... he winks. He takes the stand, points at me, and says, "She's lying. The drugs were hers. Ask anyone around. Charlotte would say and do anything to score. I fell for it... Fell for her, and she turned everything against me. She should be locked up, not me."

I scoff to myself when he spouts out the clear bullshitery, but my amusement quickly fades when I realize that all eyes are now on me. They fucking *believe* him.

When I look down, my cute black pantsuit fades into a

hideous orange jumpsuit. The row of multicolored rubber bracelets lining my delicate wrists is now replaced with a more bulky metal restraint– not the fun kind, either. When I glance at the judge with a pleading look, he simply points at me and tells the bailiff, "Lock her up, Steve."

I usually wake up around the time that I'm thrown into a small cell with a tattered cot and a fully metal toilet. When I reach out for a guard, the cell door is slammed in my face.

David plops down beside me and pats my knee in reassurance, "It's just this one last time, Charlotte. We'll nail the bastard, and then you and the rest of the town can rest easy knowing he's locked away where he can't hurt anybody else."

The words are meant to be comforting, but the dark cloud widens around the room. Thinning the air to mountain peak levels. My teeth gnaw into the soft skin of my bottom lip, and my right leg begins to shake. Nervousness exudes from my body. This isn't what I wanted. *Get it together, Charlie!*

A creaky groan is the only heads-up we get just before people start flooding into the courtroom.

Spectators fill the pews. Neat rows of nameless strangers, relation to the situation unknown, to me at least. All I know is these are strangers to me, and yet they get to be privy to the most humiliating experience of my life. They get to listen to the details of the months of horror I experienced at Priest and his buddies' hands and other body parts.

The contents of my stomach slosh about violently, my hand immediately cupping the middle of my abdomen to soothe the revolt happening below.

A hand lands on my shoulder, and I let out an unfortunate squeal of shock. "I'm sorry honey, it's just me," Mary whispers into my ear. My hand immediately goes to cover hers.

117

I'm sure she can feel the trembles that I'm trying desperately to hide. "Your dad is here as well."

I instantly whip my head around, searching for those treacherous brown eyes that match mine. I narrow my eyes at him. His shoulders sag, and his once handsome features have been battered with emotion and avoidance.

I almost let myself feel sorry for him. My face softens at my sperm donor's silent plea for connection, and then I remember what he did to our family. The once soft expression hardens to stone, *connection denied motherfucker*.

I loosen my grip on Mary's and give it a squeeze before pulling away altogether. Dejectedly, she shrugs a shoulder like, *"Okay, well, I tried"*, and leans down to kiss the top of my head before making her way to Homewrecker Harry back there.

The pews are mostly full. News crews have taken residence along the back wall of the room, all standing. Voice recorders in hand, ready to immortalize my harrowing history for the world. The greedy bastards ready to sip the pipping hot tea born of my pain.

The crowd's murmur dims all at once. Confused, I look around for the source of the change. A haughty man, maybe in his late forties, comes strolling through the door. Wealth seeps from his pores. He seems the type to wipe his ass with hundred-dollar bills.

At least ten years his junior, a breathtaking blonde trots in behind him. She's dressed to the nines. A high-neck, skin-tight, beige bodycon dress is worn like Mr. Vuitton himself stitched on it.

Behind the stunner is the sharp jaw only a TV villain should have. Dark hair perfectly coiffed. Suit pin-straight. Cold, calculating eyes scan the room as his languid gait echoes his father's.

When his gaze lands on me, a slow smirk curls up his lips. Entitlement oozes out of him, stinking up the air with false prominence and submission as he joins his family at the front pew directly behind the defendant's table.

When the defense attorney takes his place at his table after shaking Erick's dad's hand, it begins to make sense.

Poole money paid for his representation, and he's a damn good one. Not like the ones listed on the back of the Gas'N'Go's receipts.

Fuck.

A throat clears from directly behind me, drawing my focus to it.

Dr. Turner.

He came. I smile softly at him when our eyes meet. He nods in hello, his lips quirking up in a delicate wisp of a smile. My lawyer looks back to see who caught my attention and eyes Dr. Turner quizzically.

Dr. Turner pulls out his notebook and begins reading over its contents without acknowledging David. He seems almost... embarrassed. Why would he be?

We both turn back to the front, where the prosecutor has now taken his position and is sorting through several papers, making neat stacks along the tabletop.

A whoosh of air coasts over me as a body lands in the seat beside me. Startled, I jerk my head at the newcomer. A girl with short black hair, wearing a knee-length satin black dress, black tights, and black flats. She looks like she should be attending a funeral.

She's young—maybe fourteen or fifteen—but her eyes and

haunted expression age her far beyond that. I peek around for the adult who will inevitably join her, but after a few minutes, no one comes.

The jury is led in, and Judge Appleton takes his place on his grand throne of justice.

And then it happens.

The side door opens. I squeeze my eyes shut tightly as soft murmurs fill the room. I know what or rather *who* I'll see when I open them.

Barely audible, humming reaches my ears from behind me. A tune I recognize as the one I chanted in his office during the last time I kicked his ass at Tic-Tac-Toe. It's his way of telling me it's okay. That he can't hurt me. That I will make it through this. That Priest will finally get what he deserves. At least, that's what I choose to believe the hymn represents.

Priest looks different. Obviously, he doesn't have access to his nice clothes and fancy products, but his presence is just... less. Less than it used to be. Maybe it's because there are several armed guards between us, giving me false confidence. Maybe I'm just stronger than I've let myself believe.

The thing that captures my attention most is his jumpsuit. Huh. I thought they were orange. But no, his is a denim-washed blue hue with a small pocket on his left pec and, just above that, a small strip of white with numbers on it.

I feel slightly victorious that he is indeed in both ankle and handcuffs. A wave of giddiness skims over my body when the bailiff latches him to the defense table like an animal.

I can do this.

Fuck this guy. He can't hurt me anymore. I refuse to let him. This is when I take back the pieces of me that he stole. The pieces that he ripped out of my bruised and battered body.

They don't belong to him. I don't belong to him.

The girl beside me is vibrating with ragey energy. I wonder how she knows Priest.

I look over at David, who gives me a knowing nod. Yeah. We got this. It's all going to be fine.

The crowd settles as all parties take their places and are ready for the trial to begin.

Unease seeps into my skin. Pricking up my body and coiling around my lungs, a boa of malevolent energy stealing the air I desperately need.

My eyes search for the cause of the sudden dread filling my body.

Dark, demonic eyes are watching me. The same way they've always watched me with sheer hatred and apathy.

Priest nods in my direction, "Astra."

The word is a simple one, but the tone behind it says everything he can't at this moment.

Keep your mouth shut.

I own you.

I'll come for you.

You will never be free of me.

Terror fills me even still when he averts his attention back to the front of the room.

All sounds are muffled as the cloud threatens to overtake me.

I don't hear the swearing-in or Judge Appleton's instructions.

All I hear are the last words he said to me before sending me to my death, *"Fuck, what a waste."*

Chapter 18

Charlotte

Jesus Christ. Why didn't David warn me how long this shit was going to be? It seemed pretty simple to me: we show up, everybody says what he did, the jury says, "Yup, that bastard's guilty", we go home, and Priest gets carted back to prison to play flesh puppet for the top dog on the block. Everyone's happy!

It's been three and a half hours, and we are still on opening statements.

The DA laid out Caleb "Priest" Kirkpatrick's extensive dossier. Apparently, Priest has been involved in many pots around town, and the feds have been watching him for longer than anyone thought.

Possession- Aggravated charge added

Possession of drug paraphernalia

Distribution of a controlled substance- Aggravated charge added

Manufacturing of a controlled substance

Conspiracy to distribute or traffic drugs

Interstate Drug Distribution

Money laundering

Child Endangerment

Sexual Assault– Aggravated charge added

Sexual Battery

Statutory Rape

Rape– Aggravated charge added

Extortion

Robbery

Racketeering

Criminal Threats

Fraud

And my personal favorite,

Attempted Murder

If he's found guilty of even half of his offenses, he will never step foot outside the prison walls again.

David told me he did have a few lesser charges but pleaded those down in exchange for no possibility of extradition to Kentucky to avoid facing capital punishment.

A little birdy told him that Priest agreed to give up his supplier in Kentucky in exchange for leniency regarding the charges he faces here in Alaska.

I kind of wish I could go back to 1957 and not let them abolish capital punishment in this state.

However, if I were wishing to go back in time for things, maybe I'd be better off pulling a Terminator and making sure Priest never comes to exist in the first place. Tick Tock, motherfucker. You better hope that genius guy who invented the internet never finds a way to time travel, 'cause if he does, I'm coming for you.

Would I hesitate to kill a child? Normally I would say, fuck yes, you psycho. But this is kinda like the baby Hitler debate.

Like no, I would never harm a child... unless... that child is

Hitler, or I guess, who grows up to be Hitler. And in this case, grows up to be Priest.

Normally, I'm pretty against murder as a whole. Morality and all that. But I do think there are some prime candidates to be Ed Gein's new roommate, if you know what I mean.

Namely, Hitler and Priest.

"I'd now like to call to the witness stand, Charlotte Johnson." The District Attorney announces to the courtroom.

David hands me the paper with my typed-up statement. The shortened version, anyway. That way, if I totally freeze, I can reference the paper for what I need to say. The paper immediately floats to the floor and lands on top of ragey girl's shoe. When I bend and try to grab it with my trembling hand, she stops me with a hand over mine. We lock eyes, hers an intense shade of cerulean. She squeezes my hand tightly and gives me a sharp nod before letting go and looking back at the front of the courtroom.

What the fuck was that?

I settle into the hard wooden chair on the witness stand. The bailiff hands me a Bible, and I swear to tell all the truths or some shit. I wasn't really listening. The DA starts off by asking me some mundane questions.

How do I know the defendant? How long did we hang out? Was I aware of his business practices? Had I ever witnessed transactions? How old was I the first time we were "intimately acquainted"? His questions seemed to drag on and on. I never once looked at Priest, but I could feel his eyes burning a hole into the side of my head. I know what he's thinking. He's wishing that hit would've killed me. Sometimes, I wish that too.

I answer all the questions as short and direct as possible,

per David's instructions. Finally, he asks me to detail that last night for the court.

I stare at the cue notes on my lap. Come on, Charlie, just tell it like it's written. Like it didn't happen to you, but instead, you're just telling a story. A fucking demented, sick, and twisted tale.

Sweat dots my palms, and I run them across my thighs before looking up and meeting the DA's impatient stare. I've been silent for too long. Not just at this moment but my whole life.

No more.

I clear my throat, "I was at Priest's place and was chilling on the couch when he hollered for me to come into his bedroom. I wasn't sure what he wanted, but he was very insistent, and you don't say no to Priest–"

"Objection!" His lawyer shouts.

I immediately slam my lips together. Shit. I fucked up already.

"Miss Johnson, please refrain from using speculation. Stick to the facts, and use the defendant's legal name." Judge Appleton instructs me.

"Yes, sir," I nod and continue, "Like I said, he yelled for me to come into the room. When I did, I saw he had a tray of items in his hand."

"What items were on the tray, Miss Johnson?" The DA asks.

My hands twist together on my lap. Cold sweat begins to drip down the back of my neck as I try to separate the recalling of events from my near brush with death that day.

"There was a needle, a tourniquet, and a vile with some sort of liquid. I wasn't sure exactly what was in it. When I asked Prie–" I catch the slip before I fully get it out, " – I mean Caleb,

125

what it was, he informed me that it was an injectable version of the AstraMallum he had been producing."

"And what did he do with the tray, Miss Johnson?"

My heart is thudding dangerously against my chest. The ghost of that night hovers over me, ready to reach in and slow my heart just like it did before.

I gulp past the vomit that creeps up my throat, "He told me that I had to help him," I answer, my voice small. Smaller than I'd like in this vulnerable moment.

"Help him with what exactly?" he questions.

"Caleb said I needed to shoot up the new drug so he could make sure it was good and ready to hit the streets. I tried to refuse, and he said he would call someone over to hold me down if I didn't comply."

"What happened then?"

The ghost's fingers tap dance up my spine, filling my body with icy terror. I open my mouth to answer him, but my words are frozen.

"Miss Johnson? Please tell the court what happened after Mr. Kirkpatrick said he would call someone to hold you down if you didn't comply."

I blink back the tears that begin to pool in my lids, "I did what he asked. I shot up the drug. I don't remember much after that. I started having trouble breathing, I couldn't move, and eventually, I passed out. When I woke up again, I was in the hospital with a breathing tube down my throat and wires hooked up all over my body."

"Thank you, Miss Johnson. You may step down." The DA instructs with finality.

I let out a breath of relief. It's over. I did it. I made it through without falling apart.

I stand and smooth my skirt down, and as I make my way back to my seat, the Judge's words halt my movement. "Okay, folks, we will take a thirty-minute recess, and then the previous witness, Charlotte Johnson, will take the stand for cross-examination."

Fuck my life, I forgot about that part. I glance at David, he must read the horror on my face. He nods at me in a placating way, telling me with his slight smile that it'll be okay. We did go over what could happen during cross-examination, but with everything else going on, I fucking forgot about it.

"Miss Johnson, is it true that you asked to meet my client?"

"Well, yes, but—"

"A yes is all I need, Miss Johnson. Is it also true that you offered yourself *willingly* to my client – as well as a number of his friends – sexually, in exchange for drugs?"

The blood may as well be draining from my body. My lips rub against each other tightly. "I mean, willingly is a loose term when it comes to Caleb. He would've taken it one way or the other."

"Objection! Move to strike, your Honor." The Defense attorney shouts.

"Sustained. Young lady, you will keep to the facts and the facts only. Do you understand me?" Judge Appleton chastises.

I nod in dejection, "Yes, sir, I'm sorry. Yes. I sometimes gave myself willingly to Caleb and his friends in exchange for drugs." I respond solemnly.

" I have no further questions for this witness, your Honor."

"You may step down." Judge Appleton informs me with a wave of his hand.

"Redirect, your Honor?" the DA asks.

"Proceed." He agrees.

"Miss Johnson, you said *sometimes* you gave yourself willingly to Mr. Kirkpatrick and his friends. Are you implying that there were times you were *unwilling*?"

This is it. My most shameful secret. My truths flayed open before a room of eager, bloodthirsty onlookers.

My hands curl into tight fists, my nails finding their cavernous crescent homes. The pain no longer phases my palms. "Yes. That's exactly what I'm saying." My body slowly inflates with every ounce of strength I can muster, and I pray my voice doesn't betray my trepidation.

My shoulders lock into place, and I hold my chin high as I lock eyes with my monster. Let him see the words flow from my mouth. Let him feel my truth smash into him like a freight train. Let my pain etch itself into his blackened soul and become the only movie his subconscious watches on a loop when he's burning in Hell. "Caleb Kirkpatrick, along with his friends, raped me. Numerous times. I said no. I screamed no. But they did it anyway."

"Thank you for your candor and your testimony today. You may step down."

* * *

"How much longer?" I whine to David. The jury has already been deliberating for several hours. If they don't come back in the next hour with a verdict, it will go into tomorrow and possibly beyond.

What the hell could they be deliberating for so long? The bastard is clearly guilty as fuck. You can just look at him and tell what a scum bag he is.

I sip my soda and lean my head against the wall. The ceiling is low in this part of the hallway. Not as regal as they made the courtroom up to be. The ceiling tiles are cheap plaster with pockmarks all over them. There are a few random watermarks, turning the light gray into a muddied brown.

The brown splotches turn to clouds, and suddenly, I'm lying on the grass outside of our house, and my mom is beside me. *She points to the one on the right, "Rabbit." I roll my eyes. "It's clearly a shark, Mom." I correct her.* We never saw the same thing. We've always had differing opinions, she and I. God, I wish she was here. How am I going to get through this without her? Without Savvy?

Grayson is here, but I've asked Mary to keep him far away. I can't handle his bullshit on top of everything else today. So far, she's kept to her word. I don't know what she said to him to make him keep his distance, but I don't really care as long as he does.

"I'm going to grab a snack from the vending machine. Do you want something?" David asks as he stands and points down the hall where a large black vending machine sits. A line of hungry court attendees wait in front of it for their turn.

I shake my head and return to looking for errant sea creatures on the ceiling when warmness fills the space David just vacated. "That was tough. How are you doing?" Dr Turner asks in that soft, soothing way he has. I don't bother taking my eyes off the ceiling. He's used to talking to my chin when I do this in his office—or the top of my head if I'm scribbling in my notebook.

I shrug my shoulder, "Eh, I mean, it could've been worse, I suppose. But I'm definitely in no hurry to repeat it. I just want it to be over, and I want never to see him again." We don't have to define who "him" is. We both know.

With his shoulder pressed to mine, I feel the nod of his head.

"When this is over, I'd like to take you back to Starry North if that's okay with you." David picked me up, but I don't see any harm in Dr. Turner taking me back. We are going to the same place anyway, and it seems silly to make David go out of his way. "Sure. I'll let David know."

His hand comes down between our legs and gently brushes against my thigh. Whether it's purposeful or not, I'm not sure. "Actually, I'll let him know. There's paperwork we have to fill out. It's a chain of custody thing. I'll go talk to him now. Hang in there, Charlie. We'll be done with this soon." *Charlie*. Not Miss Johnson.

"What the fuck was that? How could they find him not guilty on so many charges? The justice system in this country is a crock of shit!" I swear as I slam my fist against the dashboard of Dr. Turner's SUV.

The flames of anger lick at my skin. I want to hit something. Actually, I want to hit *someone*. I want to punch Priest in his stupid, pretty boy face until he's unrecognizable.

"I hear you, Charlie. It doesn't seem fair. But look at the bright side. He was found guilty of the most heinous crimes he was charged with. Those will carry a very hefty sentence if not life." Dr. Turner lifts his right hand from the steering wheel and holds out his palm to me, "Let's take a look at that left hook. That hit sounded like a doozy." He jokes. I didn't know Dr. Turner had a sense of humor. I roll my eyes, but I place my left hand in his.

As we pull up to a stop light, the interior of the car floods with a red hue. Dr. Turner rolls my hand from side to side, inspecting the damage—spoiler alert, there is none. He hms and purses his lips. He looks over at me as he brings my hand to his lips and places a featherlight kiss on my palm. "There. All better," he whispers reverently, almost to himself.

I slowly pull my hand back, "I-it uh feels much better now, thanks, Dr. Turner."

We spend the rest of the drive in silence. As we pull up to the facility and Dr. Turner parks in his spot, I unclip my seat belt and move to open the door. A hand on my shoulder pauses my movements. I look over my shoulder in question, but his face is covered in shadow. "Dr. Turner?" I ask.

Silence.

I let go of the handle and turn my body to face him. He leans forward just enough that I can see his eyes in the stream of soft lighting from the lamppost in the parking lot.

His eyes are dark and simmering with raw desire. My pulse jumps rapidly at his attention.

"Jensen." He breathes out forcefully, his teeth gritting together.

"W-what?"

He leans forward, his face now well over the halfway point of the center console. I don't back away.

"My name... is Jensen." He punctuates the words with a soft run of his index finger along my wrist, which lies on the console.

His breath lingers against my skin, a damp, warm breeze of life. The nerve endings along my flesh spark up like lights on a Christmas tree.

He leans in closer.

"Say it." His words ghost across my lips with their proximity. "Please, say it, Charlie."

I let out a soft breath and give him what he asks, "Jensen."

I don't know who moves first, but our lips slam together. Though the motion is quick and rough, the kiss is anything but.

Jensen's lips move softly, tentatively across mine.

He doesn't kiss me passionately and domineering like Jason.

He's not kissing me like he wants to save me, and I'm the very air he needs to breathe like Zach.

He's kissing me like he wants to know my soul and take away every bad thought and painful moment I've ever had. He's not kissing to lead to more.

His lips dance delicately across mine, and when his tongue asks for entry, a small gasp comes out of me.

As he breaks our kiss, Jensen lets out a breath of air across my mouth. He brings our foreheads together for a moment before pulling away and exiting the car.

Sitting stunned, I place two fingers over my still-tingling lips, trying to make sense of what just happened and how I feel about it. I don't get to think about it for long before he opens my door and leads me into the facility.

He checks us in, silently.

We walk down the corridor towards the center, silently.

And when we reach the dorm hall, I turn to say something, *anything,* to dispel this awkwardness between us. He's already walking off in the direction of his office, silently.

Chapter 19

Charlotte

Ari walks into our shared room a few minutes after I do and immediately plops down beside me on my bed. She wraps her stick-thin arms around my shoulders and leans our heads together.

"How did it go?" she asks.

Jesus. What do I say? I know she's specifically asking about the trial, but my head is still so spun up over what happened thirty minutes ago in the parking lot. My lips still burn from the all-consuming kiss. Why did he do that? Why did *I* do that?

Sure, Dr. Turner is attractive – I'm sorry, Jensen. I have eyes. That man is built, and his toned muscles are proof of a lifetime of dedication to fitness. The silver streaks along his temple only add to the allure of the man who makes sweater vests look like lingerie. I never thought I had a Mr. Rogers kink, but fuck me, Jensen is undeniably hot. He may be pushing forty or maybe fifty, but the man could still get it, in another life.

In this life, it's fucking wrong. Set aside the power dynamic and age gap. My head is already fucked by two boys. One who doesn't deserve to be in my thoughts after the shit he put me through. And the second is someone who I don't deserve for

133

the same reasons.

But I can't help the ache in my heart when I think about those smokey eyes that day in the pool when he tossed both of us in with our clothes on, kissed the shit out of me, and asked me to be his girlfriend. No one has ever looked at me, *inside me*, like that.

But he betrayed me. He took the love I was offering, set it on fire, and then roasted s'mores on the flaming carcass of my heart with Jade by his side.

I wish I could use a magic wand to pull those memories from my brain. I don't want to think about Jason. I've tried so hard to move past him and the feelings he invokes.

Did I though? Or did I just get high about it?

For fuck's sake. Maybe I need to talk about this in therapy...

Except, oh wait! I fucked that up, too, by making out with my fucking shrink.

Why am I so goddamn broken?

All I've had is time in this shit hole to think about all my many, many, *many* failures in life. I have plenty of regrets. But I'm tired of begging to be someone's first choice. I won't throw away a chance to be truly loved.

When I get out of here, I am headed straight to Zach to ask him to give us a real chance. He already told me he loved me. I want to believe him. So badly. I want to be worthy of his love.

He deserves nothing less than my full attention. My full, *sober* attention. It's time to move on. Forget the past. I probably only have these residual feelings about Jason because I gave him my virginity. This is exactly why guys don't like to be the one to pop a chick's cherry. They linger. Fucking lingerers.

It's not real, I tell myself.

It's just my hormones messing with my version of reality.

Zach is real. Zach is my now. Zach is my future. I can love Zach... Yeah, I can do this.

My eyes close, and I shake my head back and forth, "Girl. Do we have some shit to discuss..." And I tell her everything. The trial, the angry girl, the verdict, and the spit swapping with our resident hottie therapist.

Ari, being the true friend she is, doesn't lecture me or question my choices. She simply listens, rubbing soothing circles along my back while I spill my guts.

"When is the sentencing?" she asks when I finish my recap of the day.

I shrug a shoulder, "They set a date for April."

"But that's almost three months away!" She huffs in annoyance.

I nod, "Yep. But the good news is he stays locked up in the meantime. My lawyer said with the charges he was found guilty of, I don't ever have to worry about seeing him without bars between us for the rest of my life."

"Good. Fucking jerk."

I bark a laugh at that. Ari is not big on cussing, so when she does, it always sounds strange—like a newborn speaking in full sentences.

"What am I going to do without you? I can't believe you're finally getting out of this place in less than two days," she laments as she squeezes my arm tighter, "I'm going to miss you so much. Charlie, you've become my best friend. You've given me a reason to stick around." She looks down at her bandaged wrist, the attempt on her life still fresh in her memory.

The agony of the recollection plays across her delicate

features. I turn to face her and gather her in my arms, crushing our bodies together in the snuggest of hugs.

"Aurelia, you are an amazing human. You are kind and forgiving, even when you shouldn't be. You are a beautiful soul, inside and out. Never let someone make you feel less than the badass queen you are. I love you so much. I thank the universe every day for bringing us together, even in this fucked up place. I need you, Ari. The world needs you. Stay."

She pulls back and frames my face with her hands. Her eyes flood with tears as they pierce into mine, "Ditto, Charlie. Fucking ditto."

* * *

I shake off the nerves twitching in my arms as I raise my fist up and knock on the door. "Come in," a clipped voice answers from the other side.

Twisting the knob, I press the heavy wooden door in and take in Jensen's office space, the very empty office space. What the fuck. I close the door and spin around, taking in the mostly empty shelves of his bookcase. The office box on his desk, with his diplomas and nameplate inside, edges sticking out haphazardly.

Jensen is rummaging through his desk drawers, pulling out pens, notepads, and other office supplies.

"W-what..." I start, but the words fade off my tongue. I don't really know what to say. He has yet to look at me, though he is clearly aware of my presence. "Jensen, what's going on?" I manage.

His shoulders stiffen, his head snaps up, and his eyes are

void of the softness I've come to expect from him. "Dr. Turner." He grits out in correction.

"Okay," I drag the word out, tentatively taking a step toward the studious but currently feral beast on the other side of the desk. "Dr. Turner, what is happening here?" I try to keep the hurt out of my voice, but the slumping of his shoulders tells me I wasn't exactly successful.

He hangs his head, his forearm pressing against the top of his desk, holding his weight up. He speaks to the desk, but the words are for me, "I crossed a line, Miss Johnson. A line I never should have remotely approached."

"I can't stay here. I won't let a momentary lapse in judgment demolish my career." He protests.

Um, ouch. I also agree the kiss was a mistake, but fuck did he have to say it like that?

He doesn't wait for me to interject, "I have a standing offer at a clinic in California, and I've decided to take them up on it. Today was my last day at Starry North."

"But, who's going to do my mandatory therapy? You were supposed to be my person for the next six months, remember?" I chastise, my feelings a little more hurt than I care to admit.

Dr. Turner flings a business card across the desk at me, and it lands at my fingertips. I put my finger to it and turn to read the writing across the front: *Margaret Thitters, PHD PSYC.*

"What the fuck is this? Can you just talk to me?" I toss the card back in his direction. It misses him entirely and flutters to the ground under his desk.

"I can no longer help you, effective immediately. Dr. Thitters is a colleague of mine and is willing to take you on for the duration of your court order and after if you so choose."

I fold my arms across my chest, rage bubbles in my stomach,

marching its way up my body. I bristle at the clear rejection, "So, that's it then? You kiss me, now you're running away like a little bitch instead of having a conversation like a fucking adult?"

His eyes widen in anger, and he storms around the desk and stands toe to toe with me. His hands tightly fisted and bouncing off his thighs, "What aren't you understanding? I *can't* be here anymore. I can't be around you, *Miss Johnson*. If I were more of a man, I would resign. But this has never happened to me before. I've never crossed a line. Ever. I've never been tempted to. But you," his voice softens as his hand lifts like he wants to reach for me.

I instinctively pull back from him. He sighs and drops it down with a smack against his thigh.

"I've developed inappropriate feelings for you. I should've recused myself as your therapist long before now, but I've been selfish. I've enjoyed the time we've spent together. I know it's wrong, fuck, I know–" His hands fly to the top of his head and run through his perfectly combed hair in frustration.

Dr. Turner bends down to meet me at eye level, the gentle features I've become accustomed to back on his face, "Charlie, I need you to understand that this isn't about you. This is about me. You did nothing wrong. This is my fault."

I want to tell him he's wrong, but he's kinda right. Did I kiss him back? Yes. Did I think he was hot? Also, yes. But I didn't pursue this. He's beating himself up enough for the both of us. So I'll give him this. I'll play the part he needs me to.

I bob my head up and down in acceptance, "I understand. Thank you, Dr. Turner," I bend down and grab the discarded business card of his colleague, tucking it safely inside my notebook and make my way to the door. Before leaving, I turn back to him, "You're a good man, Jensen. I know bad men. I know users and abusers," I shake my head vehemently, making sure he knows I mean every word, "That's not you. You are good. I hope you have a great life in Cali. Hit some waves for me." I smile sadly when our eyes stay locked together until the closing of the door breaks the spell.

* * *

Though I'm absolutely not going to miss that place at all, I miss Ari already. When I was walking out, I caught the Fugly Five –Roman, his lackey, and the tres twatsickles – watching me with sneers on their faces. It took everything I had not to charge into their group and kick Roman in the nuts again as a parting gift. If they mess with Ari, I will make my way back here and fuck shit up.

I've spent the last hour watching the trees go by in a blur as Mary takes us on the two-hour journey back to River View. She's tried to make small talk, but I'm just not in a talkative mood. I'm anxious as hell. I haven't seen Zach in over three months, and the last time we spoke, I was hospitalized, in and out of consciousness, and withdrawing until I got on a dose of Suboxone.

I wasn't allowed any non-familial visitors or phone calls. Mary was the only exception to that rule since I am technically an adult, I told them she was my mom, they couldn't prove otherwise. Still, I refused any visitors except for the trial. I sure as shit didn't want to see Grayson, and I just couldn't bring myself to face Mary.

Seeing the disappointment on her face would be almost

as bad as seeing it on my momma's. The first two months were rough. Between struggling to come to terms with what's happened in my life in the last year or so, the drugs, Priest, Jason, and Zach. It took the nurses a while to get a good medication dosage and type to bring me a semblance of normality, headspace-wise.

I'll never be "fixed". I know if I'm not diligent with medication and therapy, I can slide right the fuck off the sanity wagon and dive back into the deep recesses of depression and drugs.

Things aren't all sunshine and rainbows, but I have something that's always been a little foreign to me. Hope.

The metal disk sits heavily in my palm, another token of my sobriety. Ninety days. Joe sought me out yesterday and presented the medallion to me with another copy of the meeting list.

He also reminded me that the real work begins in the outside world. It's easier to adhere to abstinence when you don't have access to temptation.

I've never been happier to see the crappy, rust-spotted, beige four-door jalopy than right now. I'm sure Mom could've replaced it at any point over the years, but she was bound and determined to "ride it until the wheels fell off," and now, so am I.

I thank Mary for coming to get me and toss my bag on Savvy's bed. Thankfully I had the forethought to shower this morning and since I was being discharged, they let me have my entry outfit back. A simple pair of jeans and a tye-dye 70s band tee.

I don't care what I look like, and I'm pretty damn sure he won't, either. I'm so giddy to see Zach that I completely forgot to grab my cell from Savvy's dresser, and it only occurred to me once I was already on the way to Sky Ridge.

Pulling into the long gravel driveway of the Morris estate feels surreal. Excitement floods my body. I am going to kiss his fucking face off. And then fuck his brains out. We have a lot of time to make up for.

I get out of the car, trying to tamp down my grin so I don't scare the poor boy away. I lift my hand to knock on the door and do a little happy shimmy as I await the answer.

A gorgeous woman with sandy-blonde hair in a super cute floral sundress opens the door with a warm smile, "Hiya darlin', how can I help you?" Oh my God, she's just so cute. I want to stick her in my pocket and take her home with me.

"Hi, Mrs. Morris. My name is Charlotte. I'm here to see Zach," I tell her, giddiness weaving through my words.

Her smile falters just a little, enough to sink my heart. She opens the door wider and gestures for me to come in, "Let's have a chat, honey."

Chapter 20

January 2007

Zach

Sweat and dirt linger heavily in the air in the locker room as Coach spits out all the reasons we fucking suck and are ruining our chances at the championship title. I tune him out. My focus is solidly on my pad-covered leg as it bounces repeatedly. The motion causes my cleats to make a song of distinct taps along the cement floor.

We did fucking suck, though. We partied last night. We knew it was against the rules, but we thought we had this in the bag. So we played like shit tonight and only narrowly came away with the W, and Coach ain't gonna let us forget it anytime soon.

I'm just ready to get the hell out of here. My whole body aches. I need a cold beer and a hot bath.

Once he feels we are thoroughly dressed down, Coach dismisses us, and I head to the showers.

Walking out of the locker room, Morgs stands against the wall with my gear bag, and as soon as I'm within spitting distance, she hurls it at my face. "What the fuck, Morgs?" I holler.

She rolls her eyes at me and looks down at her manicure, unbothered by my response. "Your damn phone is blowing the hell up. It must've gone off a thousand times during your game." She complains.

Confused about why anyone would be trying to get a hold of me so badly, I pull the zipper back and grab the phone, pressing the button on the side. When it turns on, my eyes nearly pop out of their sockets. There are forty-seven missed calls and only one text. All from the same person. *Fuck.*

Little Bit: Alabama, Zach? Nice. Real fucking nice.

My gear bag drops to the ground, startling Morgan. "Hey, Zee, what is it? Is it your mom?" she asks, clearly concerned with my reaction to the contents of my phone.

I shake my head no and hand her the phone. I've told her about Little Bit. I wish I had known exactly when she was getting out so I could've called her before she found out some other way. How did she find out?

I started texting her many times to tell her, but I always deleted them. That's a fucked up way to find out that someone just up and left you. No matter how you church it up, that's what I did. I put myself and my career ahead of her. Fuck, I'm such an asshole. I should be there. She shouldn't have come home to me not being there.

"Damn, Zee. What are you going to do?" she asks as she hands me back the phone. I reach out and take it with shaky hands. I tighten my grip around the metal and look towards the ceiling, "I'm gonna fix it." I say in a more convincing tone than I feel. I have to fix it.

"Let's get on back to the dorms so I can beg for my fuckin' life."

Morgs nods, and we head to her car, bypassing all the folks trying to get my attention. Either they want to congratulate me and shake my hand, sometimes offer to shake other parts of my body— which I always decline – or they want to get on my case for whatever play they think I coulda done better at. Either way, I want no part of any of it. All I want is to get to a quiet, private place and call my girl.

I want her to know I'm not ignoring her, so I shoot a quick text.

Me: I'm gonna call you in thirty minutes. Answer the phone, Little Bit.

I plop down on my bed and attach the charger cord to my phone. Ain't no way in hell I'm letting the fucking thing die during this conversation. I told Tuck I needed the room for the night. He's lucky he's quick because when he said it was about time I took some chick to pound town, I damn near took his head off.

The trill of the ringtone grates on my already frayed nerves.

Pick up.

Pick up.

Pick up.

The ringing stops, but dead air greets me on the other end. I pull my phone away to make sure the call didn't disconnect—it didn't. The stifling silence is almost too much to bear. Then I hear it, a muffled sniffle. Oh no. I can take her anger. I love her fire. I can't handle her tears, especially knowing I've caused them.

"Aw, honey, please don't cry," I plead softly, delicately

gripping the phone as if she can feel my soothing touch through the line.

"How could you?" she demands, voice hoarse. No doubt from crying for God knows how long.

I blow out a breath. That's a great question. How could I? I've asked myself the same question repeatedly, and every possible answer I've come up with sounds like a lame excuse.

"I am so sorry, Little Bit. You got no idea how badly I want–" Her sobs increase as she interrupts me. "Y-you told me you fucking *loved* me, Zach! And you left me!"

My eyes burn with the tears gathering in them. "Baby, please forgive me. I do love you. I didn't leave you. I left Alaska. Not you. Never you."

Apparently, I'm just dumb enough to ask the wrong questions at the wrong time, "Who told you?"

"That's what you have to say for yourself right now? Not a fucking explanation, but all you want to know is who told me?"

Okay, slow down, man. I need to tread lightly here. I'm not getting my point across very well. "I just mean, I woulda rather told you on my own, Little Bit. I didn't want it comin' from anyone else. I figured you would get in touch with me when you were ready since you returned all of my letters."

"What letters?" she asks, confusion lacing her words.

Now I'm confused. What does she mean by "what letters"? Did she never see them? I just assumed she didn't want to hear from me while she was there, and I wanted to respect that.

But, fuck, she didn't even know I sent them?

"Sweetheart, I sent you a letter every week that you were in that place up until three weeks ago when I got here. Every one of them was returned to me, unopened."

145

"I don't understand. I never got any letters, Zach. From you or anyone. My therapist was in charge of all incoming and outgoing correspondence. We weren't allowed anything outside of a pre-approved list of recipients/senders. I didn't know."

"I don't know what to tell you, Little Bit. I sent them, and they got sent back. But it's all water off a duck's back at this point. I didn't have a choice but to come here when I did. My parents went behind my back and enrolled me in spring semester. I woulda lost my scholarship if I didn't come. But baby, I fought them as best as I could. Please believe me. I lost my shit when my momma told me I had three days to pack my shit and be on a plane."

"She made it seem like this is what you want, that I was kinda... holding you back." She murmurs, ashamed.

My eyes snap to an imaginary adversary on the wall, and I thrust myself into a standing position, ready to lash out at the invisible foe. "Who?" I demand.

"Your mom. When I got back to Savvy's earlier, all I wanted was to see you. I was so hurried I didn't even grab my phone. I just got in the car and headed straight to your house. Your mom let me in and told me you left for school," she lets the words dangle in the air. There has to be more to it than that.

"What else did she tell you?" I ask, trying with all my might to keep anger from seeping into my voice.

I can just picture my Little Bit sitting on the floor of Savvy's room, her back pressed against the bed, staring blankly at the wall, same as me, picking nervously at her nails. Just imagining her actions and knowing she's home and safe deflates most of my anger.

"She basically said that you needed to focus on school and

football and that distractions would just make things harder on you. She said that if I cared for you that, maybe it was best if I just let you be and that if we were meant to be, things would work out eventually."

Mama said what, now? It takes a moment for her words to settle in and my mind to make sense of them. My jaw clenches, and I tighten my hand into a fist, "Motherfucker!" I shout as I slam my fist into the drywall. Not giving two fucks about the dent now present in it. "Listen to me, darlin'. Listen up real good. I love you. I want to be with you. Not in a year. Not in two years or four. Right fuckin'now. You ain't a distraction... you're my reason, don't you get that, Little Bit?"

Her weeping is so intense that it fills the space between us, enveloping me in waves of her emotion. I wish I could reach right through the phone and take my girl in my arms. Take away her pain. She's had enough pain for several lifetimes. I never wanted to be the cause of any.

"We can make this work, Little Bit. I promise you. You are all I want. I'll do whatever it takes. God invented phone sex for a reason, ya know?" I joke, hoping to lighten the heaviness just a tad.

The sweet sound of her giggle sets my heart afloat. "Yeah, okay, Zach. Like I'm supposed to believe you've been the picture of abstinence with all those college girls strutting around." She chides, but I can hear a hint of jealousy in her words.

I laugh at her statement. "Oh, darlin', you ain't got no idea, do you?"

"No idea about what?" she questions.

I smile, my most heart-stopping, panty-dropping, play-boy smile that she can't even see, "That even though we ain't never made things official– which is your fault, by the way– you own me, baby. Mind, body, soul. Every piece of me belongs to you and you alone. I haven't so much as touched another woman since meeting you."

Crickets may as well start chirping in her stunned silence. I never thought I'd see a day when Charlotte Johnson was speechless.

"Nothing to say with that sassy mouth of yours, Little Bit?" I tease.

She stutters out some unintelligible words before making a string of them work together. "First of all, I don't remember you ever complaining about my mouth," I groan at the reminder of just how good her warm mouth feels wrapped around my cock. Just the memory has the fucker perking up, ready to feel it. "Secondly, I'm sorry."

"What are you sorry for, baby?" I ask her, perplexed by why in the world she would be sorry. I'm the sorry one.

"I haven't been deserving of you. I've been through... some shit. Zach, my head isn't a pretty place to be. But I want to be better. I want to be someone who deserves you. I want to be with you, too. I need you to be patient with me," her voice drops to a low, husky tone, "But I suppose I can keep my legs closed until your head is able to be between them again."

"Oh, girl. You got me sittin' over here with a rock-hard cock from them dirty words comin' out of your pretty mouth." I inform her, my voice dripping with sex. My hand reaches down to palm my aching dick over my sweatpants.

"And what do you plan on doing with it? Hm?"

"Why don't you lose your pants and panties, and I tell you exactly what I plan to do with it."

I hear the rustle on the other end of the phone as she does

what she is told. A little out of breath, she comes back on the line, "Okay, I'm bare-assed. Now what?"

"Now, you're gonna lay back and put those fingers where I tell you. We got some time to make up for, Little Bit."

She huffs out a breath of impatience. My girl is ever the greedy one. "Zach?"

"Yeah, baby?"

"I love you."

"And I love you. Now put your phone down to my pussy, and lemme tell her how much I've missed her."

Chapter 21

April 2007

Zach

The past seven months have been hell without seeing my girl. It's been seven months, one week, and three days since I've touched her, held her, kissed her. Even longer since I've been inside her. Way too fucking long.

We've perfected the art of phone sex over the last two months since she got home– with a particularly vigorous session last month on her birthday. I tried like hell to get her to nineteen orgasms. She tapped out at five– but now I'm ready for the real thing. I need to have my girl in my arms. Look over her and make sure she's all in one piece with my own eyes.

I can't wait to surprise her.

As much as I want to see her and be with her for my own selfish reasons, I definitely don't want her to be alone when that piece of shit is sentenced tomorrow. She's been trying to put on a brave front, but I know it's eating at her. She won't be able to rest easy until she hears exactly how fucked he is.

We've talked about the plan moving forward. She has

another four months of mandatory therapy and drug testing before she can leave the state. As long as she gets through that without any issues, she'll be free to leave in the fall—just in time for the fall semester at the University of Auburn, which, coincidentally, she is now enrolled in.

Mary kept up on her paperwork, ensuring everything was submitted on time, and worked it out with Charlotte's dad for the tuition. She and her dad have been working on their relationship in therapy, but they still have a long way to go to rebuild trust. He has traveled back and forth between AK and AL so many times, all for her.

I know she wants to forgive him but feels like she would be betraying her mama by doing so. I didn't know the woman, but if she was anything like my Little Bit, she had a heart of gold and wouldn't want someone else to suffer out of some misplaced notion of loyalty.

But I can tell some healing is happening there.

We plan to surprise her with the good news tomorrow. But tonight is just for us. There is a nice ass hotel downtown with amazing views over the inlet that I know she loves. And because I'm basically the greatest boyfriend in the world, I got us a room there for the night. I want her to experience all the luxury the SeaFort offers. The finest of dining. The softest of bedding. The most discrete of staff. These were all the things promised to me by the concierge when I booked the room.

That last part is the most important. I plan to have my girl screaming my name all night long, and I want no fucking interruptions.

"Now boarding general seating for flight 78 with service to River View, Alaska."

I hitch my bookbag over my shoulder and make my way to

151

the gate. In just four more hours, I'll get to see my girl.

* * *

"Thanks again for pickin' me up, bro." I thank my driver, Max Whitaker.

We played football together at RHS. He may get on my nerves, but he's always had my back, on and off the field.

His dad had a bad accident right before we graduated, and his mama bailed on the two of them when he was a kid, so they're all each other has. He decided to skip out on leaving state for college, essentially giving up any chance at a football career, to stay home and take care of him.

"Ah shit, it's no problem, man," he reaches out to turn the volume up on the trendy rap song that just came on the radio. His voice increases in volume to be heard above the music. "It's good to see you. I can't believe you ditched out on LSU. That's all you talked about back in the day. What's up with that?"

I focus my attention out the passenger window, watching the world go by in blurry whooshes. I knew this would be the hardest part about coming back here.

He's right. LSU was my dream. Playing for the Tigers is all I've wanted for a long time. Don't get me wrong, Crimson Tide is hella good, and I'm blessed to be a part of the team. But, a small part of me wishes I could take the field in purple and gold. Though, I'll never fucking say that shit out loud.

"Things change sometimes, bro. What can I say?" I answer with as little information as possible, never looking over from the window.

"Hm, the only thing I know to keep a man away from his dream team is money and pussy," Whitaker reaches over and pops my arm with the back of his hand as he snorts out a laugh. "I happen to know you got plenty of money, Morris. So, what's the pussy's name? Have I had her?"

My head snaps over, and I pin him to his seat with a glare and the promise of one hell of an ass-whoopin', "You better fuckin' not have." I growl, my jaw muscles ticking with barely restrained rage.

He holds his hand up in surrender, a nervous laugh bubbling out of him. "Whoa, man. I just mean, do I know her?"

I suppress the possessive beast that tends to pop out whenever Little Bit is involved. I know that Whitaker is a good dude, regardless of his mouth. I lift my chin in the affirmative, "Yeah, you know her. She went to school with us. I believe you had a hard-on for her best friend. The curly-haired cheerleader?"

Max slowly moves his gaze to me, eyes wide and mouth slightly agape, "Dude. Are you talking about Charlie?" My hackles raise at his astonishment.

River View isn't that small of a town, but it's small enough that word always travels fast. When that shit went down at the end of last year with her mom, everyone saw the change. The crowd she ran with was known to be into the hard shit. There's still a lot I don't know, but I'm waiting for her to want to talk to me about it. When she's ready.

News of the raid and subsequent shootout was the talk of the town for several weeks. Every news station covered it, and Charlotte was made out to look like some kind of drug queen pin.

Gossip filtered around about her involvement, ranging from

people defending her and saying she was just caught up in a bad way because of losing her mama and was a victim in the whole thing. To the ones who believed her to be the mastermind behind all of River View's crime problems. If you believe those, she ran a brothel out of a shed, sold drugs to elementary school kids, and moonlighted as Skipper the Stripper down at the Busy Beav. Clearly, those motherfuckers have no idea who she is.

But the worst ones are the ones who have passed rumors about her being mentally ill. Those piss me off the most. I'm not blind. I know she has her demons, and she fights them often, but she ain't crazy. The fact that the news broadcasted her court-ordered placement in Starry North Behavioral Facility fueled that particular gossip fire.

The last thing I want is for her to deal with small-minded folks who got nothing better to do than speculate on people's lives. They gonna learn, even if I have to drop-kick a mother-fucker to get my point across.

Is Whitaker's shock because he thinks she's a nutjob? I really don't wanna fight my friend, but I fucking will.

"Yeah. I'm fuckin' talkin' about Charlie. You got somethin' to say about that?" I lean into his space, my large frame imposing and rife with anger.

A large smile curves his face, showing off the work of four years of braces when he was younger. Pearly whites gleam as much as his brown eyes do as he lifts his hand up for a high-five, "Dude! Fucking nice. Give me five, bro. Charlie is fucking–" I cut a glare at him, interrupting his sentence, "Charlie is what?" I ask, head cocked in demand. "A nice girl, bro. She's a nice girl. Good for you." He stutters out to correct himself.

I nod and grunt, "Yeah, that's what I thought you were gonna say."

He laughs and reaches forward to skip to the next song, without looking back at me he adds, "It doesn't hurt that she's also hot as hell!"

I roll my eyes, "Watch it."

But I can't argue with him. She is in fact, hot as fucking hell.

When we pull up to my house, I grab my bag, thank Whitaker for the ride, and promise to hit him up on my next pass-through. I'm only here for four days, and I plan to spend every one of them buried deep inside my girlfriend.

No one is home, but both my parents know I'm coming, so I hope I won't have any bare-assed surprises. I've had enough of those to last me the rest of my damn life.

Everything looks and smells the same, but the feeling of home isn't there. I make my way to my room. It's still the same as I left it. I didn't take much to Alabama. I figured if I needed something other than the things I brought, I'd just pick them up down there.

The wall of trophies still sits proudly against the otherwise bare side wall of my room. Not a speck of dust to be seen, clearly Mama's been in here with her feather duster. I pick up the nearest one. The golden player is frozen in mid-air, both feet off the ground and hand stretched out to catch the ball perfectly. A moment of glory immortalized in metal. The marble base is engraved with my name, letting the world know I am indeed *The World's Best Wide Receiver*.

I hope to one day be kissing one of these on a Super Bowl field. I chuckle to myself and put my pee-wee trophy back on the shelf.

All I want to do is high-tail it over to my girl's place, but I've been traveling all day, and I need a damn shower.

After washing the travel stink off myself, I gussy up all pretty boy like. I grab the stack of returned letters and stuff them alongside my clothes and toiletries in my overnight bag.

Excitement thrums through my body as the anticipation of getting Charlotte in my arms approaches fruition. Grabbing the bag off my bed, I head to the door, and as I'm about to turn out the light, I catch a glimpse of the shit-eating grin that has affixed itself to my face, and I thank God I rubbed one out in the shower.

Time to get my girl.

Chapter 22

Charlotte

As soon as my head hit the pillow, I was down for the count. I haven't napped in forever, but apparently, my body just said enough.

My mind is as exhausted as my physical body. Dr. Thitters suggested I take up some sort of physical exercise to blow off steam and clear my thoughts—a metaphorical bleaching of my gray matter.

No matter how much bleach I use, I can't seem to clean the sordid filth that clings to the walls of my mind. It's more like hastily surface cleaning up before guests arrive, stuffing everything out of sight into closets and under beds. Despite these efforts, the tainted mess remains, just like the thoughts and emotions crowding my brain.

Much like when you shove those items in random locations, often, I forget about some deep, dark memory I've placed in a box in the back of my mind until I'm clearing things out and accidentally stumble upon it. And I deal with it like any rational adult would. I kick that fucking box until it falls under a mountain of other boxes, and I can walk away pretending I never saw it in the first place. May not be the healthiest way to deal with it, but it's what I'm working with right now.

Last week's family counseling session is still weighing heavily on me. It was the first time I let my dad come into the room with me to talk with Dr. T. We've each seen her on multiple occasions over the last two months. It still seems weird to refer to him as "dad" again. He's been such a non-familial presence in my thoughts for so long.

I still haven't forgiven him for everything, but I did agree to hear his version of events. I had to hand it to him. He stood in the face of my full rage and loathing and laid his truth bare before me.

I was eight when he started working with Alexis. She was a bouncy twenty-something, eager to learn all she could from such a distinguished businessman– my words, not his. He spared me a lot of the nitty-gritty details and basically said they spent a lot of time together. What started as a professional working relationship developed into a friendship and turned into a crush, and when it was reciprocated, a "one-time" mistake happened.

He had Alexis transferred to another department, but eventually, they made their way back to each other, and a long-term affair ensued.

My mom found out when she went to his office one night when he was working late. He had missed one of his favorite meals– corned beef and potatoes – I was staying at Savvy's, so she decided, the doting wife she was, to take him his favorite meal.

She walked in and saw them in a "romantic position". Like the true queen she was, Amelia Johnson simply placed the to-go container in front of them on his desk and left without a word. She didn't scream, cry, or beg.

As much as it killed me to listen to him detail his betrayal, I couldn't help but feel my chest swell with pride that my mother was such a fucking amazing woman. He didn't deserve her. My only two regrets for her are that she dealt with that all alone and that she never found her own happiness.

Dr. T brought up a valid point that got me thinking. My mom forgave my dad. She was the one who was wronged, and she forgave him. They had a great friendship and co-parenting relationship. That wasn't faked. It couldn't have been. So if she saw something redeemable in him, maybe I should give him a second chance.

I'm just having a hard time not feeling like a traitor for *wanting* to forgive him, but Savvy was right. At my mom's funeral, she reminded me that he's all I have left.

I made no promises about our future relationship but agreed to try. If I learned anything from Mom's death and my dip in the River Styx, it was that life is fleeting.

I'm not angry at my dad for finding a love that wasn't my mom. I'm well aware that you can love more than one person in your lifetime, and I fully believe you can have more than one soul tie. I'm pissed at the sneaking and hiding. Divorce was invented for a reason.

He and Tuscaloosa Barbie have decided to postpone their wedding indefinitely. I should probably care about that and want only his happiness but also fuck her. I don't forgive her. She knew he was married and pursued him anyway. She made my mom feel like shit in her last days, and I don't know if I can ever forgive her for that.

I roll over on my back and stare at the ceiling, a small smile lifting my lips at the "W" and the pot with the handle stretched along the surface in glow-in-the-dark stars.

The big dipper for me—obviously—and Cassiopeia for Savs. When we learned about constellations in fifth grade, and Savvy heard about the queen with unrivaled beauty, she came home and begged Mary to buy a set of stick-on stars.

Since then, whenever we want, we have been invited to a nightly private showing of celestial splendor, regardless of the sky's temperament.

I think I've finally convinced her to keep her ass in Florida. She has threatened several times to come back home to be with me. Well, more like to babysit me. I let many people down with my selfish actions, and I think Savvy was probably the person who was hurt the most. Not that she was judging me for what happened, but that I didn't feel I could talk to her about what was happening.

Sure, she saw the bruises, and I came home high too many times to dismiss, but I hid the worst of it from her. I made excuses. I outright lied. To my best fucking friend. She has every right to be hurt about it and make me earn back her trust.

I have no desire to be in that position again. The pull of the drugs is strong sometimes. Occasionally, something happens to trigger the craving for numbness, and I have to work through it. "Pull out one of the tools in my toolbox," as my sponsor, Tina, would say.

I've been working hard on my sobriety and my mental health since I was released from Starry North. I'm finding the two often go hand in hand.

A soft knock raps on the door before it opens, just enough for Mary's head to poke in. "Hey, sweetie, I hope I didn't wake you. You have a visitor," a sly smile spreads on her face, and she cocks an eyebrow up, "Should I send him in?"

Him?

I'm about to ask the question aloud, but before I can, she quickly steps back. Several emotions hit me at once, the top being pure and utter belonging.

"There she is," he drawls with that one-sided smile I love. He barely makes it into the room before I'm on my feet, running across the top of the bed. I leap into his open arms and wrap my legs tightly around his waist, burying my face in his neck. His hands latch right to my ass, holding my weight up.

God, I forgot how fucking good he smells. I take a long whiff, delighting in his familiar scent.

Fresh laundry.

Citrus. And... I press my nose harder against his neck. Where's the smoke?

Like he read my mind, "I quit, darlin'. Five weeks ago." I pull back and look at him in shock. Five weeks ago... "My birthday?" I question.

He answers with a nod, the smirk I love firmly attached to his beautiful, tan face. I slam my lips against his.

Our mouths devour each other, whispering all the love and longing between each connection of skin. It's been so long— too long.

I thrust my tongue against his lips, too impatient to wait for him to take the lead. His deep chuckle rumbles against my core, and immediately heat floods my body. He complies and opens his mouth for me. My hands thrust into his sandy locks, holding his head right where I want him as my tongue explores his mouth like a discoverer of a new world.

Our bodies fit perfectly against one another—his large and hard, mine small and soft. This is how we should always be— slotted perfectly together as a whole. My soul's mate, home where he belongs.

Home.

Wait.

I jerk my head back, his eyes slowly open. A drunken haze of lust coats his verdant stare. "How are you here right now?" I ask.

"Well, you see, darlin', there are these big ol' tin cans that hold lots of folks and shoot across the sky from one place to another. Ow!" He pouts at me, and I rub a gentle circle around the spot where I hit him.

"I know what a plane is, dick. I mean, what are you doing here? What about school?"

He presses his forehead to mine and places a gentle kiss on my lips. "I'm only here 'til Monday. Coach is cool, and missin' two days of classes ain't goin' to hurt me none. Besides, I missed my girl," he punctuates that last bit by using his hands to grind my crotch against him. "Speakin' of," he gently sets me back on my feet and pats my ass, "Grab a bag and throw in whatever shit you need for the night. I'm takin' you out, my love."

I grin at him and do as he asks. I shove a change of clothes, a cute matching bra, and panties into a bag before heading to the bathroom. I grab my toothbrush, toothpaste, and hair tie and shove those in, too.

Walking out of the bathroom, I thrust my bag at Zach's chest. He catches it easily with a chuckle. "Alright, Price Charming, I'm ready for my princess treatment," I inform him with a haughty stare and wave of my hand. He catches my hand and brings it to his lips, placing a hot kiss against the top. The kiss radiates want through my veins, and a fire burns between my thighs.

"You are a fuckin' queen, Little Bit," he tips his eyes up to meet mine with his lips still ghosting against my hand, "And I plan to spend the next twelve hours servin' my queen. From noon until night, when her legs can't hold her up no more, and her voice goes missin' from screamin' my name."

My mouth waters and I can't find the right words to respond, so I nod frantically, "Yes. Yes. God, yes, please. Let's do that."

Chapter 23

Charlotte

Giddiness thrums through me as I stare up at the massive structure that seems to stretch endlessly into the sky, creating an epic sight that leaves me breathless. I've wanted to witness the SeaFort up close and personal for a long time now. If the outside is this impressive, I cannot wait to see the inside.

"Come on, come on. Move your ass, Morris." I needle while swatting at his ass as we make our way into the hotel.

"Damn, Little Bit, seems like your patience just gets better and better every day." He teases but still doesn't speed the hell up.

The sheer opulence of the entry alone has me gasping for breath and grabbing onto Zach's arm for stability. A gentle breeze could blow me over at the moment.

A grand archway lined with twinkling lights creates a luxurious welcome. We follow the path into a reception area, where gleaming marble floors and intricate mosaic tiles reflect the grandeur of the regal building.

Zach leads me to a plush black chair and motions for me to sit while he walks over to the check-in desk.

I don't fight him on it. My eyes dart around the space, taking in the gilded ambiance with wonder and awe. Grandiosity fills every inch of this place.

I don't think I've ever felt so out of place in my life. I suddenly feel vastly underdressed in Savvy's cheer sweats and a band tee. I look around to see if anyone is staring at me, wondering who let the bum into their fancy schmancy hotel. I prepare myself to be shooed out at any moment.

"Alright, sweetheart, follow me." I startle when he speaks from behind me and squeak a bit before slapping my hand over my mouth. He chuckles at me and motions his head towards a bank of elevators.

Elevators in fancy hotels are fast as fuck. Seriously, we hit the thirty-eighth floor in maybe five and a half seconds. Well, Mississippi's anyway. But still, hella fast.

Zach holds a black card up to the door, with no room number but a black plaque on the wall with a golden "P" on it. I flick my head left and right, seeing no other rooms on this floor. He sees my uncertainty and pulls my hand behind him into the Penthouse space.

Ho-ly fuck.

The wall-to-wall two-story windows boast sweeping views of snow-capped mountains on the left side and the choppy waves of the inlet on the right.

I plop down on the immaculate white sofa in the living room—yes, this place has its own living room! – the roar of an artificial fire blazes in the square in front of me.

Zach leans down behind me, moving my hair off to the side, and kisses my neck. His tongue traces a line from my pulse point to just under my ear. Shivers erupt over my whole body with the action. "You see that fireplace, Little Bit?"

"Mhm," I nod.

"Later, I'm gonna eat your delicious pussy in front of it while you're splayed out naked as a jaybird on that there Persian rug."

My heart skips multiple beats as I start to envision that very thing.

"But first," he starts, and then a knock sounds at the door. He opens it, and two very large, very blonde and tan men walk in carrying large black cases.

Zach throws a robe at me and jerks his head towards what looks like the bathroom. "Come back wearin' only that," he hardens his eyes and lowers his voice, "Make sure that robe stays tight. I'd hate to pluck Sergei's eyes outta his head for takin' a peek at my girl." He shoo's me off to the bathroom with a swat on the ass and a wink.

I come back into the room, gripping the robe sash tightly. Not because of Zach's idle threat but because I've grown uncomfortable in my skin. He hasn't seen me naked in months. Pictures with flattering angles don't count. I know one of the things he's always loved about my body was the curves.

Between the drugs and the terrible food at the facility, my bones poke out in unappealing ways. My boobs seem to sag more without the proper fat, keeping them full and plump. My ass may as well be served with a slice of butter and syrup.

My hands twist into the soft terry cloth, and my eyes dart back and forth between the massage table and the door. I'm seconds away from bolting when a very sweet-looking older lady approaches me.

"Lena," she introduces herself with a pat on her chest. "Come dear. Lay. I fix." Oh, how I wish she could. Her broken English and kind demeanor endear me. Lena leads me over to a sheet-covered massage table. Zach is lying on one beside it, and Sergei is already going to town on his muscular back.

I climb on the table and lay flat on my stomach. Lena pulls the robe off my shoulders, and I flinch. She stops immediately and squeezes my shoulder, "It okay," she soothes and pulls it the rest of the way while simultaneously pulling a warm sheet over my backside, keeping it from ever being exposed.

Her warm hands land on my skin, and a cold sweat breaks over my body. My hands grasp the table's edge in a death grip, holding on to the here and now physically like it can tether me mentally as well.

Please, stop.

It's okay, Charlie.

You're safe.

Take a breath.

It's not their hands.

You're okay.

My nails cut into the soft cotton of the sheet. A scream lodges itself inside my throat. I must make a distressing sound because suddenly, Zach's head snaps over to me, his eyes wide with concern. He clearly does not like what he sees because he jumps off his massage table the next moment. Dick swinging in between his legs for all to see, but he couldn't care less.

I clench my eyes shut as a torrent of horrific memories flood in. *"She fucking likes it rough, boys; give her what she wants." I feel the clothes being torn from my body. "I'm going to enjoy this far more than you will, you pathetic bitch." I feel the scream trapped in my throat as a red-hot pain flows through my breasts with the crushing force twisting them. I feel my body being flipped with ease, like I'm nothing more than a rag doll. I feel the rugged hands that grip my ass cheeks and force them apart. I feel my soul leave my body as some nameless, faceless monster takes what was not freely given.*

"Hey. Hey. What's happenin', darlin'?" He doesn't touch me, but he hovers down so we are at eye level and keeps his voice low.

With my eyes still closed, I shake my head back and forth. I hear the words, but they don't make sense. I just want the memories to stop. *Make them stop.*

"Out!" Zach barks to the two staff members. They must think I'm crazy. Sometimes, I feel crazy. Murmured voices and movements seem worlds away. A soft snick of the door and a shuffling of a single pair of feet let me know that Zach is the only one present for my meltdown.

My eyes slowly open, staring at the expansive city view out of the impressive Penthouse window, but I don't see anything. Nothing but hands coming at me in all directions. Lines being laid out on tables before me.

I finally allow a blink when the burn becomes too much to bear. A tear drips down from the corner.

"I'm here, baby. I'm here." Zach whispers, anguish heavy in his voice as his hand slides onto the sheet beside my own. His arm outstretched from the position he's taken up on the floor beside the table. I reach out my pinky towards his. It's the only form of physical touch I can bring myself to give at the moment.

We lay in silence for what seems like forever, listening to the hum of the HVAC unit kicking on and off, doing its very best to keep up with the demands of the large hotel.

"I don't know how to do this, Zach," I say softly, surprised the words come out at all.

His pinky tightens against mine, silently urging me to continue. "I don't even recognize myself most days. When

168

I think about my life two years ago– hell, even just one year ago, I was a completely different person. How did things get so fucked up so fast?"

He heaves a sigh, not out of exasperation but of contemplation. "When my dad first got back from his deployment, I knew immediately somethin' was off. I couldn't put my finger on what exactly, but I knew he wasn't the same guy who left the two years before that," he loosens his grip on my finger, and his hand pulls down to the floor slowly.

I peek down and see him rub an invisible ache in his chest. The one caused by the man he always looked up to. The man meant to teach him right from wrong. The man who destroyed his trust and broke his family.

Zach and I are much the same in that regard. Maybe that's why our souls call to each other. Why there's a magnetic pull that keeps drawing us back together.

"I spent a hell of a lot of those first few months wonderin' what I'd done wrong. Why was he so distant? Why was he so fuckin' angry all the time? Why did he look at Mama and me like we were the cause of all his problems?"

The cracking of his knuckles breaks some of the silence radiating throughout the room. "It took a whole lotta time and a whole buncha therapy sessions, but I finally figured out it wasn't about me. The weight that lifted from my shoulders when I came to that realization was immediate and immense."

He crawls to his knees and rests his chin on the table beside my hand. My pinky instinctively finds his jaw and rubs gently against the light stubble. Zach is such a larger-than-life character. His public persona is an extroverted charmer who doesn't take life too seriously. Doesn't take *anything* too seriously. But I know better. Know him better. He feels deeply, and he has a pain locked away that still is too painful to think about opening. Maybe the bleach isn't enough for Zach's dirty brain box, either.

"Everybody's gotta face their demons in their own time...on their own terms, baby. I ain't here to rush you or make you do somethin' you ain't ready to do," he says, holding his hand close to my face, eyes searching mine for the consent we both need. My eyes immediately soften at this beautiful man who has seen through me since the moment we met. I nod once, and he places his warm palm against my cheek.

"When you are ready, *if* you're ever ready, I'm here."

We stay embraced and find comfort in each other's gaze for a while before Zach stands, kisses my forehead, and disappears.

A few minutes later, he comes back. I bring myself to a sitting position on the table, gripping the sheet tightly around my body. He stands before me and holds a hand out. I look at it, concerned as to how I'm going to stand and not lose the sheet. He heads towards the other side of the living room and comes back with the robe that Lena had laid against the arm of the chair.

I feel the warmth of his body against my back as he drapes the material across my shoulders and brings the front around my body while keeping his hands in respectful positions.

Vanilla and mint fill the air with their essence, my muscles relaxing a bit as I inhale the mouthwatering scents.

"May I?" Zach breathes the question against the side of my neck. I turn slightly to look at him, taking in just how close our faces are to one another. He gestures his arms out in a carrying position. I chuckle, "What a gentleman." I tease.

"Oh darlin', I made some promises about how this evenin' was gonna go, and I intend to keep every single one. Startin' with–" His words are cut off by the very undignified squeal I let out when he lifts my body into his arms and carries me bridal-style into the bathroom.

The vanilla and mint are concentrated in this area. I peer over his shoulder at the biggest bathtub I've ever seen in my life.

Ho-ly shit. The porcelain stretches at least eight feet in length. Gold filigree lines the outer edges, making its way down the sides in soft swoopes and down to the bronze claw feet. The intricate design wraps around the metal and marks a path along the bottom of the tub to the other foot.

Bubbles fill the tub to the brim, and suddenly, I can't wait to immerse myself in them. Zach sets me on the white marble counter with a softness you wouldn't think his muscular body would possess. He's always like that with me, though. I get the side of Zach that no one else does—the tender, attentive, submissive man that I know him to be, and it's all for me.

The cadence of my heart picks up to a breakneck pace when he stands between my legs, with his hands poised on the sash. Waiting for my permission to remove it and bare my body to the elements– to him.

A cold chill spreads from my stomach in every direction, sending misfires of nerves along my limbs. I tamp down the desire to run... and fuck, that desire is fierce. I swallow down my fight-or-flight instinct and put my hand over his, interlocking our fingers as we pull the tie apart together.

His kind, caring gaze reverently follows the movement of our hands. When the ends of the sash drape along my thighs, he brings his eyes to mine, waiting for me to make the next move. It's on my timeline with Zach. *Always.*

Embarrassment heats my skin, and a crimson flush creeps

along my neck and chest. Our joined hands come to the lapels of my robe, and begin to pull it away from my skin slowly. Our gazes lock on one another as the brush of his fingertip against my heated flesh causes a familiar ache to throb between my thighs.

Chapter 24

Charlotte

The scent of my arousal permeates the air between us. Zach's nostrils flare as the robe falls limply off of my shoulders. The weight of the material eliminates the remaining coverage off the rest of my body. I sit, completely open and exposed to him, with moisture pooling between my legs.

Bright green eyes darken to a dangerous piercing jade. Zach's focus falls on the heaving of my flushed chest. His tongue darts out to moisten his plump lips. I want to taste them. I want them to taste *me*.

Zach's earlier promise of going down on me in front of the fireplace has me creating my own friction by moving my thighs tightly against one another. Desperately chasing the pleasure he vowed to inflict on me.

My hands itch to reach out and touch his exposed skin. The tautness of his muscles seems to stand out on display like the true Adonis he is. The tightly wrapped towel around his waist leaves little to the imagination, a clear outline of his desire etched into the linen.

Bravery replaces self-doubt with the clear display of Zach's hunger before me.

I bring our joined hands to my breasts, hoping like hell he doesn't notice how much life has faded from them. The appreciative groan that bubbles up from his throat gives me a renewed confidence that he does, in fact, still find me desirable. I squeeze our fingers against my hardening nipples. A jolt of pleasure lands right on my clit. I unconsciously glide forward on the towel, seeking the pressure I urgently need.

"Fuck, darlin'," he breathes out in a low timbre between our bodies. He steps closer. His hard cock presses against the robe-covered edge of the counter. Small thrusts against the hard material tell me he is equally searching for relief.

Zach leans forward and places a kiss on the area just above where our hands are joined on my nipple. His tongue draws a path down and stops just before he hits the place where I desperately want to feel his hot mouth. He places two more soft kisses before pulling back, "You're kinda distractin', sweetheart. Come on, our bath is gettin' cold."

He tugs the towel off of his waist, letting the material fall to the ground before scooping me up and setting me down in the still-hot bath. He climbs in behind me and pulls me into his chest. We snug into each other, and muscles begin to ease immediately. Fuck I needed this.

Zach dips a washcloth into the soapy water and gently rubs my chest. Skipping my still-peaked nipples, he travels down to my soft middle, stopping just above the mound of my pussy. A huff of annoyance leaves my mouth. He picks up his movements over my hip bones, up my side, and out to my left arm. Across my chest to repeat the process on my right.

I let my hair loose from the messy bun, letting the locks dance across the top of the water as I settle myself further in Zach's chest. He lifts his legs and locks them around my center.

My hands run down his soapy, thick thighs, smoothing the soft hairs that line his legs. We lay, contented to be in each other's space. The feeling of belonging envelopes me, lighting up the dark cloud that trails behind me. Somedays, the skies are clear. Somedays, the storm rolls in, and I prepare to batten down the hatches.

Between the anti-depressant that we finally got sorted out– into something that didn't make me feel entirely numb to the world– and the regular therapy sessions, things in my head have gotten a bit quieter. The darkness hasn't completely abated. I know it never will, but when I think about sliding down and letting the water fill my lungs until it displaces the last trace of air... It doesn't bring me peace.

* * *

Zach

I cup my hands in the tub and bring water over her free-flowing hair, getting it saturated enough to take the vanilla-scented shampoo. My fingertips knead the aromatic liquid gently into her scalp. The small mews coming from her let me know that she's enjoying it.

The vibrations from the sound reverberate against my cock, which is pressed firmly against her back. Surely, she can feel the rigidity setting in. *Calm it down, kid. This is about her, not us.* I tell my dick internally, hoping he'll take the hint and chill the fuck out before we make her uncomfortable.

I don't want her to think I only want her body.

I want everything.

Her mind. Her soul. Her love.

I've had superficial. I've had purely physical. I don't want that for us. I want her to crave me as much as I crave her. I want to be her peace as much as she is mine. I want to fill the dark void in her heart and tame the beast that lives within her mind.

She wiggles her body as she adjusts her position in the water, pressing into me. I'm unsure of her intent, but I've vowed to let this all go at the pace she sets. My hard-on be damned.

I press gently on her shoulders, moving her down enough that her head can tilt backward into the water. I cup the water over her hair, rinsing the shampoo. My fingers thoroughly resemble prunes from the time we've spent in here. I lean her forward so I can reach the towel bar behind us.

I step out first and quickly dry off, wrapping the towel around my waist before reaching a hand out for Charlotte. She takes it and brings her glorious, naked, wet body to a stand. My eyes greedily take in her smaller but still present curves. Heat blooms on her cheeks. It pisses me off that she's lost all confidence in herself. Regardless of her size, she's perfect to me. Now and always. It's time I show her that.

She wraps the towel around her body, sliding her wet hair over the front of her head to squeeze the excess water out. I help her step out of the tub and lead her to the living room, where she lies on the plush blanket I laid out in front of the fireplace earlier.

Nerves and hunger fight for dominance in her gaze as she looks from the blanket to me and down to the hands gripping for dear life on the towel. She needs to understand. I meant what I said. This is her show. I'm merely a supporting character.

176

Something inside of her is broken. I may not know how to repair everything, but I do know what she needs at this moment: control.

Over her life.

Over her body.

Over... me.

I flip the switch on the overhead light, walk over to the fireplace, turn my back to it, face my girl, and drop the towel. Firelight fills the dark spaces of the room. Standing before her, naked as the day I was born, I do something I've never done in my life... I fall to my knees– for her. My head bowed and palms resting openly, facing up on my thighs. A full picture of submission.

She has to believe that she truly holds all the cards here. I am hers. I trust her implicitly. I am giving myself to her in the most vulnerable way I can.

Her voice is soft, unsure, "W-what are you doing?"

My gaze remains on the floor before me. "Waitin' on you, sweetheart. Tonight is yours. *I am yours*. Tell me what you want me to do." I answer her in a muted, urging tone.

She stands in silence for what seems like hours before timidly making her way to stand in front of me.

With my head in its current position, all I can see is the towel hanging at her shins and the bright green of her toe polish. With a whoosh, the towel falls, and she steps closer. Her delicate finger rests under my chin, and with gentle pressure, she raises it up until our gazes clash.

"Are you mine, Zach?" she asks. Her brow rises as a mask of dominance slides into place.

"Forever."

She nods and drapes her right leg over my left shoulder.

The urge to run my hand along her smooth thigh and bite the supple flesh there hits me like a tidal wave of lust and want. *Wait.*

I watch her face closely, waiting for the command to come out. My Little Bit is a stubborn one, though. She does what she wants, and when she finally allows herself to take what she wants... She is a stunning picture of broken perfection.

The finger under my chin glides to cup the right side of my jaw, which she firmly pulls forward at the same time that she moves her pussy right in front of my face. *Wait.*

Her scent drifts in the air, and my mouth waters. I pause with a barely restrained compulsion to bury my face in her delectable cunt. *Wait.*

"Stick your tongue out." She commands. I obey. She leans down and sucks my tongue into her mouth. I stay stock still. I dare not move a single muscle until she tells me to. But I can't control the twitch of my cock. She works my tongue like she would my dick, and he notices.

My girl pulls back and places her hand on the back of my head, bringing me forward so my nose is against the lips of her pussy. *Wait.*

She glides her hips slightly, up and down. Her juices coat my lips, nose, and chin. "Tongue." She demands. I instantly lay my tongue flat against her opening and wait for the next instruction. Grinding her pelvis in my face, she begins using my tongue to give herself pleasure. *Wait.*

"Stick two fingers inside me while I ride your face, Zachariah." The use of my full name sends shivers down my spine, and a heady pleasure courses through my body as I comply and insert my fore and middle finger into her wet heat.

Charlotte rides my face, using her hand to grip my hair, bringing the exact pressure she's chasing forth. I curve my fingers into the pleasure button inside her, and her legs begin to shake as her orgasm takes hold. She rides faster, her moans and pants filling the silence of the room. I finger fuck her with equal fervor and lap at the essence as it slides out of her along my fingers as they plunge in and out.

"E-enough, please. It's too much." She breathes as her legs quake from the sensitivity. I smile and place a featherlight kiss on her clit, relishing in the full-body shiver that results, and pull my fingers out of her.

They glisten with her release in the firelight, and I want to suck it off of them. Before I can finish the thought, Little Bit lowers to her knees in front of me and brings my fingers to her mouth. With her eyes locked on mine, she inserts each digit singularly and sucks them clean. *Fuck me.* I am seconds away from blowing my load and making a damn fool of myself like a pre-pubescent boy.

"Lay back," she instructs as she guides my body down until I'm flat on my back. She straddles me and grasps my chin firmly in her hand, her eyes intent on mine, "You will not come. Nod if you understand." I nod as she works her way down my body and settles between my thighs. I pray to every sex God out there that I don't embarrass myself right now. My cock is already leaking pre-cum, and not letting loose when her luscious mouth lands on it is going to be a feat fit for Hercules himself.

Warm breaths hit the tip of my dick, and I fist my hands, digging the nails into my palm. The hot tongue that darts out and licks the bead at the tip nearly sends me over the edge. Thankfully, she doesn't tease me much before taking all that she can deep into her mouth and working the bottom of my shaft with her hand. Filthy, sloppy sounds thrash around the classy room. Their juxtaposition embeds itself deep inside the lavish walls. Never to be unmarred again.

Her free hand cups my balls, and I feel them tighten instantly. She pinches the sensitive flesh, and the jolt of pain alongside the pleasure of her mouth has me gripping the blanket with all my might. *Wait.*

Her cheeks hollow, and she sucks me down with renewed vigor. I'm going to come, and there ain't a damn thing either of us can do about it. My dick begins to pulse, and she pinches my balls again. *Fuck.* The pain makes the pulsing recede. She sucks harder again, and when the tell-tale pulsating begins, she pinches. Over and over until my chest heaves with desire and frustration all in one. I'm ready to flip her over and fuck her into this floor.

She lets my cock go with a "pop" and crawls up my body, straddling my waist. My skin shines in the firelight with the sweat of restraint and yearning. My breaths pant hard as my chest rises and falls rapidly.

Charlotte places her hand over the unyielding thumps of my ticker. A smirk curves her lips as she brings them down to mine. A chaste kiss punctuated by a hard bite to my bottom lip. My dick jerks at the pleasing sting.

"Have you ever fucked someone bare, Zachariah?" she asks in an emotionless tone.

I pull my face back and twist it in disgust, "Fuck no. I always wrap it up, Little Bit. I ain't no dummy."

"Are you clean?"

I nod my head, furrowing my brows in confusion. I had my physical when I got to UA—clean as a whistle.

Her hand runs from my chest, down my abs, and underneath her pussy to grab hold of my rock-hard cock, lining it up with her core.

"Do you trust me, Zachariah?" she asks, her voice seeming smaller. She is trepidatious about the possibility that the answer could be anything but yes.

"With my fuckin' life, Little Bit," I confess, meaning every damn word. This woman has everything of me.

"I'm on birth control, and I was tested when I was in the hospital—" Her confidence is wavering as she worries that I don't want to take her raw. She couldn't be more wrong. I want my girl with nothing between us. I want our bodies to intertwine as tightly as our souls have.

And even though it's not remotely the time, the thought of her belly swollen with my child has me feeling animalistic. She has unlocked a breeding kink I never knew I had. I'm ready to lay her down and fill her full of my babies. Claim her as mine forever. One day, Little Bit. *One day.*

I reach up and cup her chin, gently pulling her face down to mine. I place a tender kiss on her lips, "With my fuckin' life, my love." I reaffirm, giving her the permission she's searching for.

As she sinks down, we both moan our pleasures.

This. This is what love is: two people coming together in the most human of ways, pain and broken pieces on display for the other, two jagged edges fitting perfectly into each other's fragmented hearts.

"I love you, Charlotte."

"I love you, too."

Chapter 25

Charlotte

My body aches in the most delicious of ways as I stretch languidly in our makeshift bed on the floor of the Penthouse.

I don't know how Zach always knows what I need, but it's like he was inside my head last night. Somehow, knowing that what I needed was the control.

I don't fancy myself a Domina or anything, but I fit into the role like it was made for me. Taking the pleasure I wanted. *How* I wanted. *When* I wanted. It was liberating.

I would've never thought that was something that I needed. And Zach? I would've never guessed that he would be willing to submit himself to someone. He's never been overly dominant when we are together, but he definitely likes to take the lead.

Seeing him bear himself to me, mind, body, and soul, last night on his knees is a memory I will cherish for the rest of my days. As well as made some incredible spank bank material.

Strong, warm arms wrap around me as Zach buries his face into my back. "Good mornin', sweetheart. Do you wanna order breakfast in or grab somethin' on the way back to Mary's?" The reminder of what the day holds sucks a bit of the wind out of my sails.

Fucking Priest's sentencing.

I groan and reach for my phone to check the time. We have two and a half hours until we are to meet David at the courthouse.

"We better grab something on the way." I sigh. Thinking about Priest is definitely a mood killer. Looks like no morning sex for me. *Fucking asshole.*

I'm stuffing the last of the salmon breakfast burrito in my face as we pull up to the familiar duplex. Zach kisses my cheek to avoid fishy lips and promises to be back in an hour after he showers and dresses at home.

Walking into Savvy's room, I dump my bag unceremoniously onto her bed and strip myself of the jeans and tee. I head to her bathroom to shower and get ready for whatever shit storm the day carries.

* * *

Walking into the courtroom this time feels more nerve-wracking than the previous time. I don't know why. I've already given my testimony. He's already been indicted. It's a done deal. This is simply a formality. But this just feels heavier on my heart. I can't explain the all-encompassing black cloud that coats the room.

I originally planned on wearing a black pantsuit. It's basically Priest's funeral, so I may as well dress for the occasion. But at the last minute, I changed my mind and snagged a white skater dress with a smattering of red roses along the bottom hem. I paired the graceful feminine piece with my stark white Chuck Ts.

Priest has stolen enough of my joy.

David slides into the pew first, Mary beside him, and then Zach slides in, and I take up the last position. There's still space for others to sit on our pew if they so choose, but most spectators stick to the rows behind us.

Just like before, people trickle in: onlookers, news crews, litigators, and bailiffs. The room is mostly full, and the noise lowers to a steady hum of chatter as we all wait for the judge.

I take a gander around the space, not recognizing many faces. The Poole family is a notable absence. I guess once their cash cow was a lost cause, there was no need to keep up appearances. I can't say I'm sorry not to have to see Erick's face again.

My dad is another notable absence. He's been traveling back and forth so much that some important meetings were pushed off until they couldn't be anymore. He was willing to say fuck it and come anyway. Consequences be damned. But I assured him, I had plenty of support and would give him a call tonight with a recap.

The bailiff announces the judge's arrival, asking us all to rise as Judge Appleton makes his way in from his Chambers and takes his place. He waves to the bailiff, a signal to bring in the prisoner.

A whoosh of air hits my bare legs as a bag is dropped beside them on the floor. A pair of familiar black flats settle beside the bag. My gaze travels up and lands on the fresh-faced, ragey teen with short black hair.

She doesn't look at me or acknowledge anything in the room. Her gaze is firmly fixed on the door that Priest will walk through any moment now. A haunted look affixed to her otherwise angelic, pale face.

I shake off the weirdness and tap my feet against the floor in an attempt to dispel my own nervous energy. The vibes in this room are totally fucked.

Whispers hit a crescendo as Priest is led into the room through the same door as before. Everything is reminiscent of that day. His uniform is the same, and the full-body chains are the same. A false air of confidence and superiority wafts off of him.

And just like last time, his eyes search for mine in the crowd, and he winks, "Astra."

I roll my eyes and subtly flip him the bird against my temple. Feigning an itch against my skin.

Judge Appleton calls the room to order and begins reviewing the charges against Priest. He entered a plea of guilty in exchange for no extradition and the removal of some lesser charges.

Ragey girl bounces in her seat, and I briefly wonder if there's a fire lit under her ass or something. I want to tell her to chill, but I'm kinda dealing with my own shit over here.

She begins riffling through her bag, her shaky hands not latching on anything in particular.

The banal recapping of the trial by the judge is droning on, and on; I find myself on the verge of screaming at him to just get the fuck on with it already.

Finally, he makes a call for any victim impact statements. I discussed the decision at length with David, Mary, and Zach. I decided against it. I don't want to rehash my trauma for these people yet again. I've been assured that no matter what, he will be going away for likely the rest of his miserable life, and it wouldn't make much difference anyway.

After today, Priest gets no more of me. Ever again.

David didn't seem to think there were any of Priest's direct victims attending, so this part will be over quickly, and we can move on to the nitty-gritty of the day.

"Miss Justice?" Judge Appleton calls, waving her forward.

To my surprise, the ragey girl leans down, grabs her bag, holds it tightly to her side, and pulls out a sheet of paper. She stands and walks toward the small podium between the prosecution and defense tables.

She sets the crumpled paper against the wooden lectern and lets out a deep, shaky breath. She shakes off the nerves and straightens her shoulders, turning her gaze straight to Priest, who looks at her with confusion. His reaction clearly shows that he either doesn't know who this girl is or why she's here—maybe both.

Ragey girl clears her throat and speaks loudly, with no trace of nerves in her voice. "My name is Mallory Justice. I am here today to tell you about my sister, Jennika. Jennika was smart, funny, and beautiful. Her smile lit up every room she went into. She always had the best grades, the best clothes, best friends. Best everything.

She was popular and kind. She would always make sure I wasn't left out of things just because I was younger. She was the best sister a girl could ask for. One day I came home, and Jennika wasn't so nice. Her grades started slipping. Her friends changed. She started keeping secrets. Staying out for days at a time, not telling anyone where she was or who she was with. Sometimes, she would come home with bruises all over her body. Fingerprints along her arm or around her neck.

The light completely left her eyes. She was a walking zombie. A ghost of the girl she used to be. And then, one day, she never came home. Her body was found in an alleyway in Palmsville.

Behind a dumpster. Her clothes were torn, and her underwear lay bloody and in pieces beside her body. And a needle was still sticking out of her arm."

Recognition seems to dawn over Priest. He may not know ragey girl. But he damn sure knew her sister.

She smooths the crumpled paper against the lectern with gentle care as though the soft caress of the words could bring back her sister.

The room waits with bated breath for her to continue her statement. But she stays stoically, staring at that paper.

Judge Appleton clears his throat and opens his mouth to address her when she whispers, "He killed her. He took Jennika away, and no punishment is enough." Her eyes snap to the judge as her voice raises, her ire for Priest laden throughout her words. "Caleb doesn't deserve to sit in a warm cell, eating three hot meals every day while my sister is buried in the cold, unforgiving earth. It's not enough." She turns her whole attention back to Priest and smiles. A chill runs through my veins. "It's not *enough*." She whispers again.

Ragey girl reaches into the bag she's kept tucked tightly against her side and points the shiny metal at Priest. Time slows throughout the courthouse as the bang reverberates off the walls. Priest's body slumps against the table, a pool of blood forming.

Another bang.

There's a flurry of motion all around. Crying. Screaming. Cursing. And all I can think as I look down at the speckles of red against my once unsoiled white Chuck Ts is, fucking hell, there ain't enough bleach for this.

II

Part Two

Chapter 26

October 2007

Charlotte

"How are you settling in, Charlotte?" Dr. T asks. It seems like such a simple question. It should be simple, I guess, for some people. The phone presses snugly between my cheek and shoulder so I can move my heavy-ass textbooks off the edge of the desk and into my backpack. If I don't leave in the next eight minutes, I'll be late for class. *Fuck me.*

Breathing heavily into the receiver from the exertion of heaving those cinder blocks that I call books around, I plop my butt down on my bed. "Okay, I suppose. Zach returned over the weekend and moved the big stuff around that we hadn't gotten to on move-in day a few weeks ago. Dad was able to get me a single. So, no roommate, which is a relief. I'd hate to have the awkward talk about my night terrors with someone new..." My sentence trails off, embarrassment creeping up my chest as heat settles in my cheeks.

I pick at imaginary lint on my comforter while I sit silently and wait for her response.

"Charlotte, we've been through this. It is perfectly normal

to have nightmares after such a traumatic event." She assures me, like always – but it doesn't make me feel any better. *I know what would... No. Charlotte, no. I don't need the drugs. I don't need the drugs. I don't need the drugs.*

Six months ago, I walked into a courtroom, ready to see my boogeyman receive his just desserts... and boy, did he ever.

A young girl, the sister of one of the many victims of Priest, was delivering her victim impact statement during his sentencing hearing.

This petite girl is wearing a black dress, black tights, and black shoes. The one who looked as though she came dressed for a funeral. Little did we know, she would be attending one and it would be the last thing she ever did.

With rage in her mind and revenge in her heart, she somehow snuck a gun into the courthouse and shot Priest dead right then and there. Though it shocked everyone, it was really no skin off my back. The world is better off with one less deplorable Priest in it.

But, when she turned it on herself...

Though, Ursula – the personalized identifier I've given to the part of my brain that craves the darkness. The numbing. The escape – still tries daily to lead me into temptation, to rid myself of the decrepit memory carousel I find myself on. I've held fast.

Watching someone be murdered right in front of me didn't hit me quite like I'd ever imagined it would. When that someone has made your life a living hell, raped you, let his friends rape you, and forced drug use on you, my moral compass starts to get a little wobbly.

Watching a sweet but murdering young girl kill herself... that's something I've yet to wrap my mind around.

I've had countless sessions with Dr. T. I've attended at least one NA meeting a week. I've even found a sponsor here in Alabama, Genevieve "Genny" Lambert.

During the day, I keep busy. Class, study, meeting, therapy, food. Rinse and repeat. But at night? The demons flood in from all sides. My subconscious forces me to relive different traumatic events from the last year or so.

My body is locked in a chair by thick ropes that cut into the skin of my wrists and ankles. So tight that the blood caused by the friction of my frantic movements pools onto my jean-covered thighs. My head is strapped to the back of the chair with an unforgiving restraining metal band across my forehead. Sharp claws of a rusty metal speculum dig into my top and lower eyelids, forcing them open in plain view of the tattered projection screen that is pinned to the crumbling red brick wall in front of me.

Flickering images dance across the screen, and a chilling sensation surrounds me. The sepia-toned frames flash rapidly, casting eerie shadows as if whispering secrets of a dark past. Each scene unfolds with a haunting moment of my life. The otherwise silent air is punctuated with unnerving whispers and disembodied cries coming from the darkness that surrounds me.

With a forced gaze, I am peering through a window into the darkest recesses of my psyche, where the echoes of bygone terrors still linger. And as the final frame fades into darkness, I am left with a lingering sense of unease and dread, haunted by the spectral fragments of what I had just relived.

Waking is the same every time. As my consciousness slowly returns, I find myself suspended in a transitional space between dream and reality. The remnants of the nightmares clinging to my mind like tendrils of shadow, refusing to release their grip. My heart hammers against its cage. Each beat echoes like a drum in the silence of the night. With a gasp, I try to sit up, to escape the clutches of the darkness that still linger in the corners of my mind.

But to my horror, my body remains motionless, as if shackled by invisible chains. Panic surges within me, a primal instinct urging me to flee, to break free from the paralysis that holds me captive. Every fiber of my being screams for release, for the ability to move, to escape the suffocating grip of terror. But still, I remain trapped, a prisoner in my own flesh.

Time suspends around me as I battle against the invisible bonds that hold me. After what seems like an eternity, slowly but surely, sensation begins to return to my limbs, like a thawing frost melting away under the warmth of the sun. But even as I regain control of my body, the memory of the nightmare lingers, haunting the edges of my consciousness.

After one of these episodes, my body is thoroughly drained. Feeling like I've gone ten rounds with Mike Tyson and somehow survived more than one hit.

I always check over my skin in the full-length mirror, expecting to see a battered and bruised reflection, finding nothing but unblemished flesh before me.

"Yeah. Normal." I retort sarcastically. I thought shrinks weren't supposed to use words like "normal". Makes the loonies itchy.

"Is the medication helping?"

I reach for the bottle of sleeping pills she's referencing, turning it in my palm. "Yeah." *When I take them. Which is almost never. They make me groggy and floaty. It's too close to how I felt back then.*

"Good. Well, I know you need to be off to class. I'll call you at the same time next week. Take care, Charlotte."

I barely utter an agreeance before the line is cut off. Dr. T is all business. Whatevs, I need to get going anyway. Checking the time on my phone, I now have three minutes to make it across campus.

Of course, I would be racing the clock for English Lit, Professor Gentry's class. He fucking hates me. I have no idea what bug crawled up his ass, but he seriously has me at the tip-top of his shit list.

I hoist the hundred-pound bag around my shoulder, instantly feeling the ache from the repetitive motions over the last three weeks. When I step out of the dorm building, I'm immediately met with the harshest torrential downpour I've ever seen.

Not having another choice, I flop my wafer-thin hood from my sweatshirt on top of my unruly blonde hair and head toward the English building as quickly as my tiny legs will carry me.

Every eye is on me as the heavy wooden door slams shut behind me. Dozens of stares latched onto the dripping rat, who is now– looking down at my phone– six minutes late. So much for sneaking in without being noticed.

I give Professor Gentry an apologetic smile. I open my mouth to pour out some lame excuse. He stops me with a shake of his head and lifts his hand in a "stop" motion.

"Miss Johnson, if this class isn't important to you, that's fine. But you will not interrupt the students who actually want to be here by creating an unnecessary disruption with your–" he flails his hands up and down my body with disgust plastered on his face. "Unpreparedness and abhorrent attire."

His gaze lands pointedly on my chest in distaste. I look down

195

and find that the rain has soaked completely through my white blouse, and my rock-hard nipples are on full display through my thin beige bra. *Fuck me.*

I quickly pull the side of my hoodie around my front, covering my borderline pornographic demonstration from the prying eyes of the lecture hall. A whispered "Hey!" captures my attention from the back row. A very broad-shouldered, dark hair man whines at the covering of the titty show. I narrow my eyes at him in warning before turning back to Professor Gentry, getting ready to put on the show of a lifetime.

"I apologize for the interruption and the unacceptable tardiness. I won't bore you with excuses. I want to be here. It won't happen again." I force a submissive expression onto my face, hoping like hell he buys my apology. This is all he's getting. I am not a beggar.

He sighs and rolls his eyes while waving me off to find a seat. I waste no time finding an empty chair at the end of a nearly empty row towards the back. I set my bag down quietly, dig out my textbook, notebook, and pen, and settle in for class.

After the longest hour ever, Professor Gentry dismissed us with a fucking ten thousand word essay due by next week as homework. I stuff my things unsystematically into my backpack and make my way down the student tiers, passing by "Leer-oy, The Giant." I give him the finger when he blows me a kiss.

Making my way into the flow of students, a hand lands on my shoulder. I immediately stiffen, ready to tell Bigfoot-Little Dick to fuck all the way off and fall short at the petite, fairly familiar, mousy brunette standing before me.

Startled, I stare at her nervous expression, frozen in place.

She tucks an errant strand of thin, pin-straight brown hair behind her right ear. Her left hand grips onto the top of her blue cross-body bag. She must have significantly fewer books in hers than I do in mine to be holding it so effortlessly.

I chuck the backpack strap higher on my shoulder as my words find their way to my mouth again, "Uh, yes? How can I help you?"

"Hey, um, Charlotte, right?" she asks, nervousness coating her words.

"Yep. That's me. And you're..."

"Rebecca Crowe. I'm Gentry's TA. I'm sorry he's been so hard on you. I don't know what his deal is." That's right, she was introduced on my first day of class. She just kinda blends in with the background, easily forgettable face, apparently.

I shrug my shoulder, "It's not your fault. I just have that charming way about me, I guess. So, Rebecca, was there a reason you stopped me or–" I let the sentence trail off, hoping she'll explain why she's deterring me from making my Calc class on time.

"Oh yes, um, so I know you're new, and I haven't seen you with any friends or anything. I'm kind of a loner myself. I was wondering if you might want to hang out sometime?"

Surprised, my eyes widen unintentionally. "Oh. Um, yeah, sure. I'm kind of busy, though, so I'm not sure when I'll be free. But, maybe?"

Rebecca's shoulders drop, and crimson covers her cheeks. She's embarrassed at my dismissal. I'm such an ass. This poor girl just wants a friend. Why can't I just be nice and take her up on her offer? I'm trying to turn over a new leaf here.

I've always been the one to have a very small, tight-knit group of friends and dozens of acquaintances. Unlike my social butterfly best friend, I am perfectly happy being alone.

But ever since the nightmares started, being alone doesn't give the comfort it once did. Fuck it. New school. New me. Let's do some friend shit.

I reach out and gently lay my hand on top of hers, pulling her attention back to me. "Hey. I'm sorry. I'm still pretty rattled from racing over here in the middle of the monsoon and being chastised by Gentry. I'd love to chill sometime. Here," I rummage through my side pocket and grab a loose pen, holding it out to her with my right hand. I offer my left palm as a paper substitute, "Jot your digits down, and I'll text you this weekend. I saw there was a pretty popular pizza place just off campus on Magnolia. I've been wanting to check it out. You down to go?"

A wide smile lifts her lips, and she nods frantically at me. Her brown eyes show off flecks of gold as the reflection from the window casts a light through them. She grabs the pen and starts scribbling across my palm. "I'm free on Saturday night, anytime after six." She says as she hands the pen back to me.

Tucking it back in its pocket, I nod my head, "Okay, so how about we meet there at seven?"

"Seven sounds perfect. See you then, Charlotte." She waves as she strolls down the hallway in the opposite direction I am heading.

"Charlie!" I holler at her back in correction, and she turns and offers another grin. "Charlie."

Internally, I high-five myself for putting myself out there. Dr. T will be so proud of me for making a new friend. This could be the great fresh start that I desperately need. Savvy might be a little jelly, but she'll always be my numero uno, my ride-or-die, *always*. But having a new friend in a new place will be nice. Rebecca's clearly familiar with the school, being a TA and a sophomore.

Yeah, this is going to be the change I needed—to heal, move on, grow, and flourish. And it all begins with my newest pal, Rebecca. Becky. Becca? I don't know what her nickname will be. We'll work it out.

Chapter 27

Charlotte

Okay, it probably should have occurred to me that Saturday night, outside of a University, would lead to any restaurant being packed as fuck. Walking up to the entrance, the line is at least ten people deep, and that's *outside* the doors.

Pulling my phone from my back jeans pocket, I hit the side button to illuminate the screen. I'm ten minutes early. I quickly scan the line and don't see the tiny statured brunette.

I join the line, so maybe we'll be close to the door by the time seven o'clock rolls around. I lean my back against the rough brick facade of the building and open up a new Snake game on my phone.

I'm just about to clear the screen when someone bumps into me, and the snake touches the edge of his motherfucking tail. *Sonofabitch!* I whip my head to the left, ready to let loose on the jackass that made me lose my game, when I'm met with a bright, shiny, and smiley Rebecca.

"Hey, Charlie! I'm uber sorry I'm late. I had tutoring before this, and it ran a little over, so I had a late start getting back to my dorm to get ready. I didn't mean to startle you. Didn't you get my text?" she asks. Of course, I didn't see her text. I was a little busy taking ass and kicking names at Snake. *Don't be a bitch to your new friend, Charlie.*

"I was a little distracted." I offer with a slight smile, shaking my phone between us, hoping it masks my irritation. If it doesn't, Rebecca doesn't let on to it. She simply smiles back, nodding in understanding.

Twenty-four long minutes later, we are finally let into the restaurant and taken to a table. We perused the menus and settled on one pizza to share—Hawaiian with chicken added—and a basket of fries to split. We also order two totally separate chocolate milkshakes because if her lips touch my straw and she backwashes in my drink, I may have to stab my new bestie. I do not share milk products. Period.

My phone buzzes on the table. I don't want to be rude to my meal companion, so I pick it up and turn the ringer on silent when the text makes my heart race. Heat creeps up my body and settles right in my pussy.

Zee: Hope my girl's ready for some phone dickin' tonight. I've had a long day, darlin', and I got an ache only you can fix.

"Oh, girl, what is that about?" I look up at her. She makes a circle at my face with a french fry.

I quickly place the phone back on the table. Nervous laughter bubbles out of me. I can't tell her what "that" is about. Zach has been insatiable lately.

"Oh, um, just my boyfriend checking in." I offer flippantly, hoping she won't ask me any details about the text. I'm not ashamed of having an active sex life with my boyfriend, whom I love, but it makes me feel itchy inside to think about delving into specifics with a stranger.

"Boyfriend, huh? Does he go here?" she asks while looking aimlessly around the room.

I shake my head no and suck down a little of my milkshake. "No, he goes to Bama."

She makes a sour face. "Oh, so you're really trying out the long-distance thing?" she asks like it's a sure thing to fail. I bristle at her question. "We are committed. I trust him. He trusts me. That's all there is to it. We make it work." I respond with less bite than I feel, making me proud of myself internally for not flipping out on her.

I have to remember not everyone has bad intentions.

Rebecca nods and takes a drink of her own milkshake, "That's great. I'm so happy for you. Most of the boys here are total dogs. They smile in their girlfriend's faces and then have their hands up a co-ed's skirt in the stacks an hour later."

She must have seen the surprised and disgusted look on my face at the reference to rampant cheating. "Oh, but I'm sure your guy isn't like that. I'm sure he's honest with you and isn't just hanging around a bunch of girls all the time." She offers, and I can't decide if it's to make me feel better or worse.

"Yeah..." I trail off and look around the room. I spot a hallway with a *Restroom* sign above it and nod my head in its direction. "I'll be right back. I gotta pee."

Closing the stall door behind me, I lay my forearm against it and prop my head on it. Inhaling the clean scent of my detergent to ground me. *Don't listen to her, Charlie. You trust Zach. He doesn't hide things from you. He's not him. He wouldn't do that to you. You trust him.* I reach down to respond to his text and realize I left my phone on the table. Well, shit, I'll get back to him when I get back to my room then.

I do my business, wash my hands, and head back out to

202

Rebecca.

"Hey, I'm sorry if I overstepped. Sometimes, I babble when I'm nervous. I truly didn't mean anything by it."

I let out a sigh and smack a smile on my face. "Don't worry about it. It's no biggie." I wave her apology off and grab another fry to pop into my mouth as I settle in my seat.

"So, what fun things are there to do around here?" I ask, changing the subject to hopefully something with less tension.

She chews her fry faster, wiping off her hands to prepare to speak. I've noticed that about her, she talks with her hands. A lot. It's a cute little quirk she has. *See, you can be nice about something that's fucking annoying.*

"So there's a bowling alley just down the street. But you want to avoid it on the weekday evenings. They have leagues, and they get uber-serious about their bowling and can be complete dicks. There's a movie theater about a mile away. They have great matinees during the week starting at ten in the morning. There's a club close by that's eighteen and up. Wait, how old are you?"

"I'm nineteen. But if you look at a certain ID that I have in my possession... I'm twenty-two."

"Twenty-two? Why not twenty-one?" she laughs.

I toss a fry at her, "Every idiot with a fake ID puts their age at twenty-one. So obviously fake. I figure no woman wants to age herself as much as possible so they'll believe twenty-two over twenty-one."

We both laugh and tuck into our food. Even though we had a bit of a rocky start, I'm starting to enjoy my night with Rebecca.

* * *

Zee: Send nudes!

  Me: In your dreams

  Zee: *Sad face emoji*

  Me: *Sends full body pic of me in the skin-tight, black bodycon dress Rebecca picked out for me to wear to the club tonight.*

  Zee: Hot damn, darlin'. I need you somethin' fierce girl. Why don't you go on and gimme a video call? I need to see what that sexy as fuck dress looks like on your floor.

  Me: Can't. Meeting Rebecca @ the club, gotta jet in five, or I'll be late.

  Zee: #1- What in the sam hell am I supposed to do about this ragin' hard-on you just gave me? #2- Not a damn person better put their hands on you tonight. You. Are. Mine. Is that understood?

  Me: LOL. Only yours, baby. What are you up to tonight?

  Zee: Good girl. Morgs and some of the guys are comin' to mine and Tuck's room for a game night.

  Me: BORING! Have fun with your Scrabble, old man.

  Zee: For your information, sassafras, we are playin' poker. Maybe strip, who knows. Could get wild in here.

  Me: LOL, a bunch of dudes sitting around naked with each other playing games... sure. Send pics!

  Me: Maybe take it a little easy on the adult bevs?

  Zee: All good baby.

  Me: KK, gotta head out. Love you!

  Zee: Love you more, Little Bit.

Every bag I own clashes with this outfit. Frustrated, I fling each of the mismatching clutches around the drawer they live in. Fuck it. This is why God gave women boobs. I tuck my debit card, coin, and fake ID into my left bra-cket and my phone into my right one. Checking over my reflection in the full-length mirror, I smooth the dress down. It stops mid-thigh. A bit more risque than my typical wardrobe allows, but I promised Rebecca she could choose, and this itty bitty excuse for a dress was her choice.

I tie up my platform MJs to complete the look. Like fuck am I attempting heels at a dance club. I'd like to avoid face-planting on that nasty ass floor. No, thank you. I can move in platforms. I have been rocking the Baby Spice's since middle school.

I pull out my phone to text Rebecca, letting her know I'm on the way to meet her in the parking lot downstairs and bypass the matching black faux leather jacket. It may be November and a balmy sixty-five degrees to these Alabamians– Alaba-mans? –, but sixty-five to this Alaskan this late in the year is freaking heat wave weather. Hell, Alaskans are still wearing t-shirts and shorts right now in our thirty-degree weather.

My jaw nearly unhinges from my face when I get a look at my friend. Ho-ly shit. Her normally mousy, straight hair is layered around her heart-shaped face in waves. Deep lines of black frame her glittery eyes. The black bandana top shows off her surprisingly taut midriff. The bottom point skims just over the top of her belly button, which is on full display thanks to the very low, hip-hugging white jeans that seem to be plastered onto her petite body. Her stature is towering higher tonight from the hot pink stiletto heels on her feet.

Who the fuck is this?

She hasn't seen me walk over yet, so I observe her in stalkery freedom through the shadows of the parking lot. Her body rests against a jet-black sports car. Whose ride is that? Has my new companion been body-snatched by a porn star?

"Damn girl, I'm gonna call you Paula 'cause you are America's idol in this getup!" I shout as I get closer, catching her attention. She pushes off the car and tucks a lock of hair behind her right ear like she does when she's nervous.

"Nu-uh. No ma'am. You look hot as sin tonight. Strut it," I dare her, cocking an eyebrow in challenge and wave my arm down the sidewalk.

Rebecca giggles and tries to brush me off. Ha. Not in this lifetime, sis. "Becky with the fly hair, you better strut your sexy butt down this sidewalk right now."

She humors me and makes a halfhearted attempt at a catwalk before rushing me into the backseat of the car as she climbs in the passenger side. Uh, WTF?

"'Sup." is the only greeting I get from the dude behind the wheel. He looks familiar. I think we have psych together.

I nod back when I catch his eyes in the reflection of the rearview mirror. "Hey."

Yep. It's definitely psych guy. Hunter. I recognize those beady eyes.

Why is Rebecca with this guy?

I scoot myself as modestly as I can to the middle of the back seat so I have a clear view of the front and windshield. Psych dude turns the volume up on some electronic mix that has my ears wanting to puncture themselves, and we fly out of the parking lot.

The club isn't too far away, maybe ten minutes at the speed of the fucking Delorean here. The lights from remaining open businesses pass by in a blur, movement from the front pulls my attention from the lightshow out of the window.

What the hell?

Psych dude just slid his hand across Rebecca's leg and landed

206

it firmly against her crotch. I know for a fucking fact he has a girlfriend. I'm subjected to their makeout sessions in class on a weekly basis. Unless they broke up four hours ago, this guy is a scumbag. And why is Rebecca letting it happen? She doesn't seem fazed at all. Maybe she doesn't know he has a girlfriend?

I'm torn. It's not my business. But man, I really want to whomp him on the side of his head for being a philandering dill hole. If we wouldn't crash and die, I just might.

Before I have too much time to dwell on it, we come to a screeching halt outside of Skin, the eighteen-and-up night-club. I fling open the door and launch myself out, wanting to get away from the sleaze ASAP. I right myself at the curb, taking in the long line. I'm glad I wore more comfy shoes since we have to stand for God knows how long.

Rebecca still hasn't gotten out of the car. The windows are tinted so dark I can't see anything through them.

Finally, she stumbles out, jerking her bandana top in place. She closes the door without looking back at the driver, who promptly tears out like a bat out of hell.

Not your circus, not your monkeys. Let it go, Charlie.

I shake off my judgment and curiosity and start to head toward the back of the line. Rebecca latches onto my bicep, her sharp nails pinching into the soft skin with a bite of pain. "Where are you going?" she asks. I point my eyes toward the end of the line like my actions are obvious. She shakes her head at me as if I'm a silly child and pulls me towards the front door.

A large, burly, biker-looking dude stands guard, and Rebecca struts right up to him with her hand on her hip. She says nothing as his lecherous gaze roams over her figure. He tips his head up in approval before lifting the red velvet rope, letting her pass. I'm hot on her heels until he reaches a hand out, stopping my movements, "ID?" he demands in a gruff, no fucking around voice.

I pull it out and hand it to him as he eyes my tits in wonder. Clearly, he is ignorant of the ways of the bra-cket. He barely glances at it before tossing it back to me and letting me pass.

It's my first time here. I thought it was both of our first times here, but apparently, Becky, with the fly hair, has got some secrets. It's like she has two totally different personalities.

She drags me through the throng of bodies gliding against one another to an empty, tall, neon-lighted table. "I'll go grab us some bevies. You have a preference?" she shouts the question into my ear, and still, I barely hear it over the pulsing bass filtering through the air.

I shake my head, "Suprise me!"

As Rebecca is absorbed into the crowd, I let the beat flow through my body. I need to chill. Between class, fitful sleep and missing the hell out of my boyfriend, and the bodily relaxation he gives, I am wound tighter than a snug hug from a nope rope as he squeezes the breath from his vermin victim.

My body gently sways with the rhythm, and my fingers drum along to the beat across the table's hard surface.

The proximity of all the bodies creates a palpable heat that clings to the air like a heavy blanket. Where's Rebecca with our drinks?

Like I manifested her return, she comes out of the gyrating horde a bit breathless as she places our drinks down. Hers is a delightful display of bright yellow and red layered slush topped with a pineapple wedge. Mine is an entrancing midnight blue slush with a swirl of neon green, topped with a lime slice.

Yum. As I pick up the crazed hurricane glass and bring it to my lips, Rebecca's hand covers the top of the drink. I pull back and look at her, perplexed. "You gotta stir it, hun."

"Oh-kay..." I exaggerate but give the little black straw a spin around the glass.

"More." She instructs, a little on the forceful side. Why is she so weird about how my flavors mix? I laugh at her and stir it harder than necessary, looking at her for approval. When she gives it, I tip the glass up and drain half of it in one go. Mmm, blue-motherfucking-raspberry.

Chapter 28

Charlotte

My head swims with a mixture of sharp pain from guzzling the frozen cocktail and bliss from the absorption of alcohol.

I normally refrain from any mind-altering substances, but I do enjoy a light drink from time to time. This thing is so tasty there's no way it has an excessive amount of alcohol.

After downing a second tasty blue thing, I give in to the compelling need to move my body amongst the sea of strangers.

Rebecca waves me off but promises to keep in line of sight. I feel so good that I have zero embarrassment about dancing solo.

I love the warmth of bodies against mine as I make my way into the mass of a never-ending galaxy of motion, and I come to a stop in a small, open space.

My eyes close, and I lose myself to the rhythm, my hands roaming over my body. The touch ignites the desire centers of my core. Fuck, I miss Zach.

I can almost feel his hands caressing my body. Starting at my midsection, curving down to my ass, where he squeezes it gently as if extracting my essence through my ass into his soul.

I wish I could feel his lips against mine.

I imagine the heat of his body rocking against the back of mine. Cocooning me in warmth and desire. His hands slide over my hips and cup my pulsing mound as his lips skim the sensitive skin of my neck. It feels so fucking good.

It feels good.

It *feels* good.

My eyes fly open and latch onto the large arms wrapped tightly around me. I watch in horror as the big paw attached to the arm works my pussy over my dress.

Immediately, I spring away, my heart thudding heavily like it's filling up with cement, each beat struggling for strength against the mortar.

I whip around to face my uninvited dance partner. His face is wrapped in a mystery, veiled in a neon kaleidoscope. I blink rapidly, trying to dispel the haze of swirling colors. My vision swims in a sea of Roy-G-Biv.

Holding my arm out in front of me to force the distance, I keep trying unsuccessfully to blink myself into a solid perception of my surroundings. "What the fuck?" I question.

His hands slink up my arm until they hit my shoulder. He pulls my body back into his. My head shakes rapidly back and forth. Saying the words my mouth refuses to voice. Why does it feel so fucking good?

Stop.

Stop.

Stop.

A burst of cool air flows against my bare arms. "Do you know what *stop* means, asshole?" a deep growl spits out from my right. I wasn't aware the words actually were being voiced.

My still hazy dance partner sneers up at me and – the very

buff, very handsome older man in a three-piece suit beside me. Handsy McGee doesn't have a prayer against this stallion. The narrowing of his eyes and huff he lets out before standing and storming away tells me he's aware he would get his ass handed to him.

A warm hand lands gently on my lower back, "Are you alright, honey?" he coos into my ear, looking down at me with soft, kind eyes. When he looks away from me, he tips his chin in the direction the man stormed away. *Who is he motioning to?*

The heat from his hand warms my whole body. I find myself leaning into it. What the hell is wrong with me? Clearly, there was more alcohol in those drinks than I thought.

Mystery man leads me to a quieter place by the bar's edge. "Hey, thanks for that back there."

He places a cool, unopened bottle of water in my hand. Where did that come from? "No problem, honey. Guys like that seem to have a way of ignoring the word no. I saw you mouth stop repeatedly, and he didn't, so I knew I had to step in."

I open the bottle and take a greedy gulp. The cotton in my mouth immediately disperses with the aqueous nectar. Draining the whole bottle, my body sways a bit. The mystery man latches on to my hips to steady me, and I hold myself up by extending my hand to his shoulder.

"You should have a seat. Did you take something tonight—?" he asks, leaving the question open for me to fill in my name. He scoots one of the leather-topped circular bar stools over for me to sit on, helping me steady on the surface.

"Charlotte. I had two blue slushy things, but no, no drugs." I reach into my left bra-cket and pull out the golden medallion with the Roman numeral one etched in the middle. "Not in a year, actually."

"Elliot." He offers his warm, welcoming hand to shake. I clasp our hands together. He places his other hand on top of our joined ones and leans close to my face, searching my eyes.

"Hmm. I don't know, Charlotte. I've done a lot of drugs in my day... The dilation of your eyes. The pleasure across your face at the slightest touch—" He trails his finger lightly up my wrist to my forearm, shooting blissful currents through my body. "Exactly."

Elliot leans over the bar, catching the bartender's attention. He whispers into his ear, and immediately, the bartender nods his head and gets on the phone.

Moments later, we are joined by another deliciously attractive older man. This one is in a more casual dark blue polo shirt with black trousers. I try to hide my shock when the polo man leans over and places the tenderest of kisses against Elliot's lips.

Elliot looks back at me and chuckles, "Charlotte, this is my husband, Sterling," I offer Sterling a meek smile and an embarrassed wave.

"Ster, can you call the car and get Charlotte home safely? I think it's best if she calls it a night."

"Wait! Rebecca!" I interject, suddenly remembering the girl I came with. I frantically look around. Not seeing her among the sea of melding faces.

After seven unsuccessful attempts at calling Rebecca's phone, I texted her.

Me: Where are you? I need to go home. I'm not feeling well.

Crickets.

I shake my head and shrug my shoulder at Elliott. "Is it the brunette in the black bandana top and white jeans?" he asks.

I nod.

"I will keep an eye out for her. If I see her, I will send her your way and tell her what happened. I'm sure she's fine, Charlotte."

"You're going to sit here all night and look for my friend... for me?" I ask, confused, why this stranger would give up his night for me.

Elliot smiles and rubs my arm in a calming manner. "Honey, this is our club. I would be here all night anyway. But I will keep an eye out, and I'll let my staff know, too."

Oh shit.

Before I can comment on his ownership and offer, a wave of nausea rolls over me. Clutching my stomach, my body bends in half. My vision dots behind my lids. I grip my head with my free hand, and strong arms hoist me up. Sterling carries me out of a back entrance to a waiting town car.

I barely remember uttering the directions. But when I wake up in the morning with a mouth covered in a pillowy veil of cotton and a horrendous headache, the last thing I care to see on my phone is the text that pisses me off.

Rebecca: Hey, girl! So sorry about last night. My phone died, and I hitched a ride back. You looked like you were having an uber-good time with those two silver foxes, so I didn't want to bother you. *wink emoji*

What the fucking fuck? Who does that?

If I didn't feel like such an utter bag of shit, I would call her and give her a piece of my mind. But if I open my mouth right now, my head might split open and purge what's left of my brain everywhere.

I roll my eyes and toss my phone back on my nightstand before curling back into my comforter to sleep the day away.

Chapter 29

November 2007

Zach

"Whoa, bro, what did that bag ever do to you?" Tuck teases. I ignore him and continue to pummel the shit out of the heavy bag. Sweat drips down every surface of my body. Beading at my hairline and marking slick paths down my skin. Skin that never seems clean enough, no matter how hard I scrub.

BANG.

Screams.

Blood.

Charlotte.

Protect. Protect. Protect.

Right jab, left jab, right jab, left jab, left jab, left jab. Twist at the hips. Kick right. Jab. Kick left. Jab. Kick right. Jab.

Harder. Faster. Better.

My muscles scream for the relief I refuse to give. At this point, I know damn well my knuckles will be swollen and bruised at the very least. Coach Reynolds is gonna tear me a new one. But that's nothing new at this point. He's always on my case about something.

"Morris! Why the hell are you late to practice again?"

"Morris! Why do you look like a bag of smashed assholes?"

"Morris! If this game ain't important enough for you to pay the fuck attention, then maybe you should take your ass to the bench."

"Morris! You smell like a gotdamn brewery. You know my rules. No parties before game night. Don't let it happen again."

Blah. Blah. Fuckin' blah.

The ding of my text alert pulls me back to now. I reach out and steady the swaying heavy bag, catching my breath. My body aches for coolness. Grabbing my water bottle off the floor, I tip it back and take a large swig before lifting it above me and pouring a bit on my heated forehead.

I shake off the excess water and dab the rest with the hand towel on the bench beside my phone.

Plopping down on the lightly matted surface, I flip my phone open.

Morgs: Yo Zee! I got somewhere for us to be tonight. You down?

I roll my neck from side to side. I can already feel the tension ebb out of my shoulders as I envision a smooth glass of whiskey gliding down my throat.

Me: Don't act like you ain't got the sense God gave a goose. You know I'm down.

Morgs: So touchy lately. Ain't been gettin' any? Thought that little girlfriend of yours was a freak in the sheets? At least, that's what you slurred out when we were at Gino's last week. *laughing emoji*

Me: Hardy fuckin' har. When and where should I meet you?

Morgs: Yeah fucking right bro, you ain't meeting me nowhere. We ain't having a repeat of last month at that kegger when you drove us home after telling me you were "totally cool to drive". We almost fucking died. I'll be there in twenty.

Fucking hell, Morgs. She never has consideration for anyone else's time but hers. It's Morgan's world, and we're all just sad little puppets attached by the short and curlies under her marionette's control. I roll my eyes but grab my shit, nod my goodbye to Tuck, and head back to our room to shower.

When we pull up to a small standalone brick building with the words *CRIMSON PAGE* splayed across the facade, I look over at Morgs, confounded. "What in the hell? Why are we at a damn library on a Sunday night, Morgs? If you needed to study, you coulda just left me the hell out of it."

She ignores me, like usual, and climbs out of her car. Leaving me behind, staring after her like a lost pup. For fuck's sake. I get out of the car and storm behind her. The windows are all dark. "Is this place even fuckin' open?" I ask, annoyed that she still ain't payin' me no mind.

As the heavy wooden door swings open, crimson velvet fills my view. Morgan presses right through the thick curtain. The door opens to a small library. Four bookshelves rest against the two side walls, with one large round table in the middle of the room.

She bypasses the table and stops in front of the lone shelf against the back wall. A brass Camellia statue is the only object on its surface. Morgan reaches her hand out and twists the top of the metallic flower.

"Are we pullin' some kinda floral heist here, Morgs?" I snicker.

"Turn around, dumbass." She instructs. As I turn, the bookshelf that was once right next to its mate against the left wall has now moved, and there is a darkened doorway in its place.

"Oh, a mystery! Call Scoobs and the gang!" I exclaim and rub my hands together like Mr. Burns does when he takes more of the residents of Springfields' money.

Morgan rolls her eyes at me and saunters off towards the mysterious door. Soft jazz fills the air around us as we enter the dimmed space. It takes my eyes a moment to adjust. When they do, I take in the crushed velvet-lined walls leading to a spiral staircase that goes one direction—down.

I follow her lead down the stairs. She has clearly been here before. At the bottom of the staircase lies yet another door, a thick wall of metal. She lifts her hand and raps on the door five times. Was that *Shave and a Haircut*? Two loud thumps echo back at us before the door swings open.

We are immediately engulfed in a thick fog. The soft jazz of the hallway is replaced with a pulsating fusion of electronic sounds. A small hand clasps into mine as Morgan drags us through the fog to a makeshift bar. "The usual?" she asks. I nod my answer and leave her to procure our beverages while I take in the spacious nightclub in the basement of a dainty library.

Laser lights bounce off of every surface in the room, immediately overloading my senses. The swaying bodies moving in perfect synchrony cast shadows that dance along the fog in time with the music.

A small, cool glass is thrust into my chest. I happily grab

onto it and take a healthy pull. The smooth, rich liquid glides down my throat. The sweetness of caramel and vanilla tempers the burn of alcohol. A sense of contentment begins to slide over my aching limbs.

Squeals fill the space around us as a tall, dirty blonde flies in front of me and envelopes Morgan in a bone-crushing hug. I stumble back a bit, my left hand instinctively covering the top of my glass, protecting the precious elixir that lies beneath.

"Mo!" The blonde shouts at the same time that Morgs yells, "Mellie!"

When the two women finally break apart, they turn to me with wide smiles. The blonde eyes me up and down, taking inventory of my features and burning them into her twat swat pot for later.

"Zee, this is my best friend, Mellie. I can't believe my two besties finally get to meet. This night is going to be the literal fucking best!"

I tilt my drink in hello to Mellie. She eye fucks me a little harder before stepping right into my personal bubble and sticking her hand between us, looking up at me expectantly.

I scoff and take her hand limply in mine, "Nice to meet you, Mellie." I offer, trying to be friendly for Morg's sake.

Her soft hand squeezes against mine as she shakes, "Very nice to meet you, Zachary, is it? I prefer full names. Feels more intimate, doesn't it?"

"Zach is fine." I grit out. That's not my fucking name, and no one calls me by full name but my mama and my girl.

Mellie steps in closer, forcing our hands to turn forty-five degrees and settle against her chest and my stomach.

"Well, *Zach*, you can call me Melanie."

Morgan must sense the tension oozing from my body because she interjects herself and pulls Melanie aside, waving me off while they head to the ladies' room.

The scent of vanilla and sugar floods my senses. My cock instantly twitches at the familiar aroma. *Little Bit.*

"Excuse me, is this seat taken?" A soft voice asks from my left. I turn, and my breath hitches for a moment. It is uncanny how much this girl looks like my girlfriend. Her blonde hair falls in waves down to her midsection.

She's dressed casually. Same as Charlie would be. A black band tee that is just slightly tattered at the edges. Light blue tight-to-ankle pants with small holes slit in both thighs. Showing just a peek-a-boo of flesh. Down to spotless white Chuck Ts.

This girl is a pretty replica, a shadowy reflection. But my girl is light-embodied, a masterpiece that could never be duplicated.

I find solace and my sense of home in her. She reminds me that even in a world full of chaos and uncertainty, beauty exists in the fleeting moments, just as there is in the serene splendor of a snowflake. My snowflake. My one-of-a-kind girl. My Little Bit.

With this twisted creation, everything is artificial. Whereas this girl has cut her own holes in her clothes to be trendy, my girl came by hers the honest way of misuse and overwear. The clothes wear this cheap echo. Charlie wears the clothes.

I clear my throat and offer my hand toward the empty stool next to me. She slides into it and leans against the bar to order herself a drink.

Her order surprises me. Whiskey, neat. Same as me. Girls don't usually go for the hard stuff without a chaser to follow it up.

I eye her suspiciously when she puts the glass to her lips. Her lips are the very same shade of light pink as my girlfriend's. But like everything else, her pout is lacking. She hums in approval as she takes a tiny sip of the whiskey.

The slight pinch of her lips tells me everything I need to know. This knockoff is punching above her weight class. But why? Why order something you don't like? Seems like a fuckin' waste to me.

She takes another small sip and manages no reaction this time. Her eyes wander casually around the club, her back straightening to lift her ass slightly off the chair as she peers towards the hallway with the restrooms.

"Lookin' for someone?" I ask.

"My friend. I was uber late getting here, and she came in without me." She responds distractedly while still searching for her friend.

I nod my head and sip my drink again. Happy to stand in silence and not engage in any further conversation.

"You here all by yourself?"

I open my mouth to answer her when Morgan and Melanie part the crowd and approach us.

"Bex! You made it!" Melanie squeals while thrusting herself at the small blonde—apparently Bex.

"Mo, you remember Bex, right?"

"Oh yeah, we ran into you at that coffee shop downtown. Good to see ya again, girl."

Bex tucks a strand of her blonde hair behind her ear. The contrast between the two women is vast. Melanie seems to be a loud, in-your-face type, while Bex seems to be more reserved and introspective.

She nods back at Morgs. "Yeah, good to see you, too."

"Another?" Morgs asks me, pointing to my nearly empty glass. I tip it back, letting the remainder of the booze slide down my gullet. "Yes, ma'am."

Melanie looks like she's about to cream her panties as she rubs her thighs together. "Oh, what a sweet, southern gentleman you are. They don't make em' like you in Jersey, honey."

"Make it a double, would ya Morgs?" I holler at Morgan. I think this night is going to require a copious amount of alcohol to get through.

Chapter 30

Zach

Buzz

"Turn the damn alarm off, Tuck," I grumble into my pillow.

Buzz

"Come on, man," I plead, my face still smooshed into the pillow. Each buzz feels like a jagged dagger in my temple.

Buzz

Motherfucker. I wince as I pull my pillow over the top of my head in an attempt to drown out the sound.

"Hello?"

My eyes snap open underneath the pillow.

"Who is this? You called me?"

I hurl the pillow across the room and stare at the girl on the phone next to me. In *my* fucking bed.

What the fuck.

"Zach? Why would you be calling for Zach on my–" she pauses as she pulls the phone away from her face, verifying that it is indeed my goddamn phone she just answered. Her blonde head whips in my direction, her big doe eyes open to their widest setting as she slowly hands the phone over to me.

Fuck. Fuck. Fuck.

Please, dear baby Jesus, please let it be Mama.

"Hel–" My voice comes out rough, the words skating across my tongue like sandpaper. I clear my throat and try again, "Hello?" Silence greets me on the other end. I pull the phone away and see that the call has ended.

My fingers tremble as I press the back arrow. My heart stops when I land on the last caller. Little Bit.

"Get out." I growl at the unwanted female in my bed, my eyes never leaving the phone.

"I said, get the fuck out!" I scream when she hasn't moved quickly enough. I don't give a fuck if she's hungover or in shock. I need her out of my space so I can figure out what's going on and how in the fucking sam hell I'm going to explain it to Charlotte.

Bex scrambles around the room. Her noisy search pulls my attention in her direction. I bite down on my lip, hard enough to break skin, when I see that she is dressed in nothing but my practice jersey.

She quickly steps into her jeans and shoes and begins to leave the room.

"Leave the goddamn jersey." I force out, my anger brimming at the surface. At her. At myself. At the fucking universe for this cruel joke.

Panic overtakes me as I jerk the sheet off of my lower half. A breath of relief expels from my lungs when I see that my boxers are still in place.

Standing up, my hands instantly fly to cup my head. A quartet of coal miners are chipping away in there. Stabbing their picks into the soft meat of my brain. The need to piss overtakes everything else.

Standing in front of the toilet, I reach down to pull my dick

225

out through the fly hole.

But the fly hole ain't there. What the hell?

I look down, confusion pinching my brows. I pull the waistband out and stare at the tag. A cold chill creeps over my body.

My fucking boxers are on backward. The only way that coulda happened is if, at some point... they were off.

Buzz

I flip open my phone with lightning speed.

Little Bit: Happy fucking birthday.

* * *

Voicemail. Again.

I've tried to call Little Bit repeatedly since this morning. She either blocked me or turned off her phone. I've also tried to get ahold of Morgan. I need to know what the hell happened last night.

You drank too fucking much. Again.

I have flashes of memory: hanging out at the underground club with Morgs and her friends, them all dancing and drinking, me just drinking. I vaguely recall getting back in Morgan's car and the two girls joining us.

But what happened after that?

"Pick up, goddamnit." I curse at my phone as the ringtone trills.

"Jesus, Zee. You know I had an exam today. What is the fuckin' emergency? I'm walking out of class now."

"We need to talk. Now. Meet me at the coffee shop in ten."

Crimson Brew is fairly empty for a Monday afternoon on campus. Finding an empty table is easier than usual. I order a plain black coffee and wait for Morgan.

"Okay, here I am. What's up?"

"What's up?" I ask, glaring at her.

"Yeah, what's up?" she replies, unbothered.

"You wanna tell me what happened last night after we left the club?"

She lifts a finger at me and darts off to the counter. The violence that begins to brew in my body is reaching a scary level, even for me.

She falls back into her seat, gulping down her choco-frapa-thingy. Impatiently, I wave my hands at her to hurry up. She gulps the coldness down faster, wincing at the brain freeze that settles in.

"Chill, dude. I dropped you and Bex off at your dorm, took Mellie home, and then I went home. What's your problem?"

"Why did you drop Bex off with me?"

"She was fairly wasted but said she had a friend in your building who knew she was coming and she could stay with."

Picking up the scalding cup, I down half of it in one go. Relishing in the pain as it burns its way down my throat and chest. I fist one hand against my thigh and lean closer into her, "If she had a friend who she was supposed to be staying with, then why did I wake up to her in my goddamn bed?"

Morgan's eyebrows shoot to the top of her forehead. "You slept with Bex?" she whisper shouts the question at me.

I glare back at her before peeking around the space to make sure no one heard her utter those blasphemous words.

"What about Charlotte?"

"Well, funny you should ask. I can't get ahold of Charlotte,"

227

I take one more gulp of the coffee, finishing it off. "You see, I woke up to a girl talkin' on the phone. In *my* bed. On *my* phone. To *my* fuckin' girlfriend."

"Oh, shit."

"Yeah. Oh, shit," I scoff. "When I took the phone from Bex, Charlotte had already hung up, and she ain't answered since."

"I don't understand Morgs. I love her. With every goddamn part of me. I would never cheat. Ever."

Morgan looks over at me, sympathy lacing across her delicate features. She reaches a hand out, gently placing it over mine. "But it sounds like you did, Zee."

"I need to talk to Bex. Can you tell me where I can find her?"

"Hang on, let me call Mellie. I don't have Bex's number." She holds a finger up to me as she calls Melanie.

"Fuck." She closes her phone with a forceful snap.

"What?" I ask.

Her shoulders sag, and she huffs out a breath. "So apparently, Bex goes to AU, and she headed back there about two hours ago."

"Oh my God. Do you think she knows Charlotte? Fuck, is she gonna tell her? Fuck. Fuck. Fuck!" My hands fist my hair, pulling roughly in all directions. Morgan's hand lands on mine, prying it off my locks.

"Hey, hey. Chill Zee. Calm down. Do you know how big the AU campus is? I highly doubt there is only one Charlotte that goes there. Besides, how would Bex even know her name or what she looks like?" she asks.

I nod along. Yeah. She's right. Bex wouldn't know Charlotte from a hole in the wall. I need to calm down.

"It just don't make sense. I think I would know if I had fucked someone, right?"

228

"Don't look at me. I may wear a penis in the bedroom from time to time, but I don't actually have one. If someone had fucked me–" she gags at the thought, "I think I would definitely know."

"Well, what do you remember? Try hard. Do you remember leaving the club?" she questions thoughtfully.

"Barely. I remember the staircase and thinking how fun it would be to sit on the rail and ride down it."

"Oh, that wasn't a thought, Pretty Boy. You fucking did. Well you tried, you fell after about three feet." I instinctively rub the mystery sore spot on my side. No longer a mystery, I suppose. "What else?" she asks.

I pinch my eyes shut, digging through the static of my memory for a glimpse of anything.

I remember the cookie in the car. Didn't do much to soak up the alcohol, clearly. The audio and video of my memory switches on and off in sporadic intervals like siblings fighting over the remote, clicking random buttons incessantly. *Think Zee. Think.*

I remember vanilla.

I remember silky blonde hair.

I remember Little Bit.

No. I remember the hollow illusion.

From there, it's blank. I tell Morgan as much. Both of us at a loss, we part ways. She heads to her next class. I head to the gym. Ready to atone for my sins with the sacrifice of my body.

Chapter 31

Zach

Nineteen days.

It's been nineteen days that she has been avoiding my calls. No more. She can't avoid me in person.

I throw a change of clothes into my gear bag and toss it over my shoulder as Tuck enters the room. "Hey, Morris, the guys and I are heading down to The Pit. Why don't you blow off whatever shit you were going to do and come with us."

"Nah, man. I'm heading out to see my girl. I'll be back on Sunday. The room is all yours."

Tuck rubs the back of his neck. Trepidation smeared across his usually playful face, "Oh shit. Man, I just assumed after I came home a couple of weekends ago to a sock on the door that you had kinda... moved on."

"No. I didn't move on. I ain't never gonna move on. I'm gonna fix this." The words burn as they leave my mouth. I will fix this. I *have* to fix this. I won't let her go. I hitch the bag higher on my shoulder and head down to the car.

The drive from Bama to AU isn't a bad one. In other circumstances, I'm sure it's positively lovely. But right now, these three hours are taking forever. My patience is nonexistent. My mood is in the shitter. My hands tremble with the need to fill my body with a smooth, aged, oak-scented single malt.

The parking lot is overly crowded, but I don't care if I have to walk five miles to get to her dorm; I fucking will. Gladly.

I hot-foot it out of the car and force myself not to run but maintain a brisk walk. The fifty-nine-degree weather offers little cooling down to my sizzling skin. Co-eds fill the open spaces on campus. I shove through the bodies, ignoring the harumphs and "Hey's!". I have one goal: get to my girl and make her talk to me. I chant the directions to myself repeatedly.

Burlington Hall, room 319.

Burlington Hall, room 319.

Burlington Hall, room 319.

Why are there so many fucking buildings? It's going to take me forever at this point. I reach out and tug the arm of the closest person passing by. A fit dude about the same age as me stares back at me with indignation. Not the time, bud. "Hey, what the hell, man?"

You catch more flies with honey than vinegar, Zee.

I hold my hands up in surrender, layering an apologetic look on my face. "Sorry bro, I'm lookin' for my girl's dorm. Burlington Hall? Can you point me in the right direction?"

He eyes me, taking in my Bama tee. His eyes narrow. Maybe he's a baller.

"Who's your girl?" he asks, folding his arms against his chest.

My jaw tightens as I grit my teeth together, "Charlotte." I grind out.

He makes a thoughtful face and taps his forefinger against

his cheek, thinking it out. "Hm, there's a lot of Charlotte's here, man. What does she look like?"

I suck in a breath of air, the coolness doing nothing to calm the raging fire brewing within my body. This kid has no clue who he's fucking with right now. I hold my hand flat out at chest level. "About yay high. Long, blonde hair. Brown eyes. Freckles all over her face."

I itch to punch the smirk that fills his smug face right the hell off of it. "Oh, *that* Charlotte. We call her 'Charlie with a body' around here."

I lunge at him and grab his t-shirt with both hands, bringing us nose to nose. The smirk slides off, and fear flashes in his eyes. That's right motherfucker, don't fuck with a man on the verge of losing the only thing he loves. I will tear this fucking world apart, stone by stone, to find my girl. I will bust down every wall. Burn every obstacle to the ground and laugh as their ashes flow in the wind. Nothing else matters. No one else matters.

"H-hey, what the hell, man? Are you a psycho? Get your hands off me!"

"I asked you a fuckin' question. You got exactly one chance to answer me. You don't wanna fuck with me today, bro. I can promise you that."

He lifts a shaky arm and points to a large maroon brick building behind my left shoulder. I follow his finger and map the quickest route in my head before shoving his body away from me. He scoffs and looks at me like he just might think about going toe-to-toe with me. Thinking better of it, he rolls his eyes and walks away. Good fucking choice.

Thank fuck no one tried to stop me at the doors. A charming smile and the little redhead turned into a damn tomato and let me waltz right in.

Room 319.

I rest my forehead and right hand against the wooden door. Inhaling like her scent will permeate the wooden fortress and soothe my wayward soul. I can almost smell the vanilla and sugar. If I concentrate really, really hard.

Vanilla and sugar.

Blonde, silky hair.

An imposter.

Tits bouncing.

Video flashing in and out. No audio.

Small hands holding my limp ones against the said bouncing tits with concentrated effort.

No.No.No. Fuck. No.

I would recognize Little Bit's tits from fifty yards. The flashing tits in my memory do not belong to my girl. Fuck.

I did it.

I fucked Bex.

I cheated on Charlotte.

In for four, out for eight.

My eyes search the wood grain for answers. Some mystical fix detailed in the deep-rooted history carved before me. Something to tell me this is a horrific nightmare. That I'll wake up from at any moment. With my girl in my arms, breath in my lungs, and a hard-on in my shorts.

The more I look, the more things stay the same. The door is just the door.

I'm stuck in a waking nightmare. My life is over. She'll never forgive this. I did the one thing I've vowed never to do.

But I have to try.

I lift my fist and pound it twice against the guarded gateway

233

that separates me from the girl whose world I'm about to shred right along the tattered edges of mine.

In for four, out for eight.

The door slowly opens. My arms brace against the frame, barely holding my exhausted body from crashing into the room as my head dangles limply between them.

Hot pink toes.

I snapshot those toes into my memory. I've never been a toes kinda guy. But these toes? Perfection. My eyes trace from her toes to the shiny silver chain secured around her left ankle with a "10" charm hanging down, resting against that perfect ankle. The chain I gave her when she first got to Alabama. She rebuffed my offer to put a ring on her left hand to let the fellas know she was off-limits. We compromised on her reppin' my number on the delicate piece of white gold.

She laughed it off, but I wasn't kidding. I woulda married her that day. Fuck school. Fuck football. Fuck my family's expectations. All we needed was each other. I woulda put a couple of babies in her belly, and we woulda lived happily ever after on a beach somewhere. Watching the crotch goblins splash about the water while we sip on cool margaritas and get lost in each other like we always do.

Her shins, marred with the consistent bruises her clumsiness awards her with, glisten in the sunlight that beams in from her one and only window.

The silkiness of her legs is cut off from view by the frayed hem of the denim skirt she wears. The waist fits snugly against the love handles I love to bite into when I take her from behind.

In for four, out for eight.

A tantalizing sliver of her belly shows between the waistband of her skirt and the cozy tank top she always wears. It's grown so threadbare you can see her bright pink bra right through it. It must have at least five holes throughout the material, but she refuses to throw it away. She knows that sometimes old, broken things need to be loved and not tossed aside for the latest and greatest thing.

The tips of her blonde hair lightly brush along the top of her tanktop and rest in a gentle wave-like movement as her breasts rise and fall with steady inhales and exhales.

The chrome heart with an "S" pendant inside the hollow space is securely in its place over her heart. Savvy wears a "C" on hers. It's their version of a friendship bracelet but "not lame as fuck" as Savvy would say.

The soft curve of her neck is interrupted by the strain of the muscles surrounding it. The curve I've traced the path of countless times with my finger... tongue... cock.

The delicate slope of her chin leads to the pursed flesh of the best set of pouty lips this world has ever seen and will ever see—lips I desperately want to press against my own. Let the world fade away, and let it just be us—together. Forever.

In for four, out for eight.

With each step my eyes take up to her face, the weight of my betrayal grows heavier, the realization of what I've done tightening like a vice around my chest. The air around us becomes insufferably suffocating in its silence. My guilt hangs between us like a thick fog, obscuring any hope of fixing this.

When I finally meet the chocolatey eyes that have always held such love and trust for me, my breath is punched out of my chest. They are hard, guarded, and disappointed. The trust they once carried lays scattered at our feet, irreparable and unforgivable, leaving me drowning in a sea of regret.

I think this is worse than tears. Tears mean hope. Tears

mean she still cares. My girl has no tears. She's as dry as the Sahara. This girl... is done. I don't think she's mine any longer. But I'll always be hers.

"Little Bit," I choke out, latching onto the door frame with all my might to keep from reaching out to her. I don't deserve to touch her, and she'd probably whop me a good one if I tried.

She taps her hand against her thigh, and her voice comes out flat, emotionless, "You know, I've been doing a lot of thinking. Trying to make sense of things," her hand flutters around the room, encompassing whatever things she's trying to make sense of. "First, I made excuses. There had to be a reasonable explanation for why a sleepy-voiced female answered your phone at seven o'clock in the morning. But try as I might, I couldn't think of one."

"Then I cried. I cried for days. Couldn't eat. Couldn't sleep. Wanted to not only jump off of the wagon but crash that bitch into a mountainside and get high off the ashes. I wondered what it was about me that made me so goddamn unlovable. So easily tossed aside. Wondering why the fuck that EMT saved me. Why he didn't just let me die like the worthless castaway I was."

The first tear falls from my eyes. I don't bother brushing it away. I know more will come. I want to grab her and shake her, tell her just how fucking lovable she is. That I love her with every fiber of my being. That I would do anything for her if she only just asked.

"Then, I saw the video."

Video?

Her words cut through my thoughts. "It was then I knew, this—" she motions her hand between the two of us, "Means nothing to you. *I* mean nothing to you. And that, Zach... That's a you problem, not a me problem. I will not let another man send me down the path of destruction."

She straightens her shoulders, armor firmly in place while she decimates my entire universe.

"No more. I'm tired of people thinking they can use me in whatever way they see fit. I'm tired of not being someone's first choice," the slap of her hand slamming against her chest makes my body flinch, "I'm fucking worthy of being someone's one and only choice, Zach."

Yes, you are.

"Just tell me one thing. If you've ever cared for me at all. If you have a decent fucking bone in your body, be honest with me about one thing?"

I can't answer verbally. My chest feels like it's caving in on itself, and if I try to speak, the rest of the walls will crumble, and I'll be lost to them forever. I nod softly. I owe her whatever the hell she needs to hear.

"Did you do it? Did you fuck sleepy-voice girl?"

I can't lie to her. I deserve whatever happens next. The tears are steadily dropping down now, obscuring her face just enough that the sharpness of her gaze seems almost softer. I latch onto the faux softness as I nod again.

She has no bodily reaction to my answer. Her eyes watch mine with detached indifference.

Breaking the connection between us, she spins around and walks over to her desk. She picks up a small silver item and sets it on top of the box to its side. She grabs the box and brings it over, holding it out to me.

Shakily, my arms release the door frame, and I take the box from her. Noticing the quickness she pulls her fingers away so they dare not brush mine. Looking into the box, I recognize

237

several things. Cards. Letters. Clothing. She's giving me our life together. Ridding herself of every scrap of me. Erasing me from her life right in front of my eyes, and I'm fucking powerless to stop it.

The thumb drive on the top puzzles me. My throat itches with the words I refuse to let it utter. I deserve this. I don't deserve her.

"Don't ever contact me again."

She doesn't slam the door in my face like I was expecting. She doesn't meet my gaze one last time with hurt and love warring in her eyes.

She softly closes the door.

On me. On us.

Chapter 32

December 2007

Zach

The whiskey no longer burns as it makes its way down my throat. I used to welcome the sting because, at least when I felt it, that meant I could feel something.

Now, I feel nothing.

I feel nothing, even as I stare down at the positive pregnancy test.

The last twenty-three days have been spent in a constant state of fucked up. I got suspended from the team indefinitely.

Apparently, Coach Reynolds don't take kindly to his star wide receiver showing up to a big game hammered.

I've been placed on academic probation. I don't give much of a shit about that one. School ain't really my jam anyway.

Tuck has spent more nights away from our room than in it. I guess I've been an ornery bastard. Couldn't imagine why.

And now?

Now, the consequences of my actions just keep on rolling in. Bex was too much of a coward to bring it to me herself, having Mel do her dirty work.

I've never put my hands on a woman, and I ain't starting now. We are both at fault for our current situation.

Mel seemed angry on my behalf. I've seen a completely different side of her than before. I haven't talked about what happened with Little Bit to anyone, not even Morgan. I can't bear to voice the words aloud. That makes it way too real.

Mel's been checking in daily, even if I don't answer or brush her off. She's persistent in making sure I'm still breathing. As much as I don't deserve to be breathing, I deserve to spend the rest of my life in a living hell regretting my actions.

Hell, she even offered to drive to AU with me to try to talk Bex into getting an abortion. But I can't do that. I couldn't live with myself if I had a hand in killing my own kid.

I won't be a deadbeat asshole like my own father. I'll be good for my kid. I'll get this one thing right in my life.

* * *

I officially resigned from school two weeks ago. I couldn't muster the give a fuck to go to classes, and when I finally broke down and told Papaw that Bex was pregnant, he agreed that I could withdraw– because no kin of his is going to get kicked out of school and smear our family name– and he would set us up with a place close to her school. She plans to finish out the semester, and then she'll be placed on a leave of absence until the baby is born.

I don't know if I'm hoping to run into *her* being so close or if I should lock myself away and never let my face be shown.

Bex has begged me to come see her at her dorm and help her pack, but I can't do that. If somehow we ran into my gir–

Charlotte, I couldn't bear to see the hurt and betrayal on her face when she finds out that, unlike our life plans that we had together, another woman would be bringing my baby into the world.

Bex hopes that one day, we will be a big, happy family. But twenty-three days ago, any hope I had for a happy family went down in flames. We will live separate lives and simply co-parent. That's it.

It's funny. The whiskey ruined my fucking life. But it is also the only thing saving it. The irony ain't lost on me.

Buzz

I ignore the first series of vibrations from my phone and continue swigging straight from the bottle. No need for glasses around here.

Buzz

For fuck's sake, leave me alone.

Buzz

"What?" I demand as I slam the phone against my cheek. "Boy, you ain't too old to get put over my knee. Don't you dare speak to your papaw that way, you hear me?"

I love my papaw, so I swallow down my snarky retort, "Yes, sir, sorry. It's been a long day. What's goin' on, Papaw?"

"Your mee-maw wanted me to give you a holler and see if you reckon our estate on Lake Wylie would be suitable."

"Suitable for what?"

"Don't be dense young man. You're better than that. You're a Morris, for Christ's sake," he scoffs in that high falutin, rich man way. "For your *wedding*, Zachariah."

Somewhere deep inside, I knew this was coming. My family is old money. Image is everything, and the prodigal son's son can't be a college dropout with a baby out of wedlock to boot.

But it doesn't make it an easier pill to swallow.

"Papaw, I don't love Bex. This was a one-time mistake. I can't marry her."

Silence fills the line, and I can picture him walking into his study, unbuttoning the bottom button of his suit jacket, and sitting at his grandiose wooden desk. Pouring two fingers of the finest bourbon into a glass and swirling the liquid with his five fingers, cupping the top of the glass.

"Zachariah, you made an adult choice. This is the way it's gotta be, son. The old adage was wrong. Sometimes, first comes baby, then comes marriage, and the love grows later—" he huffs a small chuckle before pausing to take a sip of his drink. "And if it doesn't, you hire a nanny to handle *all* your needs. You hear me, boy?"

My blood boils with the injustice of my life. This one night is the fucking gift that just keeps on giving. "Is that what you did, Papaw?"

The glass slamming on his desktop echoes on the line, and his voice gets real deep and hoarse, "You watch your mouth, Zachariah. Your mee-maw is the one and only love of my life. I've never so much as lusted after another woman."

"Then you should understand! I lost my one and only love, Papaw. Don't you get that? I don't wanna marry anyone else. I should be marryin' Charlotte!"

Papaw sighs deeply, "I know. I wish things could be different, but that just ain't how things are done 'round here."

"What if I refuse?"

"I hope we don't have to find out, but at the very least... I will rescind your trust and cut you out of the will. You will be completely on your own."

I have nothing left but my money. If I refuse to marry Bex, I won't be able to give my baby the life they deserve. Fuck. *Fuck.*

"What'll it be, son?"

"I want somethin' in return." If I'm signing away my life, I may as well get something he'd never give me otherwise.

"And what's that?"

"The 26' Macallan," I state matter-of-factly as if I'm not asking him for an almost half-million-dollar bottle of rare whiskey.

He hums, and I hear the liquid sloshing about his cup as he debates my quid pro quo. He sips on the booze and sucks a bit of air through his teeth, "Alright. You marry this girl and make our family proud, and the Macallan is yours. On your wedding night, after the certificates are signed."

"Deal."

Chapter 33

January 2008

Zach

"I wanted to offer you and your husband congratulations on your pregnan–"

"She ain't my wife." I snap out a little too harshly if the look on the doctor's face says anything about it.

Bex giggles and slaps my hand playfully, "Oh, Dr. Hughes, don't pay any attention to grumpy pants. He's uber tired from getting us all moved into our new apartment."

I roll my eyes but don't say anything else. I just want to see my baby and get the fuck out of here. I've got a bottle of Pappy Van Winkle with my name on it and a date with my video game console.

Dr. Hughes nods her head but eyes me with disappointment. Trust me, doc, ain't nobody in this world more disappointed in me than me.

"Okay, Rebecca, go ahead and lay back and place your feet here–" A long arm with a pedal-looking thing on the end springs out of the end of the table. Bex puts her foot in one and then the other when it pops out of nowhere.

The doctor rolls in between her legs and holds a giant plastic stick, and she begins smearing goo all over. What the fuck?

"As we discussed on the phone, the baby is usually only visible this early in pregnancy by an internal ultrasound. This wand will be going inside your vagina so we can take a peek inside your cervix. You may feel some discomfort, but there should be no pain. Let me know if you need a break."

Bex nods, and the doctor shoves the stick right up her hoo-ha. Damn. Being a woman must suck ass.

I watch the black-and-white screen, and when the little white blob pops up, I wonder if I'm looking at Bex's clit or something. What is that?

"That, sir, is your baby,"

"That?" I ask incredulously, pointing at the faceless white spot. Does it have a fucking tail? What kind of Sci-Fi shit is going on in this office?

"Yes. Let's get some measurements of the fetus and see how far along you are. Would you like to take home some pictures?"

Bex nods enthusiastically while I still stare, dumbfounded, at the screen.

The doctor fiddles with some buttons on the keyboard attached to the baby screen, "You are measuring eight weeks. That will put your due date at August 28th."

A fluttering, staticky thumping fills the exam room. "The heartbeat looks good and strong."

Heartbeat? That's my baby's heart I'm hearing?

Bex latches on to my hand, "That's our peanut, Zachy." I'm so enraptured by the sweet melody of my baby's life force that I don't even scold her for calling me that retched nickname.

Suddenly, I'm transported eight months ago.

Our hands are interlocked, resting on her bare chest. I stare at

245

the flickering of the fireplace. The lush strands of the Persian rug cradles our bodies in the finest wool. Maybe it's the fact that I just took her raw for the first time, but the thought of my baby growing in her belly fills me with a sense of pride. I gently glide our joined hands from her chest down to her soft, supple belly. My forefinger traces imaginary patterns on the tender flesh below.

"You know I'm gonna put a baby in here one day, right, Little Bit?"

She huffs out a laugh, her eyes still coated in that after multiple orgasm bliss, "Mmm, sure, yeah. First, we'll get married at the top of Sky Ridge– obviously, then I'll just run around your parent's mansion, barefoot and pregnant, making pickle-stuffed cinnamon rolls."

My face twists in disgust, and I playfully jerk my head back from her, "Pickle-stuffed what? That's fuckin' nasty, girl. Why the hell would you do that?"

She shrugs a shoulder and smirks at me, "I dunno, don't pregnant women like pickles on everything? They have weird ass cravings and shit. Are you judging my imaginary pregnancy needs?!" she cries in fake outrage.

Before she can even make a squeak of protest, I roll her on top of me. Our naked bodies gliding against each other. Instantly, I get hard. She does that to me.

She rests her chin on the tops of her locked hands on my chest, looking at me with affection and tenderness. Looking back at her eyes, I'm struck with an overwhelming sense of connection. In this moment, words seem inadequate. It's as if our souls are communicating in their own language, tracing the contours of each other's essence with the depth of our bond and love.

I lift my head to place a gentle kiss on her lips. The sleepy, satisfied smile she gives in return buries itself in the deep recesses of my being. I vow to myself to always keep that same smile on her face.

"I'm gonna marry you one day, sweetheart."

"Yeah?"

"Yeah. And I'm gonna watch you waddle around, pregnant with my son, apparently makin' pickle-stuffed cinnamon rolls, and count my lucky stars that some dipshit fucked up with you, causin' you to stumble into my life."

"Son? How do you know it will be a boy?" she laughs and swats at my prediction.

"I just know. The first one will be a boy, the protector. The next two will be girls, and then one more boy."

"Four?! You want four kids? Are you pushing them out of your vagina?"

"We'll start with one and go from there. How does that sound?" I coo while I run my hands lightly down her sides and cup her ass.

"One sounds good. One little jellybean to start." She responds, pressing her pelvis against mine. Looks like we are both up for the next round.

"One little jellybean, it is. I can't wait to call you Little Mama. Let's get a practice round in right now."

"Zachy?" Reality rips me, kicking and screaming, out of the memory. It's supposed to be Charlotte on this table. Belly swollen with my baby. Our little jellybean, not a fucking peanut. My teeth grind against each other as I ignore her and the judgy looks from Doctor Hughes.

"When can a paternity test be done?" I grit out the question, not bothering to look at the hurt expression that comes across Bex's face.

Professional mask back on, Doctor Hughes doesn't show any outward judgment to my question, "We suggest waiting

247

until ten to twelve weeks. You can schedule it with the front desk on your way out."

She hands Bex the little envelope with the pictures and due date and says her goodbyes so Bex can get dressed, and we can get the fuck out of here.

* * *

The South Carolina air whips across my face, and the glassiness of the lake breaks in soft ripples as the breeze glides across it. Reaching down to the ground, I pick up a handful of small pebbles. Tossing them into the still waters one by one, the concentric rings spreading wider and wider with each toss.

A perfect representation of my life. Spreading wider and wider out of my control until it's completely unrecognizable.

Footsteps against the gravel behind me alert me to an intruder of the only fucking free time I've had since Bex and I got to my grandparent's estate. I've been a forced occupant of many wedding planning meetings over the last five days we've been here.

Cakes. Flowers. Colors. Theme. Tux. Wedding Party. Seating charts. Meals. Beverages...

Mee-maw popped me a good one when I asked the wedding planner what theme goes best with the death of my life as I know it when I'm being forced to marry a girl I had a drunken one-night stand with and managed to knock her up.

"Hey, Pretty Boy," Morgan softly jests, bumping her shoulder against mine.

I nod in response, not taking my eyes off the lake. The moment I break the connection with my current distraction, I

248

CHAPTER 33

have to be back in the reality of the now, and that's not where I like to spend my time these days. I toss another pebble with more force than the ones before it, causing a quick rippling of the surface.

"I just finished the fitting for my best woman tux. Who the fuck picks brown as an accent color for a wedding?" she asks with distaste coating her words. Morgan is never one to hide exactly how she feels. She says what she thinks, and that's that.

"The bride thought it would be a good way to incorporate the muted tones of the South Carolina winter grounds and the rust that clings to the branches surroundin' the altar along the lake." I regurgitate the words I've heard repeatedly over the last three days.

Morgan snorts, "Wow. You really fucking hate this, don't you?"

"Yup."

"Any way I can talk you out of it?"

"Nope."

"Have you gotten the paternity test results back yet?"

"Nope." Jesus Christ, we just sent them out yesterday. How quickly does she think this shit happens? They told us it'll be two weeks before we get the results back.

"Are you going to be a miserable fuck-shit this whole weekend?"

"Yup."

"So, when's the big day?"

"The 31st."

"Isn't that..." Morgs' question trails off. I've been drunkenly bitching about missing the one-year anniversary of becoming official with Charlotte during our phone calls for the last

249

month. She's heard it so much that clearly, she's committed the date to memory.

"Yup."

"Uh. Why would you choose that date to get married?"

I swallow the insta-rage that fills my body. I didn't *choose* any of this. I mean, technically, I did, but my hand is being forced. I'm being *extorted* into this, there's a fucking difference.

"Apparently, it's the only date that works with the bride's family's schedule," I explain, the suspicion entwined in my answer laid out clearly for her.

I think she's eavesdropped on my conversations and wants to lay some kind of claim over the date that is so near to my heart and fucking ruin it.

Bex can't stand the fact that I don't love her. I don't want to be with her. Outside of a few blowjobs while I was drunk out of my mind and could picture a different blonde with her head in my lap, I don't fucking touch her.

The only reason any of this is happening is because of that baby inside her body. She's an incubator. If I could take the child at birth and dismiss Bex out of our lives, I totally would. Maybe Papaw could offer her some money to fuck off... No, he wouldn't do that. His "image" is too important. Clearly more important than my fucking happiness.

A muted sound of liquid sloshing breaks my connection with the lake, and I look over at Morgs. She holds out a glass bottle filled halfway with bronze liquid, shaking it from left to right in a taunt. My mouth waters at the sight.

"Okay then, how bout we get fucked off our faces and play some video games?"

I turn and snatch the bottle out of her hand, pulling the top off and taking a large pull, "Yup, let's do that." I declare as we jet off to the guest house that Bex and I have been staying in.

Chapter 34

Wedding Day, January 31st 2008

Zach

"Oh, Shug. You look so damn handsome," Mama whispers, fighting back the tears as she fusses over my bow tie. The damn thing tightens around my neck, the feather-weight noose that it is. I swallow thickly against the material as I watch our reflections in the full-length, tri-fold mirror.

"I haveta ask one last time. Are you sure this is what you want?"

No.

"Yes."

She pats my arm, straightening the material as her hand glides against it. She comes to stand beside me and hooks our arms together, both watching our reflections. "It's just one day, Shug. One day to get through. Then everybody will be outta your hair, and y'all can prep for my precious grandbaby and begin your lives."

One day. One day can change everything. One day can destroy everything. Fuck one day.

I simply nod along. I no longer push back at the bullshit that spews out of people's mouths. I'm resigned to my fate. This is what I deserve. Mama throws herself at me in a big Mama bear hug, burying her face in my neck, her shoulders shaking with the sobs wracking her body.

Quickly, she pulls back and looks me in the eyes. Her glassy ones searching my lifeless ones, she leans in and takes a deep sniff of my mouth. She jerks back, "Are you drunk, Zachariah?" she questions accusatorily. I shrug my shoulders, not really giving a shit at her judgment of how I choose to get through this day.

"It's eleven o'clock in the morning!" She protests. *Yes, I'm aware of the time.* But the thing is, time is an inconsequential construct when your life is no longer worth living.

I yank my arm away from her and button the middle button of my tux jacket, "We best get goin', Mama."

She shakes her head, frustrated and clearly not done with the conversation. But she knows I'm right. I'm expected to be standing at the altar in exactly thirty minutes.

The midday sun is at a perfect arch, hovering over the altar placed on the lush green of Papaw and Mee-maw's estate. The backdrop of Lake Wylie adds a serene element to the picturesque setup.

"You doin' alright, son?" the priest asks in a muted voice so as not to carry to the spectators dotting the space in white linen chairs.

"Just peachy, daddio. Ready to get this show on the road."

He chuckles, interpreting my disrespect as eagerness to get the nuptials moving along. And I am ready for that, not because I want to be married to Bex, but because I'm so goddamn tired of talking and hearing about this stupid fucking wedding.

253

The crowd hushes down all at once when the string quartet begins their rendition of *Here Comes the Bride*, turning in their chairs to get an unobstructed glimpse of the blushing bride herself.

My focus locks on the stunning red maple standing tall in the distance behind her. Its copper leaves flap gently with the slight breeze running through them.

In my peripheral, a vision in white begins to make its way down the aisle. The longer I stare at the grand tree, the hazier my periphery gets.

I can pretend it's a different blonde walking towards me. The one I pictured this day with a thousand times.

She would carry a bouquet of Eggplant Calla Lilies dotted with Forget-Me-Nots because "roses are super lame."

She would be rocking a black wedding dress with silver accents that remind her of the night sky.

She would've streaked her blonde locks with hot pink, a tribute to her mama, who couldn't be with us on this special day.

Savannah, not Grayson, would be walking arm-in-arm with her down that aisle. Her tall, slender frame would wear a silver tux to complement Little Bit's onyx dress. This is a true representation of their life and friendship—one full of light, one full of darkness, both needing each other for survival.

A song would flow through the crowd, something about lying together to forget the world and chasing cars. Because *Here Comes the Bride is "so cliche."*

A smile that rivals the most radiant jewels would beam at me as she hurries down the aisle. Our eyes would never leave each other, not for one split second. The love in her gaze would draw me into her light so our souls could reflect off of one another.

She would be fidgety and bouncy as we waited for the priest to get through his spiel. My little ball of anxiety doesn't care for crowds or being the center of attention.

We would read our thoughtful, handwritten vows to each other. Hers would be sentimental and demanding, while mine would be funny and borderline explicit.

She would throw all forms of manners out the window when we had our first kiss as husband and wife by flinging her bouquet behind her and jumping up to wrap her legs around me as we devoured each other inappropriately before friends, family, and God.

She wouldn't let people throw rice because she has a soft spot for birds. She believes they remember faces and would come after her if their kin died from ingesting the rice. So, people would blow bubbles at us as we ran to our waiting limo together.

Charlotte Belle Morris. Mine, forever.

"Pretty Boy!" A hushed command and an elbow to the ribcage pulls me out of my daydream. I narrow my eyes at Morgan. "What?" I quietly spit out at her. She simply nods her head behind me.

When I turn, it's not the blonde I want. It's *her*, the hollow vessel parading the guise of the one who should be standing here before me. Just the mere sight of Bex standing here in a wedding dress ignites a flame of rage that sears through the fabric of my being, fueled by the injustice of my life.

I mentally checked out through the whole ceremony. Ticking down the seconds in my head until I could be back on the couch with a bottle and a controller in each hand. Morgan had to repeatedly pull my focus back to the present so I could utter the I Do's. I refused any type of vow beyond what the priest had me repeat back to him– not her, never her.

"*Do you, Zachariah Thaddeus Morris, take Rebecca Louise*

255

Crowe to be your lawfully wedded wife?"

"*Mhm.*"

That's all they get outta me.

* * *

My hand balls into a tight fist, gently pounding against the table top as I listen to the repetitive elevator on-hold music of the doctor's office. It's been well beyond the two weeks we were told that we would receive the results of the paternity test.

Exactly nine days passed, and twenty-four days since we sent them out. Bex hadn't swapped the address on file with our shared apartment, so the results are being sent to her dorm address. I've been up her ass to check it daily, and so far, no test results.

"Mr. Morris, are you still there?" the receptionist's squeaky voice asks as she returns to the line.

"Yup. I been here the whole—" I pull the phone away to check the amount of time I've been on the phone, "seventeen minutes."

"I apologize for the long wait. I verified with the lab that the results have been sent out twice. Maybe there's an issue with the–"

BANG

BANG

BANG

The loud knocking at the door startles me enough that I drop my phone. I see CALL ENDED across the screen when I bend to pick it up. My lip curls up at the door as I stick it back in my pocket. Motherfucker.

BANG

BANG

BANG

"Yeah, fuck. I'm comin'!" I shout at my impatient visitor.

I fling the door open, and a wide-eyed dude stares back at me. Sweat pours from his face like he ran a marathon before knocking on my door. We are about the same height, but he's significantly less muscular.

"Where is she?" he demands, slapping a palm against my door to shove it open further. I broaden my shoulders, filling up the gap between the doorway and my body, and get in his face.

"Boy, you best settle the hell down and tell me what you're goin' on about?" I growl, leaving no room for debate in my words. His eyes are frantic. A desperate man stands before me. Those kinds of men are dangerous.

I quickly eye the baseball bat that I keep beside the door. I don't wanna have to whack him, but I fucking will if he don't calm down.

"Rebecca. Where is she?" he breathes out between the gasps for air. Rebecca? Oh, he must mean Bex.

"I don't know. I ain't her keeper. She comes and goes, and I don't give no fucks either way." I couldn't give a damn who this guy is. He could be her fuck toy, and that's perfectly okay with me.

"I need to talk to her now! She's blocked my calls, and I haven't seen her around campus." He shrieks, flailing his hands above his head. Then, I see the crumpled notebook in his hand.

"Alright, bro, settle on down. What is it that you need with

Bex?"

He curves his lip, and his face twists contemptuously, "Bex? No one has ever called Rebecca by anything other than her full name. She'd flip out if you tried to give her a nickname."

I've never known her as anything but Bex. That's what Morgs and Mel call her, too. This guy is off his rocker.

He shakes his head rapidly, "Wait, wait, wait. That doesn't matter. Yes. Bex. Rebecca. Who the fuck ever, I need to see her, now."

Curiosity spikes within me now. Why would someone be so adamant about seeing Bex? I cross my arms over my broad chest, "Tell me why."

"Who the hell are you?" he questions like he didn't knock on *my* fucking door. Nu-uh, I'm not playing this game. He is the one who should be answering questions.

"Who the hell are *you*?"

"Hunter." He sighs and rolls his shoulders forward, making himself smaller. A subtle sign of submission.

"Zach." I answer back, now that we can behave like civilized men. His eyes snap up to mine as soon as my name leaves my lips. His are wide, terror lacing every blink.

"Z-zach? Oh fuck. I need to talk to you too, man."

I look over him with a curious eye. He seems fairly harmless. I could kick his ass if it came down to it. As long as he ain't on that new AstraClara bullshit. Them Astra-naughts are crazy and will steal the metal right out of your pacemaker if you ain't careful.

Deciding I could probably still take him either way, I open the door and step to the side, allowing him entry.

I offer him a chair at my dinner table. As we both sit, he places the notebook between us, with an open palm holding it to the surface.

"Okay, Hunter, lay it on me." I start the conversation, trying to keep the impatience out of my tone. He seems pretty skittish.

He breathes out a long breath before looking me in the eye. The moment his question leaves his lips, it sucks all the air out of the room, "Do you know a girl named Charlotte?"

Chapter 35

February 2008

Zach

"C-charlotte?" I stutter out. Why would he be asking me about her?

"I'm going to guess yes by that stunned look on your face." He grumbles.

My eyes search his beady ones, begging all kinds of things with words unspoken. I don't know what I want to hear come out next. Is this her new boyfriend? My hackles instantly raise, and suddenly, the baseball bat seems like a good idea again.

"Look, man, Rebecca. Bex. Whatever she goes by isn't who you think she is."

My heart thuds against my chest in uneven beats as my mind tries to play catch up with his words.

"What do you mean?" Are the only words I can manage between the panic attack that threatens to take hold of me and the sheer terror I feel for the possibility that something has happened to Little Bit.

"I met Rebecca when she started tutoring me. She seemed meek and shy at first. She dressed pretty plainly and had long, mousy brown hair. She was someone no one ever looked twice at," Brown? Bex's hair has always been blonde since I've known her. I never asked or looked close enough to check if it was natural or not.

"I had a girlfriend at the time, and after a few sessions, Rebecca started flirting pretty heavily. Eventually, we started fucking in the stacks during our tutoring time. She loved the fact that we had to sneak around. Then, this new girl moved into her dorm building. Beautiful girl. Long blonde hair, short yet blessed with a body that drives men crazy. These light, adorable freckles all over her face. And an attitude that makes you want to fuck it out of her." He wistfully describes.

My fists ball on my lap under the table. As my jaw clenches tightly, I pray to all that's holy for him to be describing someone else. I wait for him to continue.

"So this girl has a boyfriend who helps move her into her new dorm room. Rebecca got a glance at that boyfriend during that visit and started hatching a plan on how to get him."

A sudden heaviness grips my chest, sending the thumping organ plummeting to the acidic deathtrap of my stomach.

"The sabotage started immediately. Rebecca was a TA for one of the new girl's classes. She told the professor all kinds of untrue things and turned him against her. She befriended the girl and stole the boyfriend's information from her phone while Charlotte was in the bathroom. From there, Rebecca stalked the boyfriend for a couple of weeks, seeing he had a female best friend. She decided to stage a run-in with that best friend at a local coffee shop."

"She knew that was her way in. She also knew the boyfriend was hopelessly in love with the new girl, so Rebecca became her. She wore similar clothes, bought the same perfume, used the same shampoo, and, my favorite, wore a blonde wig until she finally committed to the role enough to have her natural hair bleached."

"What the fuck..." I whisper, disbelief flooding my mind.

"Oh, it gets better, man. So, after all this, she starts intentionally putting thoughts in the new girl's head. Telling her long distance doesn't work, that her boyfriend is probably cheating... And so on. Rebecca went to the boyfriend's town one weekend and was finally introduced through the female best friend, though he had no idea who she was. The boyfriend got completely shit-faced at the club they were at. Rebecca doubled down and gave him a cookie laced with AstraClara and made up some excuse to be dropped off at his dorm."

Memories flash as he describes a familiar scene.

Cookie to soak up the alcohol.

Vanilla and sugar.

Blonde, silky hair.

Little Bit.

"The boyfriend was completely hammered and now high as fuck on a drug that makes a hit of ecstasy seem like a drop of a wine cooler and gives you a guaranteed hard-on at a slight breeze. She hopped right on that hard dick and rode it to completion, all while she secretly filmed the whole thing."

Bile churns in my stomach, and the rising burn of vomit makes its way up my throat. I swallow down the feeling, needing to know what happened next.

"She then purposefully took the boyfriend's phone and waited for the call she knew would be coming. You see, it was the boyfriend's birthday, and she knew the girlfriend would call at some point. So when that call came through, she answered the phone, feigning innocence when the boyfriend flipped out."

My whole body begins to shake as a cold feeling starts at my toes and works its icy claws up to my chest.

"When she returned to AU, she anonymously taped an envelope with a thumb drive to the new girl's door. Can you guess what was on the thumb drive?"

My eyes snap over to the box that sits under the end table against the couch. The box of the belongings that Charlotte packed up when she ended us for good. The box that had all the things I recognized... Except for one thing.

I stumble out of the chair, not caring when it smashes to the floor on its back behind me. My knees hit the plush carpet, and I slowly pull the box out of its hiding place. A small, silver thumb drive is still sitting there, an unknown taunt to my forgotten actions.

"We aren't quite done with this tale of single-white-female-ing, bro. A few weeks later, Rebecca pops positive on a pregnancy test. She's elated to tell the boyfriend the good news, knowing she's just locked him down for life. There's just one problem..."

My head whips back to look at him, and he waves an envelope in the air. I get up on shaky legs and return to the table. I fall into the chair and take the envelope from him with trembling fingers.

Without taking my eyes off Hunter, I begin to pull the single paper from the envelope. When he doesn't continue this fucked up story, my eyes fall to the paper. All the words jumble together in one big mess. My eyes jump from place to place, trying to decipher what I'm looking at. It all seems so foreign. Six words and two numbers jump out to me.

Combined Paternity Index: 0
  Probability of Paternity: 0%

"But.. what... I don't underst..." I can't seem to form words. "So, I'm not–?"

Hunter shakes his head, "No, man. You're not the baby daddy," and he holds out another envelope for me.

Combined Paternity Index: 533,475
  Probability of Paternity: 99.9998%

"I am." He points to his name on the top of the paper.

"H-How? How do you know all of this? How can I trust this? No offense, man, but I don't fuckin' know you."

He holds up the notebook and slams it between my arms on the table. He opens it up to the first page.

"This. This is how I know. She detailed everything, dude. I'm not proud of this, but when she wouldn't talk to me after telling me I wasn't the father but wouldn't show me the proof, I broke into her dorm room. I found this in a locked drawer in her desk with the two results sitting on top of it. I knew she still had the dorm room despite moving out. I guess to be here with you?" he leaves the statement with a question.

The cloudiness in my mind gives way to one thing...Rage.

With hard eyes and measured breaths, I reach down and pull my phone out. The line trills, "What's up, Pretty Boy? How's married life?"

"Get here. Now." I order before hanging up the line.

"What are you going to do, bro? Your girlfriend is a fucking psycho, but she's carrying my baby..." he trails off. I can tell he is similar to me in that neither of us give a damn about Bex, it's about the baby. I can't think about the baby she just took away from me, along with everything else.

"She's not my girlfriend," I bite out, clearly that news hasn't gotten out among her classmates yet. "She's my fucking wife."

Hunter's eyes widen, "Dude..."

I nod as I stare at the blank wall beside the front door. Murderous intent fills my body. Bex better fucking hope Morgan makes it here before she does. Cause right now, I'd fucking kill her. No joke intended. I will wrap my hands around her throat and cut off her airway until I watch the light from her deceiving eyes extinguish.

I press my phone to my cheek again, and his deep southern drawl comes on the line, "Zachariah. To what do I owe the pleasure?"

"Papaw, I'm gonna need a lawyer. A damn good one."

"What's going on, son?"

I filled him in on everything. Hunter just laid on me, sat back, and waited.

Chapter 36

March 2008

Zach

The last month has been a living fucking nightmare. She better thank her lucky goddamn stars that Morgan and Melanie showed up and warned her away before I ever saw her.

After telling Morgs everything, I was the one that then had to hold her back from going after the cunt.

Papaw flew in the next day with our family attorney in tow, Jordan Bates. Since our fucking marriage had been consummated thanks to one fucking drunk and lonely night, the easy route of annulment was taken off the table. Until Bates asked why the separation had occurred. Once I filled him in on everything, he said we could file on the grounds of one party misrepresenting themselves before the marriage.

And just like that, thirty days later, I am no longer a married man.

She disappeared somewhere. Bates told her if she ever came near me again, we would turn everything into the cops and press charges. I don't really care where she went or what happens to her as long as I never set eyes on her again.

My life is in complete shambles. I don't recognize myself. The anger that I feel. The rage. The devastation.

How can you mourn someone you've never met? I've spent the late lonely hours in the dark, in a drunken haze, missing the child I never had.

It may be stupid, but he was the only thing keeping me going. The life I wanted to provide for him. The things I wanted to teach him. I was looking forward to being a daddy. Even if I hated his mama. I was willing to pretend for his sake. I would've made it work.

Rebecca– I refuse to call her by anything else– was only ten weeks along at our last doctor appointment, and they couldn't see the baby's gender yet. But, they set us up with a genetic test that would tell us in a few weeks. But I could just feel that it was a boy. My boy. *Not my boy. Hunter's boy.*

I haven't left this apartment yet. I'm not sure where I will go. Probably to Papaw and Mee-maw's for a little while until I figure out my next move. But I feel tethered here. I haven't allowed myself to reach out to her. To Charlotte.

I don't know what I would say. So much has happened. It's such an incredibly crazy tale that she probably wouldn't even believe me. The cards are stacked heavily against me. I don't blame her for taking the evidence at face value. It's hard to believe there was a time when my word meant everything to her. Now, it's as worthless as my high school diploma.

What the fuck has happened to my life? A year ago, I was living high on the hog. I had my girl. I had my team. I made a new best friend. I had a future.

Now? I have nothing. I am nothing.

The front door flies open, and Morgs comes stumbling through, her arms filled to the brim with plastic grocery bags.

"Okay, Pretty Boy. I've got some shit for dinner, and then you and I are going on a recon mission."

I meet her at the door and take some of the bags off her arm. We then take the groceries to the kitchen and begin to unload.

"Recon mission?" I ask.

"Yup. So wear all black, 'cause incognito is the name of the game."

My nuts are squished beyond any sort of comfortability. This car is a hell of a lot smaller when you've been sitting in it for hours. Why we are doing this "mission" at all is beyond me. What does Morgan think we will learn in the middle of the night on a weekday, hanging outside a dorm building?

Pushing away the balled-up tinfoil from Morgs' fifth Ding-Dong, I lift my right leg and put it on the dash, trying desperately to give Bert and Ernie some pressure relief. It's only been three hours, and I'm already sick of this stakeout.

I look over at Morgs, who's bee-bopping to a 90s boy band jam; something about it's hard to say you're sorry and to make the things you did undone. I throw her a side-eyed glare. If I thought that would deter her, it doesn't.

In fact, during the chorus, she reaches over and grabs my left fist to begin singing into it like a microphone. Her hips lift off her seat to make way for grotesque gyrating against the steering wheel while she sings about needing to be told what to do because he wants her back.

When the next song comes on, and I hear the lyrics wail something about making love to her like she wants you to and holding her all through the night, I narrow my eyes and slam my finger against the eject button of her CD player.

She's interrupted mid-lyric when she slaps at my hand, "Hey! I was jammin' to that!"

268

I roll my eyes at her and look down at the burned CD. *Pretty Boy's Sad Sack Jamz* is handwritten across the otherwise blank disc top in black permanent marker.

"Dick," she whispers into the now silent interior.

"What are we even doin' here, Morgs?" I ask tiredly, tipping my head back against the headrest and closing my eyes.

"I told you. Recon. Duh." She answers like it's the most obvious thing in the world.

"Recon for what?" I press.

"Okay, so don't get mad," she cautions in an upbeat tone.

If there was ever a sentence to make sure the person would get mad, it's that one. I turn to face her, cocking my brow, and wait for her to continue. Fully bracing to get fucking mad.

"So I may have done this a time or two..." she trails off at the end of her statement in such a low voice that I'm not quite sure if I heard her correctly.

"Come again?" I challenge.

She sighs, shoves a sixth Ding-Dong into her mouth, and begins speaking over the large chocolatey confection. "I said I may have done this before. Look, you're my best friend, Pretty Boy, and I couldn't stand to see you throwing your life away on that—" she pauses to grit her teeth, trying to come up with the best way to describe the woman who ruined my life. "basic meat pocket."

"And?" I urge. I hate when she drags shit out and doesn't get to the damn point.

"And... So, I started checking in on her. Getting her class schedule– which I had to flirt with a fucking douche boy to get, by the way, so you're welcome for that. I happen to know that on Wednesday nights, she comes back to the dorm late," she looks down at her watch and then back to the building in front of us, which is now just illuminated by lamposts every fifteen feet or so. "And, if my previous recon was accurate, she should be walking up any second."

The ice surrounding my heart cracks just a little at the thought of setting eyes on her again. It's only been a little over three months, but it may as well be a lifetime. I wonder if she'll look any different. I wonder if she's thought about me at all since the day she slammed the door on us.

My breath catches in my throat, and my heartbeat thuds in my ears as I get a glimpse of a curvy blonde with much shorter hair than I saw her last. She's so fucking beautiful. All I want to do is run to her, fall to my knees, and beg her to take me back. Give me a chance to prove that she's it for me. She's all I want in this world. Nothing else matters. Just one chance, that's all I need, and I would make sure she never regretted it for the rest of our lives.

I would give her foot massages every night. Wash all of the laundry and the dishes. She would want for nothing. I would give the very breath from my lungs so she may thrive another day.

That ice in my chest ignites into a raging inferno when I look past my girl to the tall, curly-haired brunette man beside her. As they walk to the door to her building, his hand glides across the sliver of skin exposed on her back by the pink crop top she wears.

Fucking kill him. He's touching what's yours. Protect. Protect. Protect.

As if we are sharing the same thoughts, Morgan latches on to my forearm and pins it in place on the console. "Well, this is an unforeseen turn of events. I swear I've never seen that dude before. She is always alone."

A growl emits from the deepest part of me. This bastard is wrapping his arms around *my* Little Bit. How fucking dare he.

I swear to all the Gods, if his hand reaches any lower, I will be leaving this campus in handcuffs.

The knife twists in my very soul when I watch her lips press against his. From this angle, I can't quite tell if it was on the mouth or cheek. But either way, her lips have no fucking business touching him at all.

But that's not your place to say anymore, jackass. Remember? You destroyed any chance at keeping her. She can kiss and fuck whoever she wants, and you can't do a damn thing about it. Way to go, Zee. Like everything else, you've managed to fuck this up too.

Her smile is radiant when they split apart and stand face to face with interlocked hands.

"What are you doing just sitting here? Go get your girl, bro!" Morgan implores while violently shaking my arm.

What am I doing?

Every part of me wants to get out of this car and sock that dude right in the mouth for daring to press his lips against her skin. Every part of me wants to wrap her in my arms and hide her away from anyone who might try to take her from me. Every part of me wants to bury myself so deep inside her that we can't tell where she ends and I begin. Remind her that our souls are bound to each other. Remind her of what we have together. What we *can* have.

The marriage, the kids, the beach—whatever she wants, it's hers. I'm hers, now and always.

Then why? Why am I not getting out of the car?

"Zach?" Morgan calls, uncertainty and panic filling her voice.

What if she's finally finding happiness after a lifetime of darkness? Could I really be that selfish of a bastard to come barreling in and disrupt her healing?

"Zee?"

What if she's actually moving on with her life? After everything she's been through these last couple of years, God, if anyone deserves happiness, it's her.

Can I give that to her? Even if somehow I worked my way back into her life, would she ever trust me again? Would she think about my betrayal every time I held her? Would she question if it was true when I professed my love for her?

"Pretty Boy?"

Look at me. I'm no prize. Maybe once upon a time, I was worthy of Charlotte Belle Johnson. But I'm not that guy anymore. I wish like hell I was.

Now, I'm just the college dropout who fucked an echo of the woman I loved– breaking her heart. Marrying someone who wasn't her– breaking my own heart.

I don't deserve her. She needs a chance to live her life, to be happy, and to be loved wholeheartedly by someone who would never betray her the way I have. I have to be man enough to give this to her. If I can do anything for her, it's this.

"Dude, you're scaring me. Are we whoppin' ass or what?"

I can't fix the things I've broken. But I can give her this one thing. If I could go back and change the last few months, I would in a heartbeat. But I can't. This is real.

This is my penance. I have to let her go.

"Let's go home, Morgs."

Chapter 37

November 2007

Charlotte

"Hello?" A sleepy and very feminine voice that definitely doesn't belong to a southern boy says as she answers my boyfriend's phone. For just a moment, I wonder if maybe I called the wrong contact on my phone. I pull the phone away for a moment to verify. Yep, I called the right number.

"Who the fuck is this?" I demand.

"Who is this? You called me?"

My hand begins to shake as I try to make sense of what is happening right now. Please, please tell me this isn't happening. I can't do this again.

"Where is Zach?" I question between clenched teeth.

"Zach? Why would you be calling for Zach on my–"

She clearly knows him. I pull the phone away and smash my finger on the END button. I'm really missing the days when you could slam a phone down into a receiver and hear that satisfying metallic resonance in the room, giving you a sense of finality in the action.

Rage fills my body, and I type out a final message before

blocking his number.

Me: Happy fucking birthday.

Sitting motionless and unsatisfied on my bed, I try to piece together the last two minutes. Could there possibly be a reasonable explanation for a sleepy girl to be answering my boyfriend's phone at the ass crack of dawn?

Maybe it's his sister?

Come on, Charlotte. You know he doesn't have a sister.

Maybe he lost his phone somewhere, and this girl took it home by accident?

Yeah, and maybe Hell is just a hot spring.

Maybe he's in a really early study group, and nobody's had their coffee yet. His phone was sitting on the table, and she picked it up by honest mistake.

Sure. It's totally reasonable after a guy's night with his buddy, Morgan, where he didn't call or text me like he said he would, that he is now up super early... on his birthday... with a fucking study group.

After spending two hours sitting on my bed, gaslighting myself into the various plausible, but not really, scenarios in which a girl answering my boyfriend's phone would be acceptable, I finally cave and call Savs.

"Yo," she says in a lighthearted greeting.

"Savs," I choke out, my voice breaking as deeply as my heart.

"What's up?" she asks flippantly. Can't she hear that I'm falling apart? Why is she being so nonchalant about it? We've always been able to read each other's mannerisms immediately, even over the phone. Maybe the distance is changing our friendship.

"What's up? I'm fucking falling apart here, Savs, and you're just chill as a cucumber." I squeal loudly, the sound grating to my own ears.

"Oh, that's sweet," she responds to my heartache without an ounce of empathy. Who the fuck is this girl, and what has she done with my best friend?

"Well, hopefully, you realize by now that I can't come to the phone. So leave me a message at the beep. Or, you know, just text me like a normal person. K, thanks, bye!"

I almost laugh. Almost.

Instead, I ended the call without leaving a message, deciding to just give her a call later. This isn't something I want to discuss with her voicemail or through text.

I wake with a start, the room now pitch black. Fuck, I didn't mean to fall asleep. I reach over and press the button on the side of my phone, illuminating the room with the time. It's dinner time. I've slept the day away.

For one brief blissful moment, I've forgotten the events of this morning. When the memory slams into me like a freight train, I physically feel the tugging of my heart muscles. They are ripping apart, piece by piece.

A torrential downpour of salty tears stream down my face. I curl myself against my pillow and cry.

And cry.

And cry.

My eyes are puffy and raw. My nose is dripping with the snot that runs almost as freely as my tears.

I could really use some numbing right now. I don't want to feel. I don't think I can survive this round of disappointment and betrayal.

No. I am not throwing away a year of sobriety. *Think, Charlie, think. What tools are in my toolbox?*

Reach out to someone.

When I'm greeted with the same gotcha voicemail from my best friend's phone, I decide to head down the hall to the only friend I've made on campus.

Feeling defeated when Rebecca doesn't answer her door, I head back to my room and contact my sponsor.

"It's good you called, Charlie. The urges sometimes pop up at the most inconvenient of times. That's why we continue to say we *are* addicts. Present tense. This is something we have to work on day by day, moment by moment. But, you took the first right action. I'm just getting to the clubhouse for tonight's meeting. Would you like to join me?"

My sponsor, Genny, has been such a great support for me since I got to Alabama. I've been to a few of the local NA meetings. I always feel so out of place, like I don't belong. But when Genny attends the same meetings, I have at least one person with whom I feel a little comfortable. "Yeah, sure. I'll get dressed and be there in twenty."

Sometimes, I feel emboldened when I leave a meeting.

This is not one of those times. I've heard it time and time again from Dr. T, my sponsor, Savvy, that hiding my feelings only hurts me more. It's hard to break the cycle. I've spent my whole life pretending to be something I'm not. I've walked around with a mask on for so long that I forgot it was actually removable.

My body vibrates with need. The imaginary bugs are scurrying beneath my flesh, waiting, begging, and salivating for the sweet hit of oblivion.

I bump into Rebecca when I enter Burlington Hall, "Hey, Charlie! Goodness, girl, I hope you don't take this the wrong way, but you look awful. Is everything okay?"

Savvy still hasn't answered my calls. Though I don't want to dump my bullshit on a girl I still hardly know, she is the closest thing I've got to a confidant right now.

Tears well in the corners of my eyes as I swallow down the lump in my throat. Words won't come. I simply shake my head as the first tear falls.

"Oh, honey, come with me," she coos, wraps a warm arm around my shoulders, and leads me to the elevator.

When we enter my dorm room, her gasp startles me as I flip around and stare at her wide-eyed, waiting for her to explain her reaction.

"Charlie, this place is uber messy. What is going on with you, girl?" she glares in distaste at the pile of used tissues on my desk, as if they are going to become sentient at any moment and come after her.

I look around my room and can't find a single fuck to give about the state of it. I shrug my shoulders and fall onto my bed.

Rebecca glances around the room, no doubt scanning for a semi-clean space to place her perfect self. She decides to flick the pile of clothes off my computer chair and take a seat. I can't even bring myself to care about the clothes now littering the floor. Were they even clean?

I poured my heart out to Rebecca for hours. To her credit, she sat and listened to my blabbering and incoherent ramblings when the emotions welled too large to ignore with such rapt attention. I haven't felt this seen in a long time.

"Wow. Charlie, I am so sorry this happened to you. Are you going to break up with him?"

That's her first question? I just downloaded two years worth of pain, anger, addiction, betrayal, death, and hospitalization on her, and the first thing she wants to know is if I'm breaking up with my boyfriend.

The look on my face must convey my displeasure at her response because she quickly adds, "I'm sorry. I just don't know what to say. You deserve so much more. That is all I mean. This Zach guy sounds like a typical jock frat boy. I told you, they can't be trusted. They get into college and around all the co-eds and just let their penises do all the thinking for them. Jersey chasers are everywhere at D1 schools. You must've known that."

She's right. Did I really think I was going to be enough? Zach is fucking gorgeous. He's sweet and funny. A true golden retriever of a man. Throw in the deep southern accent and "darlin", and it's no wonder he sets every pair of panties within five city blocks of his smile ablaze.

Rebecca comes to kneel before me, patting the top of my hands in what I assume is supposed to be a comforting gesture. "It's just how these men are. You aren't to blame. It was bound to happen sooner or later. Did you think he'd be satisfied with sex once a month and some flirty texts and pictures? Guys like him have a deep-rooted need to stick it in everything they see. You're better off without him, hon."

Maybe she's on to something here. I mean, he is insatiable when we are together. Maybe the sexting and phone sex just wasn't enough. How did we think we'd manage four years like this? Did I really think I'd be enough, that temptation wouldn't be everywhere? I'm sure he wouldn't have to put any effort whatsoever into getting a partner to warm his bed for the evening.

Why am I never enough? *Fuck.*

"I don't really want to talk about this anymore tonight. I appreciate you coming to sit with me and listening to my problems. I just want to go to sleep." I tell her gently. I don't want to let my emotions run off the only friend I've got in this place.

"Okay, Charlie. I think some rest will do you good. Oh!" She stops and snaps her fingers, looking back at me with her forefinger sticking up in the air. "I've got this great sleepy tea that works wonders. I'll grab you a cup. Promise me you'll drink it all and get some rest."

I nod, dismissing her in the most polite way I can. It's like three am at this point, and my body has had all it can take tonight.

I tip the mug to my lips and take a healthy gulp of the barely hot sleepy tea, setting it in between my feet as I sit criss-cross-applesauce on my bed. I lean my head back against the wall and start to flick through recent memories to see if there are any signs that I missed. Any glaring red flags that the man who said he loved me would fuck me over. And goddamnit, I can't find any.

A familiar cloud settles over my itchy nerves. This tea is pretty legit. I tip the cup back to my lips, finish off the remainder, and settle into bed. The glowing stars on my ceiling dance among the edges of my consciousness, the neon green melding into explosive colors, my own Northern Lights to lull me to sleep.

The bugs are satiated. The itch has abated.

And I rest.

279

Chapter 38

December 2007

Charlotte

I cannot wait for winter break. I am so tired of feigning normal amongst my classmates and professors.

I had to beg Savvy to stay her ass in Florida when I finally spoke to her. She had many choice words for my situation. She threatened massive bodily harm to Zach. I guilted her into promising she would stay out of it and not contact him.

He made his choice. He has to deal with the fallout. I choose not to engage. Though my feelings on the predicament change as often as the winds, right now, I feel strong and resolute. Two hours ago, I was curled in a ball on my floor, wondering why that EMT saved me and whether I would've been better off simply fading from this world.

I hate that he has this much control over me. I hate that I'm so weak as to be conflicted because I fucking love him. I want to find a way to move past whatever this is. But I also want to cut off his dick and feed it to the gators and let the roaches feast on the gaping hole where his manhood once stood. Like I said, all over the place.

Rebecca's been a pretty good shoulder to lean on. Nightly, she makes me her sleepy tea and listens to me repeatedly go through the motions. My own unhinged Ferris wheel. Round and round it goes.

I've got to find out where she gets that tea. It calms me like very few things ever have before. She says it's a special blend, and she's sworn to secrecy by her grandmother. One of these days, I will sneak a peek at the packaging in her room and order some for me. If she ever lets me into her room. She never leaves me any; she insists on being the one to take care of me. She brings the mug, already made. Every time.

I can't believe it's only been twelve days since Floozy—what I've named the sleepy girl on the phone—blew my world apart. It feels like it's been an eternity and the blink of an eye all at once.

I've spent my days crying, cursing Zach's existence. Cursing my own existence. I'm certain I'm down at least ten pounds from the lack of food. Whenever I try to eat, my brain tortures me with thoughts of what Zach could've been up to that night.

Did he map her body with his tongue like he'd done to mine so many times? Did he make her scream his name like he makes me? Did he fuck her passed the point of exhaustion and demand another orgasm when her body was spent? When these thoughts creep in, my stomach revolts. Hence, the weight loss. I've been surviving on noodles and tea.

Rebecca is literally the only reason I've made it to class for the last week and a half. She knocks on my door every morning to usher me to the shower and will pester me until I follow her to our respective classes.

She insisted on a girl's night last night. The evening consisted of spending several painful hours bleaching and toning her hair to be a light ashy shade of blonde, not too unlike mine, but hers is so obviously fake. She said she just needed a change, and I get that. It's like a rite of passage for a girl to fuck with her hair when she feels like her life is out of control. At least she didn't try to go red.

Even though the heavy fog of chemical smell in my small dorm room was tedious and nauseating, it did keep my mind off of, well, everything, and I welcomed the non-narcotic distraction.

A knock at my door pulls me out of my thoughts. I know who it is. That perky knock belongs to only one person, Rebecca.

When I open the door, she points at a white envelope taped to the wood. "What's that?" she asks. Hell, if I knew. I shrug and grab the nondescript envelope. Inside is just a small thumb drive. There is no note, nothing saying who it's from or what it is.

We walk into my room, and I set it on my desk. I'd love to see what it's all about, but if we don't leave right now, we'll be late for Gentry's class, and I don't need to give him any more reasons to hate my guts.

* * *

The sounds of over-the-top moaning flood out from the speakers of my laptop. A dark, grainy video of a naked blonde bouncing up and down assaults my eyes. Her back is to the camera, and it's too dark to make out the dude below her.

Why would someone leave this for me? Maybe a hazing prank or something? Fucking gross. Her moans get louder as she rides his dick like she's being paid to. Hell, maybe she is.

I'm sure there's good money in amateur college porn.

I'm about to rip the offending technology stick from my computer when a familiar drawl sounds out, "Mmm, fuck darlin'. So good. You're always so good when you take my cock."

Stunned, I slam my hand against the space bar, pausing the video. I move the cursor back a few seconds and play the scene again. And again. And again.

It's staticky and muffled. He's slurring. Drunk again, no doubt. He always is these days. But it's definitely him. Zach. Fucking some blonde that isn't me.

If there was any doubt that tried to seep into my mind, the blonde's next words solidified my assumption.

"Oh, Zachy, you fuck me so good, baby. Tell me again how I'm way better than your girlfriend. Charlotte, is it?"

The thudding in my chest skids to a halt. Heat rises to my head, and I think I might fucking pass out or throw up.

"Mmm, better than anything... Little bit... Love... Favorite... " his drunken declaration is muffled by the blonde leaning forward, smothering his answers with her tits. Yep, I'm gonna fucking throw up.

I gargle water three more times before heading back to my laptop. I've seen enough. It doesn't matter where this came from. What matters is that he did the one unforgivable thing—the thing he knew would break me—break us.

Zach and I are done.

* * *

I've never shared my story in a meeting before, but today, I am bursting to share my truth. The first step is admitting you have a problem and are powerless.

This is my admission.

"Hey, everyone. My name is Charlotte, and I'm an addict."

The room fills with the answering greeting, "Hi, Charlotte."

I try not to think about the last time I took my place at a wooden podium before a crowd of people. Momma's funeral.

My eyes frantically search the room until they land on Genny, who gives me a gentle smile and a nod to keep going.

"My mom died almost two years ago. An aggressive cancer that took her way before either of us was ready. It hit me hard. I stopped caring about anything. I had already dabbled in some drugs, but after her death, I really dove head first with no helmet."

My nails pick at the slight splintering of the well-worn wood. Many, many sad souls have stood here before me, and many will come after, all with different but identical stories.

I detailed every dark and depraved secret that I've held inside for the last two years to a room full of strangers. When I could bear to raise my gaze to theirs, I was shocked when I didn't see one person with judgment on their face. No disgust. No blame. I saw understanding. I saw acceptance.

I clear my throat, some of the nervousness ebbed away by the admission of my shame, "I'm fourteen months clean. But I'm still on step one. I'm really struggling with believing in a higher power when I'm shown repeatedly that if he/she does exist, they clearly give no fucks about my suffering."

Claps fill the room when I step away and take my seat beside Genny. She pats my thigh, a silent encouragement. She knows exactly how hard that was for me. She told me the heart-wrenching story of her past and when she finally got the

284

courage to talk about it.

After we wrap up the meeting with a circle of holding hands and repeating the Serenity Prayer, some of us gather to chat in the parking lot. A young guy, about the same age as me, tall with curly brown hair, steps beside me and tips his coffee cup towards me, "Great share today, Charlotte. I admire your strength and resilience."

Tears instantly prick the back of my eyes. I blink them back and manage to say, "Thank you."

"I'm Reggie," he says kindly, holding his hand in offering. I shake it. "Hi, Reggie." We both giggle at my answering greeting.

"Ah, Reg. Good, you two have met!" Genny says as she steps up to us. "Reggie is also my sponsee. I wanted to introduce you guys, so this is great."

We exchanged numbers and promised to meet sometime next week to start working on our steps together.

A horn sounds around the now emptying parking lot. The sharp noise startles me. Reggie laughs and pats my shoulder, "Oh, sorry about that. My partner gets impatient sometimes when I just start blathering away. She knows I'll talk for hours."

We both wave to the black minivan waiting in the corner of the lot, "Alright, Charlotte, text me what day works best for you! See you next week!" Reggie shouts as he jogs away. A pretty red-haired woman steps out of the van to receive him, a huge pregnant belly resting between them, and they embrace and share a kiss.

It should warm my heart to see such a loving couple. But it just makes me ill. Makes me wonder what secrets hide behind the smiles. What lies are buried in half-truths? Love is

285

bullshit. Sure, Reggie seems like a good guy, but clearly, he's done something fucked up to be here. I wonder what kind of depravity he took part in when he was deep in his addiction.

A hand lands on my shoulder, giving it a gentle squeeze. "It gets better, dear. You won't always feel this way. You won't always look for the darkness in people."

I look at her, questions playing out on my face. She answers my unasked question, "The disgust you feel is palpable, dear. It's written all over your face that you've experienced deep betrayal in the ways of love and have lost all hope in humanity's ability to love in a healthy way."

"My face says all that?" I ask, crossing my arms, feeling the need to protect what's left of the meat sack in my chest from harm.

"It takes one to know one. I've been there. I know it doesn't seem like it now, but it does get better. Someone, someday, will show you that all those thoughts in your head right now were nothing but ghosts of deceit. One day, you'll find someone worthy. Someone who will choose you. Every time."

"And how do you know that, Genny?" I question sassily with my hip cocked out to one side.

She winks at me, "I have faith."

Chapter 39

December 2007

Charlotte

I've felt more like myself this last week. I no longer let thoughts of Zach consume me. The anger and hurt are still there; I don't think they will ever completely leave me. They are just another scar on my heart, a permanent reminder that it does indeed still beat and is capable of feeling.

But thanks to the constant pep talks from Rebecca, Savvy, Dr. T, and Genny, I'm feeling stronger.

I'm not the problem—he is. I held up my end of the bargain. I loved him. I was faithful. I was loyal. I would've become a born-again virgin waiting for him if I had to. His choices aren't on me.

I'm done shedding my soul for a man who couldn't be bothered to offer me the same in return. I deserve more. I deserve better. As Genny suggested, I repeat these things daily in the mirror, and today is one of the days that I actually believe them.

I *can* do this. I *can* heal. I *can* move forward *without* drugs.

I wave my hand feverishly at my wet toes, *Bashfully Yours*

is the color of the week. I've taken to giving myself weekly pedicures. Not only does it keep Ursula from appearing and wreaking havoc, but it also pumps up my self-confidence. I soaked my tootsies in a warm bowl of epsom salt and water, when they were nice and soft, I tore into them with a pumice stone. These babies are now smooth as silk, and I wanted a more delicate change from last week's *Tornado Alley Green*.

My phone beeps with an incoming text.

Rebecca: Hey girl, I'm not feeling so well. Again, I'm sorry to bail. I'm going to skip the movie tonight and just rest. I'll text you later when I'm feeling better.

My mouth twists in disappointment. Rebecca has been really flakey lately. I'm trying not to take it too personally. I know she's busy, and she probably has other friends. But she's kinda my only friend, at school at least, so when she cancels on me, it's noticeable.

I'm pretty sure she's seeing someone, but she's been very hush-hush about it. I see how she giggles at anything related to relationships and love.

If we see a happy couple, she swoons over the sight. If we watch a rom-com, she coos at the unrealistic insta-love. She is basically walking around with hearts in her eyes twenty-four-seven. It's annoying. Especially because I'm pretty anti-love at the moment.

When I asked about the pep in her step, she simply waved me off, but a deep blush set into her cheeks. I didn't press. She'll tell me when she's ready.

Me: Oh no! KK, well, I hope you feel better. Let me know if you need anything!

I toss my phone to the side, and it bumps into *the* box. The one that's taunted me for the last several days. Rebecca finally convinced me to pack up all the shit from Zach and throw it out. But I haven't been able to bring myself to throw it out.

The sight of the thumb drive makes my stomach clench violently as I try to fend off the memory of the fuckfest. I couldn't tell Rebecca about that part. I haven't told anyone. It's humiliating enough to know the rest of the story. The shame that fills me at the thought of the knowledge that video exists is enough to keep me in silence.

I shake away the dark thoughts that threaten to roll in, pick up the box, and set it on the side of my desk next to the thumb drive.

Walking on my heels to prevent my still-damp toes from touching the floor— like that would have any impact on them— I pad over to my bed and pick my legs up to rest my arms against the top of my knees while I wait for the piggies to dry.

Sunlight from my window reflects off of the shiny surface of my anklet. It's the only thing I haven't tucked away from Zach.

The white gold "10" dangles gracefully against the bone of my ankle. When I've looked at it in the past, I felt such love, belonging, and possession. Now, it just feels like an anchor around my skin. The lightness of the piece of jewelry suffocates me with the weight of its symbolism.

My phone buzzes against my thigh, looking down at the screen I see **"SAVS"**.

"Oh look, if it isn't the girl who used to be my best friend. But you can't be that girl. That girl went to a fancy pants college and got new friends and left me behind."

"Always with the drama, Charls. You know you're my one and only. You and me 'til the end, babe."

"Mhm. So, how's Florida? Please describe the hot specimens from your trip to the beach to me in great detail. I need some new fantasy material."

"Lordy Charls, they don't make 'em back home like they do here. I swear having a six-pack must be a requirement for entry into the state. If only I could make the douches stop wearing visors. It's like I'm in lust with their bodies, and then my eyes get to that lame-ass sideways visor, and the pearl goes right back in her shell, if you know what I mean."

I laugh, "I'm so jealous! How about that sour-faced bitch of a roommate? She still giving you shit?"

"Ugh, she's such a cunt. I'm pretty sure she's sabotaging me with the team. I'm the new girl and literally the only non-white, blonde girl. I'm trying to win them over with my ever-present charm, but it's been an uphill battle. Coach made us co-captains for now, but we've each been tasked with creating a routine for nationals. I have to kick her fucking ass, Charls. If she gets captain, she will make my life even more hell than she currently does."

"If you need me to come out there and give her the ol' Tonya Harding treatment, I can make that happen..." I offer, kinda joking, kinda not. I would do anything for Savs.

We both laugh.

"I have no doubt, and I love you for it. But I have something to prove to these bitches, and myself. I can handle the likes of Natasha Channing."

I can just imagine her puffed-out chest at the statement. I have no doubt that Natasha Channing is in for a world of hurt.

No one goes against Savannah Nova Mitchell and lives to tell the tale. "Okay, the offer stands anytime, boo. So, tell me, are there any boys that have caught the ever-picky eye of my best friend?"

"Girl, you know damn good and well my kitty cat ain't been pet in a hot minute. I've been so fucking busy that I haven't had time for getting fucking busy. It's a travesty, really. I'm afraid the next gentleman that visits the clam shack will be fighting off thick cobwebs."

"Come on, not one of those hot Florida boys gets your blood pumping?" I goad her.

"Oh, someone has been getting my blood pumping but not in a good, sexy way. This asshole in my music class fucking hates me for some reason and is my biggest competition for the solo performance at the end-of-the-year recital. Between him making class miserable and Natasha Cuntting making our dorm AND squad miserable, I'm about to pick up a drug habit just to chill the fuck out." Savs gasps dramatically, reflecting on her words, "Oh my God, Charls, I'm so sorry. I didn't mean that. Jesus, I'm a fucking idiot. I'm so sorry."

Once upon a time, when I had less sobriety under my belt, that statement might have bothered me. It took a long time for me to wrap my head around the fact that some people can do drugs recreationally and not make it a habit. Who knew?

"Don't even worry about it, Savs. No harm, no foul. I promise." I wave off her concerns, she doesn't apologize lightly, and she doesn't need to beat herself up more than I know she already does for the misplaced blame she's laid on herself for my fuck ups. "Anyways, I gotta jet. My toes are about dry, and I'm going to grab a coffee before settling in for a movie night."

"Love you, girl. Call me tomorrow."

"Love your face. Night."

I probably shouldn't prance about the hallways in my cheeky panties. I walk over to my dresser, grab my denim skirt, and shimmy it up my legs. I take a peek in my full-length mirror.

The denim skirt rests nicely on my hips, and my favorite tank that has seen better days still curves to my body like a glove. My hair is, for once, combed and lying softly across my chest from the length of my most recent cut.

The light in my eyes hasn't fully come back yet. I don't know if it ever will. But the haunted gaze I used to see has lessened.

Two loud thumps on my door startle me enough that I drop my phone, which slides partially under my bed.

Grumbling to myself, I walk over and turn the knob.

If my heart hadn't already shattered to pieces in the last few weeks, I would probably have a more visceral reaction to the man slumped in my doorway with his head hanging defeatedly between his shoulders.

At one time, the sight would have eviscerated any anger, and I would go to him, ready to soothe away whatever was causing him pain.

I'm no longer that girl. I can't be.

He takes his sweet time raising his gaze to meet mine. When our eyes clash together, I almost give in. Almost. *Stay strong, Charlie.* I've thought of this moment a time or two. I've imagined screaming at him. Punching him in the face or kicking him in the nuts. In my imagination, I would scream, cry, and demand an explanation.

But as I look at the broken man before me, an odd sense of nothingness washes over me. He doesn't get to take anything else from me.

"Little Bit," he rasps; the familiar nickname comes out as if it's sliding across razor blades. But still, I feel nothing.

"You know, I've been doing a lot of thinking. Trying to make sense of things. First, I made excuses. There had to be a reasonable explanation for why a sleepy-voiced female answered your phone at seven o'clock in the morning. But try as I might, I couldn't think of one."

The tears begin welling in his bloodshot eyes, but I continue steadfastly. "Then I cried. I cried for days. Couldn't eat. Couldn't sleep. Wanted to not only jump off of the wagon but crash that bitch into a mountainside and get high off the ashes. I wondered what it was about me that made me so goddamn unlovable. So easily tossed aside. Wondering why the fuck that EMT saved me. Why he didn't just let me die like the worthless castaway I was."

I steel myself, straightening my shoulders to fight the urge to comfort him as the tears begin to flow down his cheeks. This next part is going to sting.

"Then, I saw the video. It was then I knew, this–" I sway my hand towards him and back to me, "means nothing to you. I mean nothing to you. And that, Zach... That's a you problem, not a me problem. I will not let another man send me down the path of destruction."

This is it. I refuse to be yet another pawn in someone else's game of fuckery. I slam my open palm against my chest, "No more. I'm tired of people thinking they can use me in whatever way they see fit. I'm tired of not being someone's first choice. I'm fucking worthy of being someone's one and only choice, Zach."

I told myself I didn't need him to verify, but now that he stands before me, I have to ask, "Just tell me one thing. If you've ever cared for me at all. If you have a decent fucking bone in your body, be honest with me about one thing," he nods his agreement and all I can do is hope he believes somewhere deep inside that I'm owed this one truth. "Did you do it? Did you fuck sleepy-voice girl?"

He nods. Of course, he did. Any last bit of excuse for him has completely left my body. I'm done with this. He can take his shit and leave. I turn away from him to grab the box off my desk. I fling the home porn vid on the top and offer the box to him.

His hands tremble as he takes it from me. His eyes plead the case that his mouth dare not try. Not a chance. You get nothing else from me. Except... I reach down, rip the anklet from my body, and toss it on the top of the pile.

"Don't ever contact me again." I whisper as I slowly close the door.

Chapter 40

January 2008

Charlotte

I knock on Rebecca's door for what feels like the hundredth time in the last few weeks. She's been avoiding me, and I want to know why. What did I do? Did I offend her somehow? She barely speaks to me in class. She sometimes responds to my texts, and when she does, it's usually in as few words as possible.

I tried not to let it bother me, but it started to feel a little pointed at some point. She's hardly ever in her dorm anymore. Not that I've stalked her or anything, but we have similar schedules and usually bump into each other daily, but even that has been far and few between.

Giving up, I walk back to my dorm. As I go to close my door, my phone buzzes in my pocket, **"ARI"**.

"Ah! Ari, fucking finally! How are you?" I screech so loud it hurts my own ears but fuck, if she's calling me, that means she's finally out of treatment.

She was in Starry North for only a few days after I left. To my surprise, Jensen– I mean Dr. Turner, called in some favors and got her transferred to a private facility in California. It was much more extensive and strict. They take their patient care very seriously. She has only been able to call me a handful of times in the last year.

She was released a few months ago but has been settling into her new life in some podunk town in Texas. She decided to put off college, maybe indefinitely, to live on a horse ranch. If she's happy, I'm happy.

"Charlie, God, I've missed your inappropriate noise levels!" She laughs, and I bristle at the implication that I am a loud-mouth. You don't just say it out loud, even if it's true.

"How's Nowheresville?" I ask, eager to hear about this mysterious ranch.

Ari laughs and corrects me, "It's *Norsville*, Charlie. How many times must I tell you?"

"I said what I said." I tease.

"It's... um, good. I'm spending a lot of time with the horses and their trainer. He is teaching me how to care for them and read them."

"Wait. Wait. Back up. First, he? Who is this trainer? And what do you mean *read* them?"

A pregnant pause fills the airspace between us. I can picture Ari twirling a piece of her fiery locks and kicking her shoe against the dirt, nervousness oozing out of her.

"Oh, um, he's nobody. His name is Calvin. His family owns the farm. He just got out of the military and is back to help his family run the ranch." She rushes out, obviously giving out more information than she originally planned.

"Hm, yeah. He sounds like a nobody to me." I joke. Clearly, this man has Ari flustered. But maybe a big, strong, military country boy is exactly what she needs.

"Ari?" I goad.

"Yes?" She squeaks.

"Do you have a thing for Nowheresville boy?" I ask, leaving the sarcasm out of it.

"Oh, Charlie. I don't know. I don't know how I feel. This is the first time I've had the tinglies for a boy..."

"The *tinglies*?" I question, this time there's no hiding the sarcasm in the words.

"You know. Like the fluttery feeling in your stomach... And,"

"And your vajay?" I help her supply the word she's too embarrassed to voice.

"Charlotte!" She protests at my vulgarness. Well, vulgar to Ari's sweet baby ears.

A muffled whistle sounds over the line, and crinkly static blares in my ear. *"Cherry, what's the holdup? The stalls aren't gonna muck themselves."*

The crinkle sound increases as Ari presses the phone against herself. Oh, but I heard. I can't quite make out what she says to him before she returns to the line. "I've got to go, Charlie. I'll call you next week."

"Cherry?" I cackle at the sweet nickname from Nowheresville boy. I can just see "Cherry's" deep crimson blush from here.

"Oh, shut up. I'll call you." She whispers into the phone before disconnecting it.

I've become somewhat of a creature of habit as of late. I have classes on Monday, Tuesday, and Thursday. Meetings on Wednesday and Friday nights. Weekends are spent between the library and The Coffee Cove, a small, not very busy coffee shop on campus.

I have a few hours until Wednesday's meeting starts, so I might as well get some studying in. I grab my books, shove them into my backpack, and head to the library.

A cloud of rose-scented perfume chokes me as a petite blonde collapses in the chair beside me. I try to keep the distaste off my face. I know I have a resting bitch face that scares most people off, but I am trying to branch out. Just a little.

"Hey. You're Charlotte, right?" she asks in heavy pants of breath as if she ran a few miles before busting in here and deciding to sit beside me.

"Um, yeah…" I respond, extending the yeah in question. She looks familiar, but I can't quite place her.

"I just wanted to give you a heads up. Your friend? The mousy TA. Ain't what she presents herself to be."

"What? Rebecca? What are you talking about?" I ask, confused.

"Yeah, *Rebecca.* She pretends to be this little nerdy, innocent girl, but she'll stab you in the back in a heartbeat. I've seen you with her on campus, and I just wanted to let you know what kind of person she is." She warns. Realization dawns on me. This is psych boy's girlfriend. The douche who was feeling Rebecca up a few months ago.

"Look, I'm sorry if your boyfriend was a cheating a-hole, but that's no reason to go smearing a nice girl's name around school. He was the one who was committed to you, not her."

My defense sounds hollow even to my own ears. As someone who has been cheated on *twice*, I want to jump over to her team and say fuck the homewrecker. But the other part of me feels compelled to defend my only friend.

"Nice girl, my ass. She knows exactly what she's doing," she sneers, lifting herself into a standing position. She leans down, placing her hands against the tabletop before whispering in my ear, "Mark my words, Charlotte. That girl is going to ruin your life. Get out while you can."

With that ominous warning, she storms off towards the exit. Leaving me reeling and unable to focus on my studies.

* * *

A flash of bleach-blonde hair enters my periphery as I close my door, getting ready to head to class. I march after her and catch her door before it fully closes. Rebecca turns to me, eyes widening in surprise as she fumbles for words.

Hard to avoid me when I'm standing in your face, huh?

"C-charlie, hey. Um, I was going to call you soon. I've been uber busy and," she nervously rubs her hand against her stomach, "I've got some news."

I cock my head to the side and cross my arms, waiting for this ground-breaking news.

"I'm pregnant." She breathes out in a huff. Excitement coats her words and face. Clearly, this is good news to her.

Stunned, I gape at her. *Say something, Charlie.* "O-oh. Um, I didn't even know you were seeing someone."

A brilliant grin forms across her lips as she holds her left hand up. A rock the size of Pluto gleams back at me from her ring finger. "I'm not just seeing someone. I'm getting married. Next week. I would've invited you, but it's literally just going to be the two of us and a witness. He's very private and wants this special day to be just for us. I will officially be a wife on the 31st."

The air punches from my lungs at my connection to that specific date. I shove it deep inside. This isn't about me. Even

299

if I think she's making a horrible mistake, this is her life to live, not mine. I put on my best fake smile and congratulate my friend. "Oh Rebecca, that's great news. I'm so happy for you. When do I get to meet this mysterious fiance of yours? What's his name?"

Her smile falters ever so slightly, "Oh, um, his name is Za-Zane. I'm not sure when a good time would be to meet. He's uber busy, and now we've got the wedding, honeymoon, and–" she looks down and rubs circles around her belly, "baby planning. But we'll pencil something in for sure. Soon."

I nod along, clearly she has little interest in sharing this part of her life with me. Maybe we weren't as good of friends as I thought we were. Looking around her dorm, it's very bare. "Where's all your stuff?" I question, gesturing around the near-empty space.

"Oh! That's the other news. We got an apartment just off of campus. My Zane can't stand to be away from me for a moment longer than necessary. He left his school and moved closer to me but insisted I move in with him. I'm keeping the dorm for another month or so just in case I need somewhere to nap or change during the day. I'll take a leave of absence when the baby comes, so I want to prepare things as much as possible."

"Oh. Okay. Well, um. I'll get out of your hair. Congratulations on... everything. I'll see you later."

As I leave her room, I remember the tea. I've been having some night terrors lately, but when she shared the sleepy tea with me, I didn't have any.

"Hey, do you think I could get some of your sleepy tea?"

Rebecca nervously looks around the room, twisting her hands together before looking at me, "Funny story, I actually lost the recipe in the shuffle of the move. Darn it, I'm sorry about that." She responds with a quivering voice. Strange.

"Oh, okay. No worries. See ya."

I try not to think about the significance of my friend's wedding day. The 31st would have been Zach's and my official one-year anniversary. I had so many plans, and I imagined marrying him on that date one day.

Then, he smashed all those hopes and plans in one fell swoop.

Now, that date can be significant to someone else.

Zach no longer gets to hold that space in my heart or my head.

Never again.

Chapter 41

February 2008

Charlotte

"You are a godsend, Charlie!" Reggie gushes as he grabs the folded manuscript from his backpack. He is a theater major and hasn't had someone to run lines with since his partner Sariah has become too exhausted from being hugely pregnant and nesting. I was happy to offer my lame acting skills. He's become such a great friend over the last few months.

I haven't seen Rebecca in weeks. It's like she fell off the face of the planet. Maybe that's just her MO. Some girls only keep friends around to bide their time until they hook a man. Then it's sayonara chicky and hello dicky.

I'm grateful for Reggie and Sariah. They've opened their home and their hearts to me. We've come up with some weekly traditions. Game nights. Pizza nights. Movie nights. You name it. Anything that doesn't involve drugs, partying, or sushi. Who knew preggos couldn't eat sushi? Maybe I'll just never get pregnant. It sounds like a giant list of shit you can't do for nine months.

I take my place in front of Reggie as he hands me a copy of

my own crumpled manuscript. "Okay, you will read the red parts, and I will read the blue parts."

Nerves begin to take hold, as if we will be performing this train wreck for a stadium full of people and not his two cats, Johnny and June.

I take a large bite of my Hawaiian pizza and nod my head at him.

We spend the next hour and a half trading dialogue back and forth. I suck. He's actually pretty good. I don't know anything about acting, but I'd try to stay awake through it if he were in a movie.

Life is starting to look a little less bleak. I've been consistently on the go, and the busyness helps the dark thoughts stay at bay. Thankfully, we've got a good mix of meds going on, and I'm no longer living in a fog.

Most days, I can function as a regular, neurotypical human. And thanks to therapy and meetings, I have an arsenal of tools to fight off the darkness on the days I can't.

Reggie wraps his arm around my shoulder as he gently takes the manuscript back, "Don't take this the wrong way, Charlie. You know I adore you. But you are an awful thespian. Please never pursue a career in acting. Promise me." He jokingly implores.

I shove him off with a fake huff, "Well, not after that silent dissent...thanks for crushing my dreams, jerkface." I tease back.

Sariah walks into the room, her arms loaded with greasy snacks. We all post up in our various spots in their living room for movie night.

Walking into class the next morning, I'm stunned to find an empty auditorium. Professor Gentry is resting against his desk with one of the campus security guys. When the door bangs behind me and alerts them to my presence, Gentry straightens up and gives me a very curious look. He's had it out for me from day one. I'm used to his glares, sneers, and sassery. But this look frightens me a bit. It's full of regret and compassion.

"Miss Johnson, please come in." Gentry pulls the chair out opposite his for me and gestures for me to take a seat.

"Uh, what's going on? Was class canceled?" I pull out my phone and begin to pull up my email. "I didn't get a notification or anything."

"Well, that was by design. Yes, class has been canceled. But we needed to speak with you about an urgent and confidential matter."

Uh, okay? What the fuck is going on? He's acting like someone died. Oh fuck.

"Did Rebecca die?" I gasp out urgently. My heart pounds with the beat of a thousand drums. It makes sense. I haven't seen her. She hasn't been in contact with anyone I know. She hasn't responded to any of my communications.

Gentry pats my hand in what is supposed to be a comforting gesture, but after months of animosity, the comfort is lacking. "No, dear. But this does pertain to Miss Crowe. Did you two have any sort of falling out or ongoing issues?"

"Uh, not that I'm aware of. She's been pretty distant lately, and..." I bite my lip and debate whether or not I should say anything about the pregnancy. She seemed excited about it, but it's definitely not my news to share. But... if something's wrong or she's gone missing, maybe that's important information to have. "Last time I spoke with her, she was getting married in a week and had just found out she was pregnant."

Gentry doesn't seem surprised by my revelation. Maybe as her mentor, he was already privy to that piece of hot goss.

"And when was that?" he asks as the security guard pulls out a little yellow pad and black pen.

"The last week in January."

"You're certain about the date? That came to you awfully fast." He asks, not accusing but uncertain.

Yeah. I'm certain that she told me a week before she was getting married on what would have been my anniversary. That date is seared in my brain, as I hoped it would be my wedding day one day.

I clear my throat, "Positive."

Gentry nods and rests his behind on the edge of the desk. "Has Miss Crowe ever prepared your food or beverages?"

Well, that's a weird fucking question. I mean, she's brought snacks and stuff to my room, and I have to hers too, so I guess, "Yeah?" I respond with question.

"Did you ever notice feeling off after ingesting the items prepared by Miss Crowe?"

Feeling as though I've been slapped, my head whips back as I stare up at him with furrowed brows. "What?"

"At any time, did you feel like something wasn't quite right, or did you feel sick or maybe really tired?"

"This is super weird, Professor. Can you just tell me what is going on?" I plead, done with the fuck-fuck games and ready for some answers.

Gentry sighs, "An anonymous source has made me aware of some inappropriate and possibly illegal actions by Miss Crow. Against you, dear."

Huh? "I don't understand." I sigh heavily, exasperated by this circle jerk of non-information.

"It's been alleged that Miss Crowe was giving you small doses of something called AstraClara for a number of weeks."

A torrent of memories threatens to take me under at the mention of the newest version of a familiar drug. This can't be happening. What? Why? This doesn't make sense. "I think I would know if I was given drugs, sir."

"We are aware of your past, Miss Johnson. But we have strong evidence to the contrary," he motions to security, holding his hand out. The security guard hands him a small, clear cup with a light blue lid. He places it in front of me on the desk. I look up to him and see the apology in his eyes.

If he knows my past, then he knows I'm clean, and this is not only a slap in the face to my character but could change my whole fucking life.

"How long have you been clean, Charlotte?"

"Sixteen months, sir," I reply firmly. There is no room for debate with my sober date. I've worked too fucking hard for it to be called into question.

"I believe you. But with these allegations, we need to be certain. We are going to need a urine sample."

I can't believe this is fucking happening. I'm used to giving my fluids at the drop of a hat, but I thought all that shit was behind me. Something dawns on me, "I haven't seen Rebecca in weeks, and it's been longer than that for any food preparation. My pee would be clean."

"The urine sample is to exclude the possibility that you are currently partaking in drugs. This−" He pulls out a thin, long, clear plastic bag and lays it next to the cup. " −is for the follicle sample we will test for the history of usage."

Defeated, I grab the cup and look around. "You may use my private lavatory," he oh so kindly offers.

I place the cup full of my mellow yellow on his desk. The security guy has gloved up and takes a few strands of my hair from the root to put in the baggy.

"We've marked this as urgent and have been assured results in the next forty-eight hours. Are you sure there's nothing you can think of that seems suspicious now?"

I think back over the course of our friendship. We've studied. Had movie nights. Gotten take out. Made ramen. All the normal college things. But.. now that I think about it. There was that weird night at the dance club. I definitely felt high, though I had only had two drinks. I just assumed they were hella strong. If she put something in those drinks...maybe she put it in others. Fuck.

"The tea!" I exclaim, slamming my hand against the hard surface of the desk.

"Tea?" he asks.

"Yeah, for a while, she brought me this 'sleepy tea' that she swore was a secret recipe from her grandmother. She was real squirrely about it and would never leave me tea bags or share the recipe. I didn't notice much because I drank it right before bed. I just thought it had a bunch of Chamomile or some shit in it."

He nods his head, "That tracks with the information we have. A small bag of the AstraClara was found next to a pad with your schedule. A calendar was marked with 'AC' and your name on many occasions."

"What the hell..." I whisper in disbelief.

"Charlotte, this next part is going to be a little difficult to hear." He warns.

I huff out a laugh with no joy in it, "More difficult to hear than I've been micro-dosed by someone I thought was my friend and has thrown sixteen months of sobriety out the damn window?"

"Yes, I believe so."

I sit ramrod straight, eyes wide, begging him silently to continue, though I don't want to know.

"A diary of sorts was also found with the items. It seems Miss Crowe may have been stalking you. For what, we aren't quite clear on. But she detailed all of your comings and goings. She talked about wearing the same scents you do and dying her hair to match yours. She noted that she would quote 'take everything that you thought belonged to you'"

I feel like I'm gonna fucking hurl. She was stalking me? How did I not notice all of this? I mean I thought it was weird she wanted to bleach her untouched hair suddenly but what girl doesn't fuck with their hair in times of mental crises?

"We aren't sure to what end this all took place, but I assure you, we will contact the proper authorities and will press charges should she return. Even if you decide not to do it of your own accord."

I nod, not sure what else to say. They finish up my statement and assure me that all will be well, subtly asking me not to place blame on the university and claiming they are totally on my side.

I walk back to my dorm in a mental haze, replaying every interaction, conversation, and subtle dig. How did I not see this? Am I so full of myself that I didn't realize what was happening in front of my eyes? And what did she mean she would take everything that belonged to me? It's not like I'm rich or anything.

Entering my bathroom, I stare at the girl in the mirror. Ghosts of my past threaten to come forth. The bugs in my skin begin to crawl. I need to do something. I can't just fucking sit here.

My hands fist my long locks, and I tug them sharply, reveling in the sting of the pain. *No. Stop. We can handle this. What are the tools? What is a healthy way to deal with my dark thoughts?*

I pull my phone out of my back pocket and press it to my ear. I stare myself down in the mirror, looking at the wisps of my hair as they brush against the middle of my chest.

"Sariah, do you have the number for that hair stylist friend of yours? I need a change. Right now."

Chapter 42

February 2008

Charlotte

"OMG, I love it, Charlie!" Sariah gushes over my new lob. The weight that came off when the stylist took those scissors to my long, luscious hair and begged me to reconsider when the almost two-digit inches fell was both metaphorically and physically a load off.

I feel like a whole new person. My hair has always been long. I never thought I could pull off a shorter cut. But here I am, killing it.

I dramatically flip each side of my hair back and forth, "Why thank you, it is pretty rad, huh?"

As Sariah drives us back to my place, I lose myself in the blurring of the trees as we pass them when her voice breaks the comfortable silence. "So. Did you hear back from the university?"

I sigh deeply. Yeah, I heard alright. I nod, "Yeah. I was called in for another meeting yesterday. This time with the Dean and a police officer. The urine was clean."

"Of course it was." I love how she is so steadfast in her belief in me that she has zero doubt as to whether or not I have been using again.

"The hair, however, showed minor traces of AstraClara. She fucking did it. The cunt drugged me. She smiled in my goddamn face while planning my downfall. She had apparently also been in Gentry's ear since my first week of school. Telling him I've cheated on tests. That I seduced another professor. Even said I was planning on seducing him. So when I walked into his classroom and accidentally gave everyone a titty show, he thought that was purposeful on my part."

"What a horrible girl. I hope the police find her. Is there still no word?"

"Nope," I respond, popping the P.

I wave goodbye to Sariah and walk into my building when my phone rings. Without looking at the caller ID, I pick it up.

"So?" Savvy impatiently asks.

"Let me get into my room, and I'll tell you everything."

We've missed each other for the last few days, but I texted her a brief Cliff Notes version about everything that happened with Rebecca and the drug testing.

When I get back to my room, I spill it all. Including my new 'do.

"She fucking Jennifer Jason Leigh'd you? That fucking cunt. I will come there right now, Charls. I will stomp the hoe right out, pregnant or not." Savvy snarls. And I have no doubt she would. God love my best friend, I know she would do anything for me. I can't help but laugh at her *Single White Female* reference. "Also, I bet it's super cute, and I want pics ASAP."

"Yeah. So that's my life." I laugh. Because what else can I

do? This shit is bananas. Like, fully b-a-n-a-n-a-s.

We catch up for a while before her busy social life pulls her away as usual. This guy in her music class has gotten under her skin. People never get under Savvy's skin. I'm curious if there's more to it than the hatred she claims.

My next call is to my sponsor, Genny. I need to inform her that my clean date is no longer accurate. My fault or not, I can't in good conscience tell myself and a room full of people that I've been clean for over a year when that's no longer true. Genny assured me all will be well, and we will discuss it more at the meeting tonight.

Sariah promised I could be the one to tell Reggie. She swears no one will look at me differently or judge what's occurred, but the guilt I feel over the situation is immense and, if I'm not careful, could be debilitating.

As I stand at the podium and gaze out among the sea of my fellow addicts, a cold sweat works its way down my spine, and my hands begin to tremble. There's no getting around it. I need to rip the bandaid off and confess the sins that don't actually belong to me, but I'm being punished for them anyway.

I don't know what I expected. The crowd to turn into an angry mob complete with pitchforks, Bibles, and flaming sticks of condemnation? Shouts of judgment and anger? Being kicked out of the group and banished forever?

None of those things happened. As a matter of fact, at the end of my very long-winded share, Genny and Reggie pulled me aside, and we had a good, long talk. I'm in charge of my clean date. Whether or not drugs were forced in my body –ah-fucking-gain–, I remained clean. My soul is clean. My intentions are clean.

I decide whether or not to reset my date—no one else. Though the sentiment does make me feel better, and I see where they are coming from, I still struggle with deciding how I feel about it.

"I know you usually walk home, Charlie, but would you mind riding with us so I can run some lines with you? I am so nervous about my audition tomorrow." Reggie asks with a sweet, pleading face only he could get away with. Complete with bottom lip stuck out for childish effect.

I agree, and we hop into Sariah's waiting minivan. Reggie's actually getting really good. He handed me the only copy of the manuscript to follow along, and he hasn't missed a single beat. He has absolutely nothing to worry about, though there's no telling him that. I don't know if it's all actors or just him who needs to be one hundred percent perfection. There is no room for error in the world of Reggie.

Walking down the sidewalk on campus heading to Burlington Hall, we rehearse the scene he's most uncertain about.

He plays a working man in the 1950s who has been courting a young girl, but she doesn't know he's actually very rich and doesn't need to work at all. She has been working herself to the bone ever since she could remember, just trying to scrimp and save every penny she can to take care of her ailing father and much younger brother.

He wanted a wife who didn't want him just for the money. He pretended to be destitute to make sure his bride was pure of heart. Tonight, if her response is favorable, he will tell her the truth and ask for her hand in marriage.

Reggie delicately wraps his arm around my lower back as we walk. Getting into character, he leans down and says, "Stella, I have something to tell you."

I try really hard to remember my lines, but for the life of me, I have no idea what I'm supposed to say. So, I improvise.

"Tell me what's up, big boy?" I say dramatically breathy.

Reggie smiles and shakes his head at me but doesn't break character. He continues with his next line. "I know I told you I was a bus driver, but that's actually not true."

I gasp loudly, "Oh shiz! Why you lie, bro?"

"You see, I'm actually from a very wealthy family, and I have been unlucky in the ways of true love. So, I came up with this test of sorts. To make sure you loved me for me and not the riches I can provide you."

I lean close and whisper conspiratorially, "But you spendin' them dollars, right?"

"I want to give you the moon, my darling. But only if you'll have me, as I am." He turns us, and I beam a wide smile up at him. Feeling so proud of how awesomely he is nailing this scene. He is going to blow this audition out of the water.

"Hells yeah boo, rain them benji's down on me!" There's supposed to be a big romantic kiss, but yeah, no, so we hold hands as I lean up on my tip toes and place a nice chaste kiss on his cheek.

"You are going to crush this, Reg. I mean it. You've worked so hard, and you know these lines backward and forward. Don't fuss about it. Take Sariah home, maybe bang out your nerves a bit, and get a great night's sleep."

"I can't thank you enough for going through this with me. It truly means so much. You're a great friend. I feel ready. I'm going to kick names and take ass, or whatever it is you always say." He laughs as we pull apart.

"Call me first thing when you hear! I want to be the one to take you and Sariah out for a celebratory dinner. And I won't take none of the bullshit you pulled last time we went out and secretly snuck your card to the waitress," I poke him in the chest so he knows I mean friendly business, "I mean it, mister."

"Yeah, yeah. You got it. Have a good night, and we'll talk soon." He says as he begins walking back toward the lot where Sariah parked.

As I push the large front door of my dorm building open, a loud squealing of tires startles me. My head whips towards the lot on the other side of where we walked in. A small car is speeding away out of the parking lot.

With my heart pounding in my ears now from the fright, fear instantly turns to annoyance. "Slow the fuck down, you psycho. You could kill someone." I grumble to myself and make my way into the building.

My phone pings with a text just as I begin to drift off.

Savs: Call me first thing in the morning. We have something urgent to discuss.

Chapter 43

March 2008

Charlotte

Fucking humid.

That's my very first thought as I deboard the plane. Florida air is thick and wet. And smells weird. Like mud. And bugs. And gator shit. With just a spritz of fish.

I miss my crisp Alaskan air. My hair is already frizzing up, and I've been in the state for seventeen seconds. How am I going to last a whole week?

When Savvy tried to convince me to spend spring break in the Sunshine State, I almost told her to shove it. But I need the break, and I miss her something fierce. Besides, no one says no to Savannah Nova Mitchell. She was having no part of any excuse I tried to come up with.

She was oddly persistent. I tried to convince her to come to Alabama, but that was an instant no from her. She was pulling every hat trick out of her ass to get me on this damn plane.

I swear if she bails on taking me to the theme park like she promised, I'm going to punch her right in the tit. Hard.

When I make my way out of the gate, a tram pulls up in front of me. I guess I'm supposed to get on this thing. The signs are a bit confusing, and there are people everywhere, shoving and hip-checking me left and right.

I get onto the speeding bullet death trap and hold on to the disgusting, fingerprint-laden pole to keep myself from falling on the lovely foreign family speaking their native language in rapid-fire succession at my back.

Finally, I make my way to baggage claim after fearing for my life in the shuffle of bodies. I eagerly watch as my zebra-printed suitcase comes across the conveyor belt.

The black-and-white stripes curve around the bend, and I begin to reach down when someone snatches it out of my hand. "Hey! That's mine!" I shout at the body next to me, my suitcase firmly in their tight grip.

The sparkling brown eyes of my bestie light up as she gives me a look at the pearly white of her dazzling smile.

"Finder's keepers. Love the hair." She whispers as we embrace and nearly knock each other over. Grumblings from other passengers trying to get their bags sound from around us, but fuck all of them. I haven't seen my best friend in person since just before I left for Alabama.

She had come home to see Mary and help me pack and pre-pare to leave for AU. A week before she arrived, Mr. Seymore passed away, so we made it a point to attend his funeral. In true Savvy fashion, she made that a spectacle.

We lock arms and walk up to the open casket. Poor Mr. Seymore. I know he was an old man who lived a full life, but death is always difficult, especially when it's unexpected. As much as a heart attack in your eighties can be unexpected.

Looking down at the sweet man, his face is frozen in a slight, serene smile. "That's a little creepy." Savvy whispers. I bump her hip with mine, "Savs! You can't say shit like that. He's been stuffed or embalmed or whatever. Would you have rathered he had a scowl for all eternity?"

She shrugs her shoulder, "I'm just saying. Sending him off like the Joker to the afterlife seems kinda like a dick move."

"It's not that dramatic. Stop being an ass. Do you have any final words for our dear, sweet Mr. Seymore?"

She leans down, whispers something to the man, and tucks something between his arm and his side.

As we turn and let the next set of folks come to say their final respects, I lean to her and whisper, "What did you just do?"

Savvy shrugs a shoulder and, as if it's the most normal thing in the world, says, "I wanted him to have something to remember me by."

"So..." I coaxed.

"So I tucked my panties in the coffin so he goes to the afterlife like a pimp."

"For fuck's sake, Savannah. You brought an extra pair of panties with you to a fucking funeral? What is wrong with you?" I chastise in a hushed tone.

"Oh no, I took them off right before we came in here when I went to the bathroom."

"You put used panties in that man's coffin?!"

"Well, yeah, he wouldn't have bragging rights if they were new. Use your head, Charls. Now, let's get out of here. Funerals give me the creeps."

"Fancy car, Savs." I compliment the sleek, black convertible as we pull onto the turnpike. The wind is flowing through my ever-frizzing hair, but sitting next to my best friend, I couldn't care less.

She's worked so hard academically that Mary and my dad got

together and decided she deserved her dream car. So, due to their busy schedules, they surprised her with it for Christmas, virtually. They had the dealership drop it off at her dorm, with a giant red bow on it and everything. I wish I could've seen her face when she realized what it was.

"So, what's the plan?" I ask. Savvy never has a shortage of plans. I'm sure she's got the whole week mapped out to the minute. But I need it. After the year I've had. Shit, after the last several years I've had. I need to be able to just let loose with my best friend. She can take the reins and just tell me where and when to be.

"Oh, a little of this and a little of that." She answers. Is she being obtuse on purpose?

"Okay. You know I hate surprises, Savs. You don't have to give me a detailed itinerary. Just a general idea of plans is sufficient."

"Don't be a buzz-kill, Charls. We are going to drop your stuff at my dorm. Thank God Cuntasaurus Rex is in Mexico for spring break, so we don't have to worry about her during your trip. Then I figured we'd go to this little cantina on the beach and get dinner and maybe a daiquiri. Is that *sufficient* enough for you, princess?"

I cock a brow at her sass, "I'm a fucking queen, and you know it. Sounds good. I just need to shower first. I'm fucking pitting here already. I thought Alabama was humid. This shit is on a whole new level." I whine as I hold my arms up straight in the air, basking in the cool breeze that flows through my hands and my pits.

"Jesus, Charls. Do they not have deodorant in Hicksville?" she teases, pinching her nose like I'm stinking up the open-air car. Wait, do I stink? I not so discretely lean my head down to

319

my armpit and take a whiff. *Coconuts*.

I pop her lightly in the arm, "Liar! I smell amazing."

An old school ballad comes on the radio, something about how true love won't desert you, and he still loves her even though they touched and went their separate ways.

I reach over and turn the knob up. We spend the rest of the drive singing to 80s hits at the top of our lungs.

A breathtaking facade of sleek lines and glass expanses greets us as we pull into the main campus lot. The building resembles a presidential estate more so than an institution of learning. The windows stretch toward the heavens like eager arms embracing the light. With the sun radiating across them, you know that they reflect the brilliance of day and the stars of night.

Savvy whips into a parking spot and holds down a button to close the convertible's soft top.

Some students mill about the campus grounds, but clearly, many of its inhabitants have fled for more trendy pastures for the break.

It's a picturesque campus. Complete with tall palms placed around the area. Students seek the slight shade they give from the unforgiving sun. A couple of frat boys toss a football back and forth, trading insults and challenges. Iced coffee is being sipped. Gossip is being spread. This is the American dream right here, in living color.

"Jesus, Savs. No wonder you got them gams on ya. This is a hike!" I whine about the trek from the parking lot to her dorm building while simultaneously giving my bestie a prop for her hot legs.

It's like a mile longer than mine. Okay, that's probably an exaggeration, but it's far, and my legs are burning almost as bad as my lungs are burning from sucking in the humid air.

Florida is trying to suffocate me. I'm certain of it. Fuck you, too, Florida. Once I see Mickey and friends, you can kiss my ass with your heavy weird air.

Savvy strolls ahead of me with her athletic body, clearly not struggling nearly as much as I am with the unexpected cardio.

"What's the rush?" I huff out between struggles for breath.

She simply turns and winks at me, "Pick up the pace, sister. We've got shit to do. I know you're short, but put them little stumps in overdrive. Go, go, go!"

I flip her off but try my best to pick up the pace. The sun is frying the delicate skin of my neck. My hair has always been long enough to cover the area, so I've never had to worry about burning it the fuck off. Guess I'll need to pick up some sunscreen after all.

We enter the large building, and an instant wave of cool recycled air hits my face, and I damn near faint from relief.

Eyeing a water fountain to our left, I make a beeline toward it. "Ugh, what the hell? Why does the water taste so weird? It's like rotten eggs or maybe Swamp Thing's nuts! Fuck, I hate this place."

Savvy tuts at me and leads me away by the elbow like an insolent child throwing a tantrum. To be fair, that's kind of what I am and what I'm doing. She's never embarrassed, though. She still struts through the place with her head held high, dragging me behind her.

She stops in front of a large set of stairs that makes zig-zags upwards for what seems like forever. I glare at her in disbelief. "You've got to be fucking kidding me. There's no elevator?" I demand, a little entitled even to my own ears. But good lord, I haven't had this much exercise in like... ever.

"Nope. Get to it, toots." She says as she shoves me towards the stairs and gives me a little pat on the ass for encouragement.

Four floors later, we burst through a door, and I collapsed on the floor. Panting for air. My heart is racing at dangerous levels. It's kinda like the one time I took five caffeine pills and swallowed them down with an energy drink. I was pretty sure I was going to go into cardiac arrest that day. This is much like that.

"Are you done?" Savvy questions from behind me.

I turn my head and press my left cheek against the carpet of her hallway. Her golden sandal is right in my face, but just past that, I see a metallic rectangle.

"You are a fucking asshole." I fume through bouts of breathlessness. That metallic rectangle is a very real and very in-service elevator. I know that because a set of students just walked off of it and are now giving me very judgy looks as I lay here fighting off the cold breath of death.

If I had any energy, I would flip them off.

Savs bends down and boops my nose, "Come, come. Things to do, remember?"

"I hate you," I grumble as I pick up my exhausted body from the floor and begin to follow her down the never-ending hallway.

"No, you don't. You love me."

"Mhmm. Ask me tomorrow when I can't fucking walk." I lob back at her.

Undeterred by my tude, she giggles. "You trust me, right, Charls?" she asks over her shoulder as she continues walking.

"Uh-huh," I respond.

"You trust that I always have your best interest in mind?"

322

"Yes. Savs. Why are you being so weird? You're the only person in this world I can trust wholeheartedly. I know you would never do something to hurt me."

She stops walking, and I assume we are now in front of her room. She looks at me with a soft, loving gaze. Her finger comes up to move a piece of my hair that has smashed against my sweaty forehead and was dangling in my eyes.

"I'm so glad you put it like that, Charls. Keep that in mind."

I don't get time to respond to her weird comment before she flings open her door and shoves me through it. I stumble and catch myself before I completely biff it.

I turn around, ready to open the door and give her a tongue lashing for shoving me, when a throat clears behind me. I slowly turn, and the stuttered breath I was already struggling for is snatched from my body.

"Hey, Sweets."

Epilogue

The girl with bright brown eyes,
She believes they veil her deepest lies.
Her smile, a mask she wears each day,
Conceals the truth she hides away.

Freckles dust her tender cheeks,
A voice that rises, never meek.
I yearn to taste the tears she swallows,
To trace the path of pain she follows.

She wears her mask with practiced grace,
Deceiving those who know her face.
But, pretty girl, your eyes reveal
The secrets that you try to steal.

Let me in, and soon you'll see,
You don't need to hide with me.
Since we met, I've searched the sky,
High and low for my favorite starlet.

Don't you know? I see you, Charlotte.

Afterword

Thank you for continuing on this wild ride with me. If you are anything like my Beta team (shout out to those five amazing ladies!), you are probably pretty upset with me and may have screamed at that last line. All I can say is things go the way they were always meant to go. Trust the process. **The fuckery continues in book 3!**

In the meantime, you are welcome to join my Facebook group. We talk all things Charlotte. Members get first dibs on ARCs. I post teasers and give exclusive looks at my WIPs and new covers! See you there!

Facebook Reader Group

For signed paperbacks of currently available books, visit my website

Store — cltaylorbooks.com

Follow me on socials for Bookish content

Tiktok

Instagram

9 798989 367559